Always
Be My
Bibi

x x

Also by Priyanka Taslim

The Love Match

PRIYANKA TASLIM

Always Be My Bibi

xx

Simon & Schuster

London   New York   Amsterdam/Antwerp
Sydney/Melbourne   Toronto   New Delhi

First published in Great Britain in 2025 by Simon & Schuster UK Ltd

First published in the USA in 2025 by Salaam Reads,
an imprint of Simon & Schuster Children's Publishing Division,
1230 Avenue of the Americas, New York, New York 10020

1 3 5 7 9 10 8 6 4 2

Simon & Schuster UK Ltd
1st Floor, 222 Gray's Inn Road
London WC1X 8HB

www.simonandschuster.co.uk
www.simonandschuster.com.au
www.simonandschuster.co.in

The authorised representative in the EEA is Simon & Schuster Netherlands BV,
Herculesplein 96, 3584 AA Utrecht, Netherlands. info@simonandschuster.nl

Simon & Schuster Australia, Sydney
Simon & Schuster India, New Delhi

A CIP catalogue record for this book
is available from the British Library.

PB ISBN 978-1-3985-0517-9
eBook ISBN 978-1-3985-0518-6
eAudio ISBN 978-1-3985-0519-3

This book is a work of fiction. Names, characters, places and incidents are either the
product of the author's imagination or are used fictitiously. Any resemblance
to actual people living or dead, events or locales is entirely coincidental.

Printed and Bound in the UK using 100% Renewable
Electricity at CPI Group (UK) Ltd

MIX
Paper | Supporting
responsible forestry
FSC® C013604

Always Be My Bibi is my book about sisters, so I would be remiss not to dedicate it to my own pesky little sister, who always makes time to listen to publishing gossip or help me bounce titles off her until I can devise the punniest one.

But also: this one is for the Bibis of the world, who make mischief and mistakes in the course of growing up. It's okay if you're "too much" or "too messy" sometimes. In a society that is far too harsh toward women, especially teenage girls, especially brown girls, just know that there are those who will root for you even when you fall off the pedestal. You're allowed to remain on solid ground—and there's nothing wrong with shaking things up every now and then either.

CHAPTER ONE

After sixteen years, the reign of Daddy's little princess has finally come to an end.

That much is clear from the way Abbu is currently glaring over my shoulder, stocky arms crossed over one of the neatly pressed button-ups he insists on wearing every! Single! Day! Even though:

A. it's *July*;
B. fryer grease makes the kitchen at least twenty degrees hotter than it is outside, leaving stains under his armpits and the faint stench of BO in the air (gag); and
C. wearing a Brooks Brothers dress shirt in a fast-food joint is practically a crime against fashion.

Do you see what I have to deal with?

"Don't just *throw* the pieces into the box, Bibi"—his

voice drops a decibel as his eyes skirt past the drive-through window—"and you're giving him too many breasts."

Several snarky retorts sit on the tip of my tongue, but I settle for rolling my eyes. It's not like I don't know each Royal Family Value Bucket is supposed to get "one breast, two thighs, two drumsticks, and a smile." I've had the menu memorized since I was four. It's just that I couldn't care less.

Oblivious to my saintlike restraint, he thins his lips under a thick, bristly mustache. "Enough of the attitude, young lady. Working for me this summer is so much better than being grounded at home, and it's time you start appreciating it. When I was your age, I . . . "

I tune him out the second he starts down memory lane.

If being stuck in the house was the frying pan, Royal Fried Chicken is the whole freaking fire.

He's acting like our house is some hovel next to the highway and not a seven-bedroom mansion with a home theater. I am so sick of my battered and fried jail cell and its authoritarian warden that I'd even sacrifice my new Louboutin boots if it meant I could serve out the rest of my sentence in the comfort of my own home. In fact, a rom-com and popcorn in those overstuffed armchairs and ice-cold air-conditioning sounds *heavenly* right about now.

Instead here I am, in a two-sizes-too-large red polo with a crown stitched onto the breast pocket that I'm forced to tuck into baggy tan corduroys. Black orthopedic sneakers and an RFC baseball cap complete the look.

Barf!

To top it off, I can feel a layer of airborne grease totally clogging up my recently facialed pores. Do you have any idea how many showers it takes to wash that deep-fried stench out of your skin, clothes, and hair?

(Spoiler alert: infinity.)

When I don't take the bait, my dad fixes a smile onto his face and busies himself with tidying a toppled pile of soft drink lids. He reeks of forced enthusiasm and french fries. "Besides, it will be fun to have my little princess here with me. Just like old times."

I stifle a snort and finish packing the order into a white paper bag, tossing in several more RFC sauce packs than strictly necessary before handing it to the driver outside. Being Daddy's little princess only means so much when your father's a tyrant sitting in a castle made of chicken bones and a secret Bengali spice blend that has the entire country eating out of the palm of his hand.

To think, only a few weeks ago I was making plans with my friends to visit Cape May over summer vacation. I even picked out a supercute outfit—though, considering the reason for my punishment, the adorable Anthropologie sundress, strappy sandals, and floppy straw hat I hoped would catch a certain someone's attention would have made Abbu pop a blood vessel. I was going to tell him it was a STEMinist summer program. No boys, only biology.

"Welcome to Royal Fried Chicken," I mumble into my headset when another car rolls up, sparing me more guilt trips from my dad, "where our portions are king-size and your every wish is our command. What can I get you?"

"An order of Bibi, please, with a side of fries."

My head snaps up. Normally a scathing "Ew, as if!" would fly off my tongue, but I'd know that voice anywhere. "E-Enzo," I squeak, too startled to choke out anything else. His familiar red Benz pulls around on the video monitor, and soon I'm face-to-face with the boy himself. "What are you doing here?"

"I was craving some chicken," he replies, revealing a row of perfectly even white teeth. Blinded by their gleam, I look down and realize he's not wearing a shirt. Paterson, where my family lives, isn't exactly his scene, so he must've come straight from the North Jersey country club pool. I immediately forget everything else: my dad, my summer-long punishment, RFC— heck, the fact that I'm dressed like a total loser. . . .

When you're in the presence of a boy like Lorenzo Romano, it's physically—no, *cosmically*—impossible to think of anything else. Enzo has a halo of thick burnt-gold curls around his sculpted, sun-kissed face, an entire galaxy of light brown freckles gracing the high bridge of his nose and cheekbones. The kind of boy that can get you in trouble.

The kind that *did* get me in trouble.

He's the reason I'm in this mess in the first place. The boy who will never see the sundress and floppy hat I picked out just for him.

4

"I haven't seen you since prom," I accuse, even as I wrap my arms around myself and wish I were dressed in *anything* other than a sweat-drenched Royal Fried Chicken uniform.

Enzo's megawatt smile dims. "Uh, yeah. Y'know, senior year was pretty wild . . . but I texted you. Your parents took your phone, right? Yelli told me what happened."

I nod, though there's more to the story. Enzo is my best friend Nayelli's older brother, and I've had my eye on him since we were in middle school. On the first day of seventh grade, I walked into a locker face-first because he was doing handstands in the hallway and his shirt had slipped to reveal a stomach already toned by five different sports.

By high school, he and Armani Abimbola were already the "it" couple of Hillam Academy . . . but when they broke up right before their senior prom and he asked *me* to be his date instead, it seemed like fate.

Except, I knew my parents would *never* let me go. As soon as the *B* word enters the equation, Abbu's brain short-circuits. "No boyfriends, or even boy *friends*, until your sister is married!" he'd cry, effectively ending the conversation.

Technically we're Muslim, and it's true that you're supposed to be very Victorian with guys who aren't family. But neither of my parents have ever been *that* religious. These days it seems like Ammu and Abbu only bust out their piety when it's convenient.

And if there's one thing they've realized, it's that I didn't come installed with the same *good* daughter power-ups as my older, more beautiful, smarter, perfecter sister, Halima, who will most likely take *centuries* to find a guy. She refuses to so much as start looking till after she graduates from law school in another *three years*. By then I'll be ancient.

So I went to my school's nineties-themed prom anyway. It's basically a rite of passage to lie to your parents, right?

I told them I was staying at Nayelli's for a sleepover. My best friend agreed to remain glued to her phone in case my parents reached out.

Which they did. The elder Hossains are nothing if not predictable.

But it wasn't actually Nayelli they called. I didn't anticipate Mrs. Romano gushing about what an adorable couple Enzo and I made and how she'd add Ammu and Abbu to her shared digital album so they could see the kajillion photos she'd taken of us.

One minute, I was spinning in Enzo's arms to NSYNC's "(God Must Have Spent) A Little More Time on You," moonily pondering the precise shade of green of his eyes while his face lowered close to mine. I was *so sure* this would be the moment. My long-awaited first kiss.

The next—"Bibi Hossain, come up to the stage immediately," the principal was muttering into a megaphone, my incandescent parents standing beside him while the entire twelfth grade giggled at and recorded my public shaming.

Sure, I hid my face behind my MacBook for the remainder of the term, but I was still around. Enzo certainly could have tracked me down if he'd *wanted* to.

But he didn't.

"I heard you and Armani got back together," I reply with an overly bubbly smile, which makes him tense up. "Congrats, I guess!"

"Yeah. . . ." He rubs his neck a bit awkwardly. "But I'm leaving for the Cape soon, and it didn't feel right not to check in first. You know, to say sorry and all that."

"What do you mean? I'm, like, totally fine." I continue to beam at him until it feels like my face might get stuck that way. "Seriously, Enzo, it's not like I was in love with you or anything. Ego much? Let's be so for real."

Enzo blinks those beautiful Bottega greens, then bursts into laughter. "You really are a heartbreaker, Bibi Hossain. Those other Hillam boys better watch out."

"Oh, I know," I respond airily. Suddenly unsure what to do with my hands, I settle them on my hips in a way I hope looks casual, willing him not to notice the cracked and yellowed French tips on my manicure.

Before we can end our sort-of breakup on a mature, amicable note, the bane of my existence manifests next to me, glaring daggers at Enzo. "Can I help you with something, young man? You're holding up the line."

There is no line for the drive-through. We all know it.

Enzo's eyes lock with mine for the briefest instant, brimming with pity, before he shakes his head. "No, uh, sorry, sir. I just realized I shouldn't be breaking my diet. Coach would have my head."

He speeds off, but not before Abbu shouts "Good! No shirt, no service!" loudly enough for half of Paterson to hear.

Heat scorches up my neck until it feels like steam might billow out of my ears. "Oh my God!" I shriek, stamping my foot. "He'll never talk to me again! Are you happy now?"

"Ecstatic," answers my father, not missing a beat. "American boys are nothing but trouble. Does he think this is his thatha's restaurant, walking around all but naked?"

I cut him off with a screeched, "Arrrgh, you're ruining my life! I hate you!"

"You'll thank me one day," Abbu calls after me, but he wisely refrains from following me when I stomp toward the kitchen.

My luck runs out on the way home. Since the dictator thinks I'm not responsible enough to get my learner's permit, I'm stuck in Abbu's (admittedly spacious) Escalade for the fifteen-minute drive. As difficult as it is to tune out his endless attempts to strike up a conversation, it's much harder to ignore his gaudily crowned, twenty-feet-tall, smug face on the billboard we pass on the way to our neighborhood in the fancier part of Paterson.

As much as Abbu loves to flex his success, he could never bear to leave Paterson, where he opened the first of the now more than one thousand Royal Fried Chicken locations in the United States—probably because the local Bangladeshi population rolls out the red carpet wherever he goes. He employs a good third of them at his restaurants and is always there when the mosque needs a new roof or the community picnic needs more prizes donated. The emperor loves to be adored.

There's a car parked in our driveway when we arrive.

The entire time I pick my way through our front lawn to the porch, I eye it suspiciously. Ammu must have been on the lookout for our arrival through the Ring cam, because she throws the door open before Abbu finishes fishing out the right key.

My mother's face glows with delight. "Bibi, look who it is!"

Whichever auntie or uncle is inside, I certainly don't want them to see me in my sweaty, smelly, chicken-coop-core glory.

But the voice that pipes up from the couch in the foyer behind her is an unexpected one. "What's with the long face? Don't tell me you and Abbu haven't made up."

I gasp and do a one-eighty at the familiar teasing. My older sister rises to her feet, smiling down at me. Before she can utter another word, I close the distance between us and demand, "Halima Afu, what are you doing here?"

She huffs a nervous laugh, and then I realize there's someone else coming to stand next to her, still gripping one of the magazines from the coffee table that has an article about Abbu and RFC in it. A male someone. He's tall, with the broad shoulders and narrow waist of an athlete—that Captain America Dorito-chip kinda bod—a dark Viking's mane and beard framing his handsome face.

Sunny, my brain supplies.

A "friend" from Princeton who made it a point to introduce himself to us at her commencement ceremony in May. I sensed

9

the vibe between them then, since he couldn't stop smiling dopily at her, but even though my romance radar is rarely wrong, even though Halima made a hasty excuse to stick around Princeton instead of coming back home to Paterson right away, I cast the thought aside because my sister isn't the type to be tempted by a gym bro.

As my gaze flicks between them both now, my eyes grow round. No freaking way. . . .

"Abbu," Halima starts, pivoting toward my father as he slowly joins us in the foyer, "I wanted to bring Sunny here to meet you because the two of us are in love. We'd like to ask your permission . . . to get married."

My jaw is literally (okay, figuratively) on the hardwood floor.

Abbu's lands right beside it. He flaps his lips like a gasping fish as his eyes dart to take in every inch of Sunny. I can't blame him—never in a million years did I think *Halima* would be the one to pull the Surprise Boyfriend™ card.

Beneath Abbu's wary gaze, Halima's secret halal (or not-so-halal?) beefcake falters, Adam's apple bobbing. She gives him an encouraging look that I suspect is the singular reason his sturdy knees don't knock together.

After a long moment our father says, "You— At graduation you said you were—"

"Yes, sir," Sunny answers at once, shoulders straightening as if he's a soldier saluting his general. "My father is Anwarul Rahman. The Rahmans of Sreemangal."

"They run the tea estate near our bari, Abbu," Halima adds. "His family lives just minutes from where you grew up. Isn't that funny?"

Abbu shuffles past them to slump heavily onto the sofa. "Hilarious."

Sunny gulps again while my sister chews on her lip, waiting for Abbu's verdict. Ammu glances among us all, then drops to Abbu's side, prodding him along with an encouraging "Isn't this a pleasant surprise?"

"The biggest," I contribute, which only earns me a *Don't you start* look.

"With your permission, sir," Sunny finally musters, "I'd like to take Halima home to be married in Bangladesh this summer."

This summer? Oh, this is about to get interesting.

"But what about law school, Halima?" my father asks.

Halima continues to nibble on her bottom lip, fingers locked nervously in front of her. "Well, we talked it over, and . . . plans have changed. We want to live in Bangladesh, at least while we settle into married life. So, for the time being, I think I'll defer my acceptance to Princeton Law."

"The form isn't due till a couple weeks before the next term starts," Sunny reminds her. "There's no rush, babe."

Abbu squints straight ahead like he's trying to decide whether to boil Sunny alive or string him up by his toes. I cross my arms and raise my eyebrows at my father. Is he about to give *her* the "no boys" lecture too?

"And you say you love each other?"

Sunny nods solemnly. "Very much, sir. I will spend the rest of my life making your daughter happy."

At this, Abbu lurches to his feet, and Sunny braces like he might get punched. All of us deflate in relief, however, when my father only gathers the younger man up in a bear hug and thumps him energetically on the back. "Welcome to the family!"

Halima laughs, eyes shiny with tears, and barrels into Abbu's expectant arms next. Sunny looks on with a grin while Ammu fawns over him. Although I plan to do a thorough investigation and interrogation later, I grin back when my supposed future brother-in-law's glittering eyes meet mine. After all of Halima's hard work, she deserves a smoking-hot Viking of a man. Especially since this is the best news of the year—nay, century—for moi. I'm all too eager to remind my father of a certain rule he loves to hold over my head.

The second that Halima and Sunny turn their attention to Ammu, who is conducting them into the dining room for dinner, I spin to face my father. "I seem to remember you saying I could date when Halima got married, Abbu. Well, she's about to tie the knot."

His bushy eyebrows furrow before he lets out a loud snort. "Don't count your chickens before they've hatched, my Bibi zaan. They're not married *yet*."

Key word: "yet."

12

CHAPTER TWO

A week later I bid a tearful good-bye to Rosho Gulla, my grumpy purebred Persian ball of fluff, dropping him off at the Emons' next door, and then we make our way to JFK airport. The trip to Bangladesh will take nearly two straight days, including a brief layover in Dubai.

I stream practically every movie available on my personal flat screen and do not one but *five* face masks to keep myself moisturized in the pressurized air. As I pull my cozy duvet up to my chin in my pod, popping gourmet chocolates into my mouth and washing them down with sparkling water, all I can say is, Alhamdulillah for first class.

After more than a month of being grounded following prom, and a brutal week at RFC, I think I've earned a little pampering. If not for my parents coming over to check on me every thirty minutes, my pod time would be *divine*.

I grouse when another rap sounds on my divider just as Geet chases Aditya off their train onto a random station in the movie I'm watching, but it's my sister who asks, "Is that *Jab We Met*?"

"Yup," I answer after a second of fiddling with my earbuds.

"Our favorite Bollywood rom-com." She's been too busy to spend much time with me since returning from Princeton with her big news, but her hopeful smile seems like a peace offering. I scoot over at once, a wordless invitation for her to snuggle up beside me that she instantly accepts. It takes until Geet misses her train a second time for Halima to say, "You haven't asked about Sunny much. That isn't like you. Are you mad?"

"Nope," I reply, popping the *P* . . . even though an itsy-bitsy teeny-weeny part of me is. "You let me yap on and on about Abbu without once mentioning your burly boo when we FaceTimed the night before you came back, so I figured you didn't want me poking my nose into your business." When she winces, I shrug. "It's cool. You probably didn't want me opening up my big mouth, huh?"

Although I never could have predicted the bomb she dropped, I would have cheered on her romance from the sidelines if I'd known. I've set up loads of my friends, including Nayelli and her boyfriend. Plus, I've always supported my anxious sister through other periods of existential crises in her life, like when she decided to start veiling and transfer from Hillam to a less prestigious Islamic school.

But . . . after all the ways my own sneaking around has blown up in my face recently, maybe she was worried I'd screw things up for her, too.

The thought stings a little.

"Oh, Bibi, no!" My sister tows my stiff form closer to her.

"I wanted to tell you so bad, but until I felt ready to be Sunny's wife, I didn't want to upend everything."

"How did you know you were ready?" I press, deciding to spit out the question that's been eating away at me for the last week. "You've always had a plan. To become a hotshot environmental lawyer and save the world someday with your big, glorious brain. I'm happy for you, but—"

"But you're wondering why I'm giving it all up?" A fond smile smooths out the worry lines her face is far too young to have already. She sighs, but it's more swoony than world-weary. "Because Sunny never asked me to."

"Huh?" A half-chewed chocolate truffle almost spills out of my open mouth. "What does *that* mean?"

"Sunny and I may seem like an odd pair," she explains, "but he's always been so supportive of me. I've never felt like I had to choose between him and my faith. He let me make the rules and set the boundaries when I agreed to give us a chance, never minded if I asked for some of our friends to join us so we weren't straying out of halal territory. When he told me he wanted to marry me, he made it clear that his family expects him to come back and run their tea garden after graduation. I had the hardest choice of my life on my hands."

I give her one last push, just to be sure *she's* sure. "And you chose him?"

"I chose him," she confirms. "He told me he would never make me go if I didn't want to, and I—" Her breath hitches as her eyes flick to the snatches of sky and clouds that float by in the window. "I knew then, if I didn't already, that I *love* him too much to bear letting him go. So, even though I've always dreamed of becoming a lawyer, even though he didn't ask me to, I started doing my research on what it might mean to be the wife of a tea garden heir. I found out how much good I could do for the world, even the environment, *with* him, even if I never go to law school. So, I don't feel like I gave up my dream for him, only that it's changed because the two of us have grown together. Does that make sense?"

"Yeah," I whisper, Geet and Aditya's fictional love story taking a back seat to my sister's very real one. After all, if there's one thing you should know about Bibi Hossain, it's that I love love. Halima squeezes my hand. I squeeze back. "Let's get you two married, Afu."

Many, many, *many* hours later, the pilot announces at long last that we'll be landing soon at the Osmani International Airport in Sylhet. *Eep!*

I'm practically vibrating in my pod while peeping out the window at the endless hills of green that peek through the clouds. I was a toddler last time we visited, too young to remember much. Halima's Big Fat Bangladeshi Wedding means this time will be extra special!

The sweltering heat greets us first. As we walk through the terminal, my shoulder-length hair is already growing poofy from the humidity. I envy Halima, who manages to look impeccable in the silk urna draped over her head. The great thing about wearing the hijab is that bad hair days are basically a thing of the past.

The vibe inside the airport is . . . chaotic.

I goggle as a bunch of men make a beeline for us the second we deplane, clamoring to carry our bags to their taxis and offer us drinks.

Abbu takes out some twenties to tip the men, but Sunny stops him with an outstretched arm. "No need, sir. My driver is already waiting for us."

As if summoned by his words, a short man materializes and introduces himself, collecting our luggage at once. "Assalamualaikum, sir. Amar nam Ekhlas."

My father acknowledges the greeting with a dispirited nod, annoyed that his opportunity to grandstand was robbed from him. He stews in silence while the rest of us offer hellos and thank-yous. Sensing that the argument about whose wallet is the biggest might commence again, Ammu and I trade an eye roll.

At home Abbu is one of the wealthiest, most well-respected Bangladeshi men in Paterson, if not the country, so he's rarely one-upped. Only one other Bangladeshi family—with a hot son a few years older than me—even lives in our neighborhood, and they own a few upscale restaurants compared to our fleet of chicken shops.

I used to have a crush on their son Harun, who would stretch on their lawn, in perfect view from my bedroom, before his morning swim. Last I heard, the Paterson Auntie Network gossip was confident he and his girlfriend would tie the knot after college. RIP, eye candy.

Before my father can blow a gasket, I sidle up to him and take his arm. "Are we visiting Thathu? I miss her!"

"Not yet," he grumbles. "I wanted to, but—" He gestures melodramatically toward Sunny's chauffeur.

"But," Ammu cuts in, shooting him a look, "we *all* agreed that it'll be better to unwind from the journey first. Your grandmother will be coming soon, I promise. The Rahmans have a guesthouse to accommodate everyone."

"That sounds more like a guest *mansion*!" I do an about-face to inspect Sunny in a new light. When he and Halima mentioned inheriting a tea garden, I was imagining a quaint little farm. "Ooh la la. You're not secretly a prince or something, right?"

"Only technically." He grins. "You'll love it, Beebs. The guesthouse is part of the resort we run—a hotel, really. It's where tourists stay while visiting the tea plantation, but it's closed to the public for the duration of the wedding."

Excitement bubbles inside me—enough so that I give him a pass for that atrocious nickname. If Sunny hears Abbu's snort, he doesn't let on, and Ammu is quick to drag my father away toward customs to get our checked bags. Sunny follows, whistling an off-key tune.

Before long we're all distracted by the sights and sounds of Bangladesh coming to life as the Rahmans' driver directs us to three classic estate cars lined up in a row. My eyes flash to the medallion—vintage Rolls-Royce. Whoa. It's bougie to the max, especially in a country where not many can afford personal vehicles. It was a major deal when Abbu bought a van for his village to *share*. Are the Rahmans, like, *rich* rich?

What in the Crazy Rich Asians are we walking into?

In spite of my best efforts, jet lag takes a toll on me, and I nod off during the drive. Ammu shakes me awake sometime later. "Bibi, we're here."

I rub the grime out of my eyes and think I must be dreaming as the estate begins to take shape through the haze of mist.

All around us is lush foliage. Rows upon rows of the most fragrant yellow lemons I've ever seen peek out from branches and leaves like tiny suns, alongside bright green limes as big as my entire hand, encircling a landscaped path that leads up to an absolutely enormous colorful mansion with majestic arches and pillars. There's even a fountain at the center of the paved courtyard in front of the stately building.

"This place is ridiculous!" I exclaim, bouncing in my seat and recording already with Halima's phone—since my parents haven't returned mine. The road is narrow and uneven, jostling some of my footage and knocking my elbow into a grunting Abbu, but I can't complain when it means the view is that much closer. "This summer's going to be très magnifique! Nayelli will be soooo jealous when I post pics!"

Sunny chuckles. "I'm glad you approve, Bibi."

"It looks the same as ever," Abbu announces, indifferently fiddling with the shiny ribbons on some boxes of mishtis he must have picked up from a dessert shop on our way here. "Your father hasn't come up with any new ideas to revitalize the place?"

Sunny shakes his head, but Halima cuts in, "You've been here before, Abbu? I knew it was near our village, but—"

"Of course," he scoffs. "The estate overlooks your grandfather's bari. Back then this was the only place within a hundred-mile radius to find work. I spent some time helping here while your thatha ran the guesthouse for the Rahmans." He pauses and then adds under his breath, "I never imagined coming back. It's as if I've stepped through time."

Sunny nods along and admits, "It's mostly the same. My family is, er, a bit traditional. But, please, treat this place like . . . home." He hesitates before the word in a way that is at odds with his previous golden retriever attitude. "Anyway. Here we are."

The car trundles to a stop. I incline my body toward the mansion—so big, it makes our home look like a garden shed. It seems like the entirety of the staff has gathered in front of it. At the center of a crowd of about twenty uniformed people, there's a smaller group. They must be Sunny's family. Traditional, huh? Try *Downton Abbey*. I hug my trusty Louis Vuitton Speedy a little closer in my lap, glad I changed out of my pj's into a flowy crepe de chine dress on the plane. At least I can count on my exemplary sense of style to look the part.

At the very center of the group is a man with a salt-and-pepper beard in a fanjabi. He looks like a more stern, older Sunny with gray at his temples and less muscle definition. A pretty but unsmiling woman in a simple shari of exquisite, shiny silk stands on one side of him, tiny white flowers in her bun. On his other side, an old man who must be about three hundred bends over a cane.

They're not what I expected at all.

If I lived in a house like this, I'd probably have at least one pet tiger on a diamond leash and a bunch of peacocks running around. I'd invite rappers, pop stars, and Hollywood starlets to come hang out and film here. No one at school ever knows where Bangladesh is when I bring it up, but if you gave me the reins to a place like this, I'd put it on the map.

The Rahmans, by contrast, somehow feel like black-and-white characters in the Technicolor natoks my grandma likes to watch. Maybe even a Gothic horror about an unsuspecting American family visiting a haunted manor, never to be seen again.

We step out of the car on stiff limbs. The house staff greet us first with a chorus of salaams. Abbu strolls right past them, up to the man at the very heart of the gathered crowd, and snatches up his hand to shake, then pumps it up and down with so much boisterousness that Sunny's poor father sways from it.

"Assalamualaikum, Anwarul Bhai," he bellows. "I can call you Anwarul, can't I? After all, we will be family soon." His booming laugh cuts off any response. "Allah Subhanahu wa ta'ala certainly has a sense of humor, doesn't he? When I left this place thirty years ago, I never thought I'd come back for a wedding between our children."

If he notices the incredulous glances and surreptitious whispers of the staff, he doesn't let them faze him. Sunny's frazzled father clears his throat. "Aaah, yes, of course. Welcome back to my home."

I raise my eyebrows. The tone of his voice sounds anything other than welcoming, but Abbu doesn't appear to notice that either as he retorts, "You'll have to come stay at ours next summer" with a theatrical pat on the man's shoulder.

Sunny's father makes a face like he's sucking on a lemon but adds in a passably polite tone, "Your flight landed too late for supper, I'm afraid, but the servants will prepare a light meal for you."

"Gee, thanks," I mumble under my breath, not sure whether I'm more thrown by the fact that he treats us like guests who showed up without calling or that he calls his staff *servants*. Sunny's mother shoots a look in my direction, giving me a once-over. She purses her lips, her dark, angular eyes frosty. I shift my weight, sensing that I've failed some unspoken test.

My sister steels herself and steps forward to interrupt my father's babbling. "Assalamualaikum, Ma, Baba. Thank you so much for hosting us."

After a long moment Sunny's mother nods while his father says, "We'll speak tomorrow night at dinner, Bow Ma."

Although it's usually a sweet pet name for a new daughter-in-law, his tone sounds curt and dismissive. "Go get some rest."

"Shariq, come with us," directs his wife.

It's only when Sunny casts an apologetic glance over his shoulder at Halima and moves to follow them that I realize his real name must be Shariq. They clearly have him well trained, even after four years away at Princeton.

It didn't occur to me until now that *Halima* might be the one in danger of rejection from Sunny's parents, because Halima is—well, Halima. She's perfect. The aunties in Paterson would trip over their shari pleats in their haste to introduce their sons to her. The Rahmans' stony reception makes my blood boil. Nobody gets to treat my sister that way. *Nobody.*

Before I can ask Halima if she feels as snubbed by the exchange as I do, we're mobbed by the staff. Several of the older employees recognize Abbu, and salaams are offered all around. My father is back in his element, clapping shoulders and cracking jokes.

We have to split up to take baby taxis—a cross between a golf cart and a rickshaw—decorated with adorable painted flowers over to the equally gigantic but far more rustic guesthouse.

Beyond the luster of the glamorous estate, I'm starting to feel a sinking sense of dread about this whole situation. Sunny might seem great and clearly worships the ground Halima walks on, but spending the summer with his stuffy family as they try to ice out my amazing sister might not be much better than Royal Fried Chicken.

It was one thing when Halima set aside her law school plans for *him*, for *love*, but I've watched enough scenes in Bollywood movies about evil in-laws that I'm able to see red flags cropping up through the rose-colored glasses.

Is this epic summer rom-com actually a horror feature?

CHAPTER THREE

The next morning a skittish teenage girl wakes me up and draws a bath. Even though it's a little bit too *Bridgerton* for my tastes, I pad from my four-poster bed into the en suite, where an enticing claw-foot bathtub full of steaming water and rose petals awaits me. Some sort of spiraling incense burns in a clay bowl near the door, suffusing the room with a heady scent that keeps mosquitoes at bay, while cool air slices through the muggy heat from air vents. I slip into the water and feel three days of travel melt away. Okay, I take back the *Bridgerton* comment. I could get used to this.

"Bibi!" The *thud, thud, thud* and Abbu's head-splitting voice at the door make me sink further into the bath and blow frustrated bubbles, not awake enough to deal with him yet. "Get dressed! We're going to visit Thathu!"

This gets my attention. I *love* my grandmother and have been dying to see her since I first heard about this trip. Water sluices all around me as I climb out of the tub.

"It's about time you American girls get to see where you

come from!" he calls from the other side of the door. "Wake up!"

"Ready in a minute!" I call back.

Okay, "a minute" might be ambitious. If I'm visiting Thathu, my outfit needs to be *perfect*.

You wouldn't think a sixteen-year-old girl and her seventy-year-old grandma could have much in common, but Thathu is not like most old ladies. Back in ye olden times, she was one of the rare Bangladeshi women of her era to go to college, which is why she can hold a conversation with me in English.

A certified badass.

You'd have to be, in order to raise four kids as mulish as Abbu and his siblings while your husband worked from dawn till dusk and then eventually passed away. I adore Thathu. Someday, when I'm that old, I can only hope to be half as cool.

The tea garden is even more magical in the daytime, I'll give it that.

Rolling hills, abloom with rows upon rows of tea plants, glisten beneath the rays of the sun like a Nakul Sen shari studded with emeralds and dewdrop crystals. People in conical hats, sharis, lungis, and the formal uniforms of the tea garden staff stoop in the foliage. Tall fans tower over the trees but don't do much to quell the heat. The entire estate glimmers in the morning mist like a mirage that might scatter into dandelion puffs at the faintest breeze.

I press my face to the window while Ekhlas drives us down the mountain to a smattering of wooden buildings on the horizon, explaining that he, too, lives nearby with his wife and three sons. The air smells like earthy tea tinged with lemongrass, the imminent drizzle that rustles the leaves all around us, and an aroma I can only describe as *dirt*. But pleasant somehow? It starts to cool slightly when we reach the base of the cliff overlooking the village.

Children crowd around the car the second we cross through the open gates leading into this place. We spot their parents hovering in front of their homes, smiling and waving. The village is humble compared to the grandeur of the tea estate but far more pleasant. The ground has been paved over with soft gold sand, leaving only a few fruit trees to provide shade between an assortment of homes in all sorts of shapes and sizes: small huts made up of mud and sticks, brick bungalows with shingle roofs, gated-off areas accompanying busy farms. Stray dogs and cats and loose livestock weave between them all.

"Eesh, if only I'd had time to buy sweets for the children," Abbu laments, before snapping his fingers and retrieving his wallet. He rolls down the window as the car continues its slow descent, holding bills out for the excitable kids to accept. "Buy yourselves Cokes and chocolates, then meet us at Shuki Bibi's," he declares in earsplitting Bangla.

I slide down my seat with a hand over my face, wishing not for the first time that his default volume wasn't the highest setting. Noticing my embarrassment, Ammu nudges me and tuts, "Oh, let him. It's been too long since he came home."

Okay, fair.

Whooping villagers follow us as if we're the first float in a parade, all the way to one of the largest bungalows. There's a baby goat and some chickens grazing in the yard, overgrown with sprigs of fresh herbs, a backdrop I remember from plenty of glitchy video calls. The clamor summons my grandmother, who shuffles out in her white shari barefoot.

"Shuki Bibi!" Abbu thunders again.

She scowls, bony arms crossed. "Leave it to you to make such a scene. . . . and calling your own mother by name? Beshorom!" Everyone freezes at her scolding tone, looking between Abbu and Thathu, but there's a wobbly smile growing at the corners of her wrinkled mouth, and her eyes are swimming with a telltale brightness. "Asho, asho!"

Abbu barrels out of the car and gives her a bear hug, hiding his face in the crook between her thin shoulder and neck. It seems the last few years of not seeing his mom have taken more of a toll on him than he let on.

Finally Thathu says, "That's enough, now," and extricates herself, wiping his face with the drape of her shari. Abbu clears his throat gruffly. Thathu smiles up at him before wandering over to the rest of us. She sets one hand on my arm while the other rises to cup my sister's cheek. "Halima, shuna, I can't believe you're getting married. Thumi ki kushi?"

My sister nods. "I'm *so* happy."

"Good." Thathu's smile etches wider. "Inshallah, this boy will never make you sad."

Halima gives her a hug.

I let them have their moment before cutting in, "What about meeee, Thathu?"

My grandmother laughs. "How could I forget my stylish girl? Have you gotten taller, moyna faki?" I nod with a grin, even though it's not true. I haven't grown a single inch past five-one since I turned thirteen, having inherited Ammu's munchkin genes. Thathu grins back. "That means you need to eat to properly to fill out. Asho, asho."

She shoos us into the bungalow with both hands as if we're her chickens, before bidding the onlookers to give us privacy.

Walking into Thathu's house feels like I've stepped into an old photo. It's filled with the comfortable clutter associated with age, almost too many things for this amount of space—hand-carved wooden furniture, tablecloths that must have been repurposed from her old shalwar kameezes and sharis, with faded prints that were once vibrant.

Abbu stands beside a small round table, clutching the back of a chair and peering around with a faraway glaze over his eyes. He had everything in the house upgraded when his business took off, and grumbled at Thathu's refusal to let him tear down the current building to construct a much larger one. I wonder if it's still pretty similar to his childhood home.

"Bosho, bosho," my grandmother says.

We all lower ourselves into the chairs, though I sit backward with my knees drawn up and my arms on the backrest to watch Thathu while she putters toward the kitchen.

"Don't go out of your way, Ma. We already had breakfast," Abbu calls after her.

"I've never had a single visitor leave my home without at least brewing them some tea," Thathu counters, which shuts him right up.

In spite of her words, she returns in the next ten minutes with a variety of dishes that make my mouth water. Ammu sighs as Abbu and I dig in, while Halima politely picks at the food. Abbu hums in pleasure at the taste of the naikol fob, a perfectly crimped pastry with coconut inside its crispy half-moon shell. Meanwhile, I inhale bright yellow noonor boras with gusto, barely tasting the onion, ginger, and turmeric.

"Nothing beats your cooking, Ma," my father declares when he's stuffed, loosening his Loro Piana belt and patting his belly. "Not even the five-star chefs at the Shopno Saa Bagan."

"Who do you think taught a big shot like you his way around a stove, Mr. Chicken King?" she jibes, but she's clearly pleased.

Ammu shakes her head. "It's as if I'm not even here."

"Oh, *errr*," Abbu sputters, realizing he's accidentally offended her with his enthusiasm for his mother's cooking. "Your cooking is *also* my favorite, Rohanna, my mishti zaam. A man can have two favorites."

That's a bald-faced lie, and even Ammu knows it. Unlike Abbu, Ammu grew up in America and didn't spend much time learning to cook from Nanu, her mother. Abbu has always been the better chef between the two of them. Jars of Patel Brothers insta-curries are her best friends and his worst nightmare.

Ammu harrumphs and crosses her arms, sticking up her nose. "Maybe you should stay here with Ma since you're so happy."

"N-no, that's not what I—"

Halima and I giggle at our father's attempts to pacify her, and then glance over at Thathu when she snorts, "Those two haven't changed a bit." She lifts her cup to her lips, eyes twinkling at me over its brim. "So, Bibi, tell me. Now that Halima is settling down—"

"Ma!" Abbu protests before she can finish whatever she was going to say, growing a particularly unique violet hue in the cheeks. "Things aren't like they used to be. Bibi is—"

"Not a baby anymore," I cut in, my own face flushing. "I'm almost seventeen! You said I could start dating when Halima Afu—"

"I said *perhaps* after she marries," he interrupts, "which hasn't happened yet!"

A flare of indignation rises in my chest. "Abbu! But you did say—ugh, you're changing the rules. That's not fair!"

He opens his mouth to retort, but Ammu slams her palm onto the table before he can, giving us both the Look. Abbu does nothing to quibble when she suggests, with an exaggeratedly chipper tone, "Why don't we clean up since Ma made the food?"

Ignoring my sister's scandalized expression, I stick my

tongue out at Abbu's back while he trots after Ammu, his arms loaded with plates.

"You should chew him out, Thathu," I tell my grandmother, pressing myself to her side so I can drop my head onto her shoulder. It makes me feel like I'm five years old again, clinging to the pleats of her shari. "Tell him to stop acting like a tyrant. He has to listen to you!"

Her chuckle vibrates through me before her hand lands on my head. "Your father has always been the blustery sort, but he means well."

"Not you too," I complain, groaning.

Thathu tsks and shakes her head. "I think your mother and I, and even you girls, do a good job of keeping him modest, but he's right for wanting something different for you two. My parents didn't ask for my approval before arranging my marriage to your thatha. By pulling me out of school to marry him, they left me unprepared for what life would be like as a widow. Your parents want you to find love. Just look at Halima. But they also want to make sure you're educated enough to stand on your own two feet. Is that so wrong?"

"No, but—" I pout and cross my arms. "Ugh, whatever."

Even though Halima was always so overzealous about college, the prospect of having to finish high school *and* trudge through another four years before so much as looking at a boy makes me want to wither away like last season's Birkin in Kim Kardashian's closet. Do I really need a PhD in chemistry before I get to explore some of my *own* chemistry with a crush?

Thathu must see the disappointment on my face because she pats my head again. I look up in time to catch her wink. Her smile is impish, identical to the one I often find in the mirror. "Even when I was a young girl," she whispers, "we didn't always listen to our parents."

"Thathu," I gasp, at once delighted and aghast. "What does *that* mean? Were there *guys* before Thatha? Did your parents marry you off to get you away from some swoony Bengali Heath Ledger–type bad boy?"

"Bibi!" Halima exclaims.

"Ma, what are you telling them?" Abbu interjects, hurrying back and clutching at his chest in abject horror. Meanwhile, Ammu bites her bottom lip to swallow a startled laugh.

"Abbu, you need to chill out," I tell him at the same time that Thathu says, "Calm down, Lukman, or you'll give yourself a heart attack."

She rises creakily to her feet, making a *Scoot* gesture at him as she passes him to a coffee table in the nearby living room. She retrieves a binder under it at a pace so languid, I can't help fidgeting in my chair, itching with the urge to see what's inside.

She sets the binder down with a resounding *thump*.

I can hardly hear her over the pounding of my heart in my ears the entire time she explains, "After word spread about your visit, many were disappointed that Halima had already chosen a husband. But even more were curious about our Bibi."

"Ma, you didn't!" Abbu groans. "How? We planned the trip on such short notice!"

"Word travels fast," Thathu replies blithely. "I agree that she's much too young for marriage now, but these things are no longer arranged so quickly anymore. Some of your cousins have been looking for suitable matches for their own children for *years*. While you're here, why not let Bibi meet some nice Bangladeshi boys? You're always complaining that the ones at her school are too American."

Abbu begins to choke on air, but I'm not listening to him. Carefully, as if it might crumble beneath my touch, I open the binder and find—*boys*. Pages upon pages of them, providing detailed information about their heights, aspirations, hobbies, even blood types and complexions—yuck. Some of the pages are handwritten; some are typed and printed. Most have accompanying glamor shots, small and square like my passport photo.

A great big book of *biodatas*.

Or is it "data"? Eh, I prefer how "biodatas" rolls off the tongue.

I've seen them pop up occasionally on Abbu's phone for Halima, information about all of the guys interested in applying for the much-coveted position of Mr. Hossain, but since my sister was prioritizing her studies, no one ever paid much attention.

All these boys want to be . . . with me?

Smiling from ear to ear, I glance up at Abbu. I can practically see the cogs spinning in his head, but he shakes himself out of his doom spiral the second I say, "Can I bring this back with me, Abbu?"

"No!" he barks, snatching the book away from me. "Boys like this only want to meet American girls for a green card, *not* because they like you!"

Which, ouch.

I suppose he's got a point. These guys don't know a thing about me. Heck, considering the way Halima gets matches from aunties who randomly snap candids of her without her knowledge, the Biodata Boys might not even know I exist.

But what if some of them do?

CHAPTER FOUR

We bring Thathu back to the resort to settle in before the big family dinner.

It takes some convincing from Abbu and my sister, but my grandmother agrees to remain at the resort throughout the wedding festivities.

When we return, the guesthouse is abuzz. Staff members are running around holding freshly laundered towels, carting luggage, and dusting the vases lining the halls. Several of the doors leading to rooms that aren't ours are now cracked open.

"All this for me?" Thathu jokes.

Abbu frowns and reaches to stop one of the uniformed men pushing a trolley of bags. "What is going on, bhai? Why all the commotion?"

"Rahman Shaab's sisters have all returned to meet their new bow ma," the man explains, gesturing to my sister, the bride-to-be in question.

"Oh!" The color drains from Halima's face. "I—I knew we'd be meeting Sunny's extended family eventually, of course, but I thought it'd be only our immediate families tonight."

"How lovely that none of us were informed," Abbu grunts. "We have relatives of our own we could've invited. We could have brought back some of your aunts and uncles from our bari."

Even Ammu nods, a growing trench between her brows.

"Tik ache, sintha khorben na, they can drive up now," Thathu suggests, trying to allay their doubts. "This fancy estate has phones to call them, doesn't it? I see no reason why the Rahmans can't send a car back out to pick up Halima's sasas and fufus."

Abbu grimaces. "This is a deliberate slight. They don't want more of us here. If we're such a nuisance to them, we could have booked a suite at Grand Sultan instead."

I can't help agreeing with him for once.

If the entire Rahman gushti is here, it's clear we need to pull out all the stops for this dinner. We retreat strategically to our rooms. Halima chews on her already short fingernails while watching me drag her bags into my room, until Ammu and Thathu arrive with their own belongings and pluck her hands away, tutting at the uneven cuticles.

Throwing her luggage open, I begin rifling through both of our things, holding up outfits, considering each in the mirror for a few seconds before ultimately tossing most aside. Ammu and Thathu provide their own input while Halima stands there posing like a hijabi Barbie.

Finally we're all satisfied with a long pearl-accented white-gold dress, paired with a matching scarf, pinned to Halima's freshly washed hair with a Swarovski clip Sunny apparently got for her birthday. After I apply her makeup, all shades of shimmery bronze, my sister smiles up at me, looking like such a bombshell that the Rahmans will have to eat their hearts out.

"That's enough, Bibi," she says. "You should start getting dressed too."

I tap the tip of her nose lightly with the flat of my makeup sponge, making her crinkle it to avoid sneezing from the puff of powder. "Don't worry, Afu. We've got loads of time."

Okay, "loads" might've been an overstatement. By the time I put the finishing touches on my makeup in the now empty room, the sun is already creeping below the tree line. I glance at the antique alarm clock next to my bed. *Crap.* I'm late. The halls of the guesthouse are eerily quiet on my way out. There's not even a staffer in sight.

"Guys?" I call out. "Where are you?" But the only answering sound is the clack of my Manolo slingbacks on the marble floors. When I get to the courtyard, all the baby taxies are gone. I can't believe they left without me!

I curse under my breath. Because Abbu took my phone, I don't even have a way to contact them. Thunder crackles in the distance. Overhead, a large gray cloud hangs low in the sky. I whimper a little bit, already mourning the hair and makeup I *just* spent an hour getting absolutely perfect.

Grabbing a plain black umbrella from a stand next to the

main entrance of the guesthouse, I start the trek to the main house on foot. Aside from the way my heels sink into the soft earth, it isn't so bad. In fact, the walk is really pretty. I've never been a nature girlie, but Bangladesh might change my mind.

That is, at least, until rain begins to fall in heavy sheets. A distant memory of Abbu bemoaning monsoon season tickles the back of my mind. I whimper again, louder this time, knowing the moisture will flatten my hair until I look like a drowned rat, then fluff up like a baby poodle's upon drying.

Thunder rumbles above and wind lashes at my clothes. I clump up as much of my lehenga as I can with one arm while holding my umbrella with the other. A gust of wind catches the umbrella and it inverts, blowing out of my grasp and landing several inches away, where a path lined with palm trees up to the manor commences. FML.

"Pardon me," someone calls out. "Can I h—"

I release an undignified squeak-shriek combo at the unexpected voice that crept up right behind me without me noticing. Flinging my body forward, I attempt to use the trunk of a palm tree as a shield. Through the blur of motion and the heavy torrent, I notice an ominous figure on the other side of the tree—like a scarecrow come to life—whose fingers tighten far too close to mine on the wood, inches from making contact.

"Hey, wait!"

He moves as if to copy me, a note of irritation in his voice now, face so shadowed by the conical straw hat on his head that

I can't make out any features except that he's *tall* and annoyed with me—a bad combination.

Heart thumping, I throw myself hard in the opposite direction to evade his extended hand. My panicked brain won't catch up with my legs long enough to force them to leave this spot below the tree and book it toward the house, despite—or maybe because of—all the warnings Ammu and Abbu drummed into my head about never running off alone in Bangladesh. Was I wrong to assume the tea garden was safe?

"Why are you following me?" I demand.

He lunges in my direction. "If you'd just—"

We repeat this awkward dance once more, but when I attempt to dodge him for the fifth time, even as I mentally ask myself what the hell I think I'm doing, something snags behind me and drags me back a step. I yelp, hands reaching automatically for my throat as I come to the sinking realization that the black urna draped around my neck has somehow gotten wound around the prickly bark of the palm tree.

I glance over my shoulder and meet Scarecrow's eyes. Although I can't tell whether they're black or brown, they're equally round and dumbstruck beneath his now-askew hat and the thick fronds of the tree. They narrow as fat droplets of cold rain start dripping onto my head and shoulders, prompting a shiver I can't suppress.

When he ventures forward, my fight-or-flight kicks in, and I tug hard on my trapped scarf. Just my luck—in Bollywood movies, girls only get their urnas caught on the button of a gorgeous guy's fanjabi sleeve or his watch, *not* on a tree while some scarecrow-looking creep looms over them. Why did Shah Rukh Khan lie to me?

"I know karate!" I warn Scarecrow. Even with the hat tipped over his face, I feel like he's eyeing me incredulously— which, rude. I actually do have a white belt!

I tense as he ventures closer, then gawk when he says, "Would you quit it? You're going to tear your urna if you don't stop." For some reason, this gives me pause. I suck in a sharp breath as he closes the distance between us, but he only takes the hat off his head and plunks it onto mine with a droll, *"And you're getting wet."*

Before I can splutter a response, he pulls the brim down over my eyes—but not so fast that I don't spot the smirk that curls his lips. I squawk in indignation, lifting my hands away from my scarf to fix the hat so I can see again. The sight that greets me isn't the one I expected.

Scarecrow is kneeling in front of me, uncaring of the fact that his pants are getting soggy and muddy. He holds my scarf taut in one hand, while the long, slim fingers of the other carefully remove it from the palm tree without damaging either the embroidery or the bark. Once it's free and returned into my custody, he looks up at me with a pair of flashing brown eyes.

"Are you mad?" my savior and/or potential kidnapper inquires.

I mean to ask "W-what?" but instead my traitorous mouth supplies, "Hot?"

Because he is.

Hot, that is.

He's all angles, save for the soft, disapproving set of his full pink lips, the bangs that swoop onto his forehead, notes of russet glinting through dark strands, and his matching warm earthy-brown irises. Tall and slender and almost pretty, with enviably dewy golden-brown skin that's probably never seen a pimple in his life. The flush and slight breathiness from the exertion of our impromptu dance only makes him more attractive. Considering he looks like a teenager, perhaps my age or a year or two older, that is decidedly unfair, but as I know well from my sister, God plays favorites.

His brows furrow as concern replaces displeasure. "Are you having a heat stroke?"

"No!" I retort, my senses returning just in time for me to jerk away from the back of his wrist when he stands and makes a motion to, presumably, press it against my forehead. What happened to Bangladeshi boundaries? "I'm—I'm fine! And—and—and—just because you look, er, nice, doesn't mean you are, so you'd better keep your distance or else!"

I snatch up my dropped broken umbrella and wield it like a sword, though I'm not sure that'll amount to much if he does prove to be a kidnapper.

"I look . . . nice?" he asks, puzzled. "Thank you?"

Heat rises all the way to the tips of my ears. Of course a

guy who looks like him would be full of himself, but I wasn't quite expecting him to come right out and agree. "You are *so* not welcome. You never told me why you were chasing me."

"Ch-chasing you?" he parrots, affront lifting his brows into his hairline as he splays a hand across his chest. "I was *not* chasing you. What do you think I am, some pervert?"

"I don't know you," I counter, "so maybe you are!"

Shooting me a dirty look, he moves to stoop behind the tree and retrieve something. I stiffen and withdraw another step into the rain, grateful for the straw hat even if I'm wary of him. Despite his assurances to the contrary, I still harbor some doubts that he won't pull out something like a machete, the preferred weapon of the headhunting kuskors from the stories Thathu used to tell me and Halima.

Most of Thathu's stories were scary, in fact, in her effort to ensure we were always safely chaperoned by one of our adult relatives. They were tales of zinn and buuth, tigers who'd swallow you whole, kidnappers who would hold you for ransom if they knew you were from abroad, or traffickers who'd sell your organs for money.

I always envisioned them as menacing when I was a kid, but it makes more sense that they'd be disarmingly handsome, like the boy kneeling in front of me. Most people would let their guards down in his presence.

Not me, though!

The boy in question eyes me as he slowly, ever so slowly, holds up—an umbrella? A parasol? Is there a difference? I'm so surprised that I let my own useless umbrella tumble from my lax fingers, which he takes as a sign to step closer and open his above both of our heads.

"Um," comes my intelligent reaction.

"I was not *chasing* you," he repeats, exasperated. "I was minding my own business when, to my surprise, I saw an unfamiliar girl standing under a tree in the pouring rain. Obviously it's monsoon season. Anyone in their right mind would keep a functional umbrella on them, or at least know not to stand beneath tall trees that might attract lightning."

I look up at his umbrella. It consists of several watercolor shades of green, shinier than any I've ever seen before, a see-through lacquered material with painted flowering branches visible when held against the lightning that illuminates the sky, each spoke attached to what looks like a carved leaf. *Cute*, my malfunctioning brain supplies, an utterly unhelpful thought.

The boy, who isn't a kidnapper, sighs and places the handle of the umbrella in my listless hand, even moving to close my fingers around it when I don't do so myself. It's chilly out here, I realize, the downpour worsening by the minute.

We stare at each other for a moment, his eyes expectant. When it becomes apparent that Bibi.exe has stopped functioning and won't reboot anytime soon, he gusts a long-suffering sigh and deftly removes the conical hat from my head, returning it to his. "Well. I'll be off, then."

"You work here," I blab just as he makes to amble toward the main house.

He turns back reluctantly. "Yes . . . ?"

I want to smack myself. Obviously he works here, when he's wearing the deep emerald green uniform of the rest of the hospitality staff, nearly black beneath the cloud-cast sky, with a small, golden tea leaf over the left breast pocket, matching the trim on the collar and the cuffs of the long sleeves. Even his graceful fingers have dark smudges on them, though those might be my fault for making him stoop on the ground, rather than because he was plucking tea leaves.

My face scorches from the humiliation of that revelation as I mumble, "Um, I'm sorry about earlier. Ithoughtyouwereakidnapper!"

"You thought I was a . . ." It takes him a minute to decipher the rapid-fire jumble of words, and then he barks a laugh so loud, I jump and almost whack him with the umbrella. When I realize he's laughing *at me*, I wish I *had* whacked him. He must see the dawning fury on my face, because he wipes the tears from his eyes and clears his throat. In a more somber tone of voice, he continues with a hand on his chest, "I apologize for scaring you, but . . ."

"But?" I prompt when he doesn't complete the thought.

His eyes flick over my frame briefly before he shrugs. "I don't think you have to worry about any kidnappers here. We have security. Only ticketed guests can enter, though currently the resort is closed for a private party."

My grip tightens on the umbrella as displeasure ripples through me. Oh, so he doesn't think I'm worthy of kidnapping, eh? Just because he's so tall and pretty, and with that lilting (British?) accent I'm only now realizing is very fluent compared to most of the staff.

He blinks when I continue to death glare at him for several seconds straight. "What could I have possibly done to upset you *now*? Did you get concussed by a falling coconut? That's why one generally avoids dancing under palm trees."

I could tell him to buzz off since the umbrella's in my possession, but . . . he did bring it to me out of genuine concern for my well-being, freed me from the tree, *and* let me borrow his hat.

I plaster on a simpering smile that makes Not a Kidnapper do an alarmed double take. "Can you please help me, sir? My family is supposed to have dinner with the Rahmans tonight, but I'm late and don't know where to go." I bat my eyelashes.

His own eyes narrow with healthy, calculating skepticism, even as he mouths the word "*Sir?*" like it's sour on his tongue. He looks like he might be considering reporting me to security but ultimately concedes with a begrudging, "Right then, come along, *miss*. I'll make sure you make it there safely."

He starts walking ahead of me. I stand there for a second, fuming at that last jab at my expense, then hurry to match his long-legged strides so I can lift the umbrella over both of our heads. My shorter arms strain from the effort. Not a Kidnapper side-eyes me. He shakes his head like he can't quite believe he's in this predicament. For an instant I think a more authentic smile of amusement might be spreading across his lips—but by the time he takes the umbrella from me, the smile is gone, no more than a figment of my imagination.

We step through the ginormous double doors side by side.

CHAPTER FIVE

The grand foyer is empty. Other than a single employee who rushes to take the pretty leaf umbrella and dripping hat from my personal tour guide, we're all alone.

I inspect the massive space. Two spiraling staircases and countless winding hallways lead to an impossible number of rooms on either side of them, a chandelier glittering like a million Tiffany diamonds far above. Despite my guide's snark earlier, it's as if I've walked straight into a movie. One of those historical ones with breathtaking sets for Keira Knightley to run through in a fluttering gown—and of course I'm practically an out-of-place peasant girl after that storm.

"Is dinner already over or something?" I whisper behind a raised palm.

Not a Kidnapper snorts. "No, the dining room is farther in."

I start listening for quiet voices in the distance and slink after him in their direction, up one of the staircases and through several twisting hallways. I observe his back as we walk, noticing that his hair is still glossy from the deluge earlier. Unlike my hair, it rearranges itself artfully, but parts of his uniform are darker than others due to the wet patches.

I want to apologize again, but instead I skip to close the distance between us and peek up at his face. "Have you been working here long?"

"My whole life," he answers, lips twitching.

My brows pinch together, wondering how that could be possible. Maybe this is his way of getting me to shut up because the staff aren't supposed to fraternize with guests.

"That must mean you have all the hottest tea about the Rahmans, right?" I press.

"Hot . . . tea?" he deadpans, like he's closer to eighty than eighteen and has never been online in his life. "It's a tea garden. There's plenty of whatever kind of tea you like."

"No," I huff. "I mean, like, the juicy goss about the Rahmans." At his sharp look, I scramble to explain myself. "It's just—I don't know how much you've been told, but my sister's marrying into the family and moving into this big old house"—that is kind of scary, I don't admit aloud, in that way places this ancient usually are—"so I—I'm sort of worried about her. I want her to be happy, but all of this"—I indicate vaguely around me at the grandma-chic floral-print wallpaper that's probably been here since the 1800s, and the almost suffocatingly pleasant smell of the freshly cut flowers that bloom in every available crevice between paintings—"is a bit, um, much. Will she be okay?"

He continues to frown, but his eyes are pensive now.

For a moment, when he parts his lips, I think he's about to reveal something useful, a secret he'll entrust me with. I catch myself leaning closer to him, close enough to smell a hint of lemongrass and mint and something I can't identify that's as rich as chocolate or coffee, even as I hold my breath.

Then his eyes snap forward and he comes to a halt in front of another wooden door, sweeping an arm in its direction. His smile is all customer service. I know from a lifetime as the princess of Royal Fried Chicken.

"Well, this is where you're expected," he replies matter-of-factly. "If that's all?"

I nod. "That's all. Erm, thanks."

He gives me a brisk nod and holds the door open for me to enter, clearly not intending to follow.

Steeling myself with a deep inhale, I saunter through the door. The voices stop immediately. The long table taking up the whole center of the huge room seats at least twenty people. Sunny's aunties and uncles, my family, and Sunny's parents all stare back at me. I plaster on a smile, trying to distract them from the fact that my hair and overall appearance are giving off drowned rat vibes.

"Bibi!" Abbu announces, breaking the silence. "This is my younger daughter."

I recognize Sunny's father next to my brother-in-law-to-be, who smiles at me nervously, looking very unlike himself with his hair slicked back into a neat ponytail, wearing a brown fanjabi with gold embroidery. He looks like some prince plucked out of a storybook and dropped into the middle of war talks.

Which, fair.

I wouldn't want to be sitting between his father and mine either. The old man from earlier, Sunny's grandfather, doesn't deign to look up from the cake rusk biscuit he's diligently chewing on, but all other eyes are on me.

I bow my head as graciously as I can. "Assalamualaikum. Sorry I'm late."

There's a beat of awkward silence, until Sunny's father clears his throat and says, "Wa alaikum salam. Have a seat, young lady."

"Come sit beside me, Bibi," Abbu directs, patting the carved wooden arm of the otherwise plush empty chair next to him.

I hurry to comply and draw close just in time to hear the old man grumble, "What a discourteous girl."

For a second I'm so stunned by how open he is with his dislike that I freeze up. Then, even though I know my sister will be pleading with her eyes for me to keep my mouth shut if I bother to meet them, I peer into Sunny's grandfather's instead.

"Excuse me, sir?" I say, attempting to keep the fuming out of my voice. "I already apologized for being late. Is that not enough for you?"

Everyone is gawking at me again.

"You haven't done anything wrong," Sunny says quickly,

flinging a reproving glance at the miserly old man, who only scowls at my boldness.

What more does he want from me, anyway? A pound of flesh?

Abbu gives my knee a squeeze under the table, leaning close enough to explain, "Sunny's family is traditional when it comes to manners. Next time, if you're late, you don't need to interrupt a meal or conversation to salaam."

I'm suddenly reminded of playing that *Minesweeper* game in class anytime the Wi-Fi stopped working—the one where most of the clicks led to explosions. I never understood why anyone found it fun.

I bunch my fingers tightly into the material of my lehenga skirt. As I sneak peeks at the pained faces around me, I notice that no one seems eager to pick up where they left off before I got there. I can't help wondering if I've added fuel to what might already have been a brewing grease fire. The almost constipated expression on Sunny's face confirms my suspicions.

"Um, so American," I say to diffuse the situation, rapping my knuckles on my head and sticking out my tongue in an *Oops, my bad* gesture.

Sunny's father grimaces, clearly not disarmed by my adorably clumsy charm.

Jeez. Will every night with the Rahmans be so formal? Will my sister have to flutter around pleasing her uptight in-laws for the rest of her life? The thought alone makes me want to crawl out of my skin because I *know* I'm not cut out for all these rules, and I sure as hell don't want my meek sister to have to deal with them.

On the bright side, Sunny's family is probably thinking, *Alhamdulillah, at least it's not* that *one.*

My fingers drum on the table involuntarily. Thathu frowns at my fidgeting, but even she can't dampen my annoyance right now. I'm so preoccupied, I don't notice when someone else drops into the empty seat on my other side, until Sunny's father pipes up and says disapprovingly, "Sohel, you're late. You know how important tonight is."

"Sorry, Baba," answers a familiar voice, sounding wholly unapologetic. "I couldn't decide what to wear for such a special occasion."

"Sohel!" Sunny's mother scolds—the first time I've heard her speak tonight.

My head jerks up to find my guide from earlier. "H-hey!" My finger shoots out to point at him.

This elicits appalled whispers from Sunny's aunts, but my seat neighbor merely gives me a polite, bemused look with a quirk of his head. "Hello?"

A sting of indignation pricks me at the realization that he's pretending he doesn't know me. He has the gall to look somehow hotter in the crisp white button-up shirt he's wearing now, his inky hair lustrous like he just showered. His shirt is very casual compared to everyone else, not helped by the fact that he has his sleeves rolled up and a couple of buttons undone at the collar. I do my best not to sneak peeks at the sharp hollow of his throat. Sunny's mom—*his* mom—is doing enough glaring at him for the both of us.

"Now isn't the time for your smart mouth, Sohel," she reprimands.

My cheeks turn beet red when it sinks in that I was asking him to spill the tea about his own *family*. "You've worked here your whole life, huh," I say in a hissed whisper.

There's something almost taunting about the twitch of his lips. "You could say that."

"You did. You did say that." My eyes narrow, but then the staff begins to enter the room holding plates of food—I suppose because they were waiting for me and Sohel to arrive. When the scent of rich spices hits my nose, my stomach grumbles.

The assortment of dishes is carefully placed from head to toe of the table, every single kind of main course you could imagine: sliced ilish maas arranged to resemble a whole fish, swimming in a thick golden broth with green chilies. Chunks of bhuna beef and chicken. Plump shrimp with green beans and potatoes. Even cooked jackfruit seed curry, three varieties of greens for shaag, and multiple bowls of dahl using different lentils for anyone on a vegetarian diet.

The table immediately comes to life as everyone starts chatting and passing around the plates. I grin and pile mine high with everything in reach, delighted that good food can even bring people together in a situation like this. Maybe if they're just hangry, they won't be so bad when their bellies are full.

The smile fades when I catch Sohel observing me out of

the corner of my eye, his cheek cupped in one raised palm and his eyebrows arched.

"Um, is there something you want me to pass you?" I ask, doing my best to remain civil.

"The kitchen staff worked very hard on this," he says, low enough that no one else hears him over the din.

"O . . . kay?" I reply, trying not to squint at him like he's some sort of inexplicable science experiment. "It looks great? My compliments to the chef."

"You haven't tried it yet," he answers in a way that almost seems like friendly ribbing.

Almost.

He keeps eyeing me with his eyebrows rising higher and higher until, out of spite, I tear off a giant wad of ruti, use it to wrap up a particularly large piece of chicken and curry, then shove it into my mouth.

Thathu kicks my ankle under the table none-too-gently, almost making me choke on the defiantly huge, spicy bite I took.

"Allahumma barik lana—"

I go ramrod straight in my chair, not daring to breathe, much less chew, as I realize everyone else has gone quiet in deference to Sunny's grandfather, who is loudly praying over the food. They all have their hands lifted up to their faces and are repeating it more quietly.

Shi—dam— Oh, heck! I might get struck by lightning if I so much as mentally curse while the rest of the room is prostrating themselves in devotion. It's not like I didn't know better. Ammu is always clucking at me for forgetting to pray before I eat.

Sneakily, *oh so sneakily*, I shift my own hands away from my plate and lift them up in front of my face, positioned perfectly so that no one can see how my cheeks are currently puffed out like a panicking chipmunk's. No one except for Sohel.

I wonder if I can pray to have him choke tonight.

Thankfully, everyone else is intent on Sunny and Halima. From the far end of the table, one of his aunts says, "Halima, I hope you know how lucky you are to win our Shariq's heart. He's the precious eldest son of our only brother. Why, when our nephew was born, our father had a solid gold spoon imported from Dubai for him to use at his rice-eating ceremony."

"I'm very lucky," Halima agrees, even though her round eyes and too-wide smile speak to her internal hysteria. "Sunny—er, Shariq is wonderful."

Next to me, Sohel muffles a snort behind his glass, and I have to resist the urge to raise an eyebrow at Sunny too. He has the decency to grimace. "No, I'm the lucky one, Alhamdulillah. Halima is so patient with me. She is a precious blessing in my life."

"Our daughter is equally precious to us," Ammu adds in her evenly toned way where you have no idea whether she wants to invite you to tea or pour a whole steaming pot over your head. Abbu barely manages to restrain himself to a nod beside her.

Sunny's mother pauses midbite before clearing her throat and turning to her son. "Tell your fufus your plans now that you've graduated, Baba."

"Other than marrying the most beautiful woman in the world," Sunny starts with a lovesick smile, "I don't know yet. I'm excited to be back here. It's been too long."

"Sure has," Sohel agrees with that acerbic undercurrent again.

It flies right over Sunny's head because his responding grin is blindingly bright. "Aw, Sohu, I missed you, too, little man."

"Hardly so little anymore," one of Sohel's aunts says, beaming with pride.

Sunny's father raises a hand that silences everyone else. "Shariq, it's time you grew more serious. You're set to inherit the estate any day. Now that you and your wife have graduated, there's no reason to delay."

"I guess you're right, Baba," Sunny relents, rubbing the back of his neck. "That was always the plan, and"—he smiles over at Sohel, who tenses up—"that will probably be a load off your back, right, bro? Amma is always worrying that you're not focusing enough on school because you're too busy here."

Beside me, Sohel's grip tightens around the rim of his plate, but his voice remains level when he replies, "Sure thing. Bro."

"Sohel should go into medicine or law," suggests one of his aunts.

"A respectable field for a second son," another concurs.

A third adds, "Engineering is lucrative too. That's what my Shahriar is studying."

"Why not accounting?" a fourth chimes in. "That way he can be useful to his brother one day." Her remark sends a ripple of endorsement through the table. "You should have kept him enrolled at Eton, Atiya. Sohel is so bright that even the best Bangladeshi schools can't challenge him. Is it any wonder he's bored? A university like Princeton would be good for him."

"I'm staying in Bangladesh," Sohel spits out before his mother can defend herself. "I've already been accepted to the University of Dhaka. That's as far as I'll go."

Sunny coughs up a strained laugh while their aunties gasp in tandem. "Sohu can do whatever he likes. I don't need him to choose a degree for my sake." Sohel frowns down at his barely touched meal like it contains the secrets of the universe, ignoring his brother's olive branch.

I find myself unable to tear my gaze away from the back-and-forth. The Rahmans act more like actors hired to play a family in some melodramatic reality show than an actual family. Maybe that's why I can't help noticing that my sister has also gone rigid, her eyes glazed and a small frown contorting her painted lips. She mentioned on the plane that she and Sunny had the "inheriting the tea estate" talk already, but will she actually let running an empire thousands of miles away trample over her lifelong dream?

"Bibi, is it?" Sunny's mother says without warning.

My head snaps up. "Yes, Auntie?"

She smiles tightly. "You must be around my Sohel's age. Your sister's pedigree is quite impressive so surely your plans are too. Will you study at Princeton as well, or perhaps a university closer to home? There are several adequate schools in New York."

"I don't know," I admit, twisting the napkin in my lap. "Halima got all the genius genes in the family. I prefer mine designer." When the joke flies right over her head, I begin to babble, "B-but I might take a gap year to travel or try to grow my makeup channel or—"

My sister motions desperately for me to zip my lips as the people around us grow more and more visibly horrified.

"No university at all?" Sunny's mother parrots, dismayed by the concept.

"Well, not right away—"

"These days no boy from a good family will settle for an uneducated girl," an auntie interrupts, looking meaningfully between her sister-in-law and me. "How can she raise intelligent children if she's a rube?"

A rube? What kind of insult is that? My hackles rise, but I keep my tone light. "It's just, after spending practically my entire life in school, is a break such a crime?"

The dour expressions directed at me answer plainly: *Yes.*

"Do you know what a privilege it is that you even have these opportunities?" Sohel demands in their stead.

"W-well, duh, but—"

"Duh?" he repeats, never taking his fiery gaze off me. "Plenty of people can't afford schooling in Bangladesh and around the world, but you can and don't want to go? It was only under my father's management that the tea garden even built a school for the laborers here. The majority of people in this country would give anything to have the privileges you have."

How do I even respond to that? I know I'm lucky to grow up in America. It's not like Ammu and Abbu haven't said the same thing a million times in their lectures whenever I've brought home a less than perfect report card. Then again, who is *he* to call me privileged from his thousand-acre estate?

"Talk about pot-kettle, tea boy," I hurl back. "Get a grip."

"What?" His brows shoot up, his lips flapping like a fish in shock.

This sends a tidal wave of dissent through the table as Sohel's aunts leap to their nephew's defense, while his parents and the old man watch me with muted disapproval like *I'm* the one who decided to cause a scene.

Sohel, on the other hand, looks gobsmacked, his jaw working but no words coming out. I decide I like him better when he's stunned silent, even as he sputters, "You, you—"

"Me what?"

Abbu swoops in before he can find his words. "Step off the high horse before you injure yourself, young man. If my daughter needs a little extra time, she certainly has it. She has another year left of school, and I'm fortunate enough not to need her to work, Alhamdulillah. It may be a privilege, but it's a privilege I worked to give her."

I stare at him, suspecting that the conversation would go very differently if I told him my plans for after graduation back in New Jersey. But it's nice to know, even if I would have hypothetically gotten an earful then, that he has my back now, despite all our bickering.

Halima, on the other hand, is as white as a sheet. Her eyes are flickering to her soon-to-be in-laws with alarm. Uh-oh. I guess it's time to do some damage control. . . .

"Look," I say to the room. "I'm not saying I won't *ever* go to college. It's just that I'd like to see a bit more of the world before I handcuff myself to my laptop for another four years. I've been looking at some schools in New York like the Fashion Institute because I'm thinking about studying design."

I'm really hoping some semblance of a future plan helps get the aunties and Sohel off my back. Pasting on a winsome smile for the latter, I punctuate my speech with a thumbs-up. Sohel's face becomes a red so garish, my Nº1 de Chanel blush would pale in comparison.

His mom audibly gasps.

"She didn't mean—" Ammu starts to say.

"She doesn't know—" Abbu begins at the same time.

Next to me, Thathu is cackling under her breath.

"Bibi, that's Bangladesh's version of a middle finger," Sunny explains from between his hands, sounding like he's speaking through gasps—stifling laughter or tears, I can't tell.

Oh, crap. . . .

I've really made a mess of things now.

CHAPTER SIX

Halima is pissed at me.

At me! As if I didn't spend the entire evening doing damage control with the most miserable family in Bangladesh.

The short drive back to the guesthouse feels a thousand hours too long since my sister keeps staring broodily out the window. Even the kind smile the driver gives me isn't enough to make me feel better. As Halima trudges toward her room, I reach out to grab her by the sleeve.

"Afu, I'm . . ." I catch my lower lip between my teeth. "I'm sorry. I didn't mean to set that Sohel guy off, but you don't know what he—"

"Bibi." The fury burning in her eyes stops me in my tracks. "Ya Allah! Do you have to be so *Bibi* all the time?" Her chin begins to tremble, and her next statement is softer. Somehow it's even more of a stab to my heart. "Maybe our families are too different after all. Maybe we're just too loud. Too American."

"What? Th-that's not true!" I exclaim, finally finding my voice. "They were plenty loud!"

"You're blaming *us*, Halima?" Abbu explodes.

Wincing at his unironic volume, I snap my jaw shut with a click of my teeth. Perhaps we're proving Halima's point, since the staff are now none-too-discreetly watching us argue in the middle of the hallway, whispering behind their hands.

Abbu doesn't read the room. "They spent that entire dinner looking down their noses at us. Were we meant to keep our traps shut in response?"

"I never asked for that," Halima replies at a much more reasonable decibel, her voice wobbling. "I just don't want to do anything to make them hate me, that's all. Is it too much to ask that no one goes out of their way to offend my future in-laws?"

"How could your sister possibly know—" Ammu steps in and holds up her hands to stop them both.

"Forget it," Abbu continues. "I'm going to bed! Hopefully my snores won't disrupt the Rahmans' esteemed ears!"

The next morning I'm woken up by a hair-raising "COCK-A-DOODLE-DOO!"

I slept so fitfully the night before, unable to get Halima's disappointed face out of my head, that I burrow deeper into my duvet with a groan.

Please be a dream. Hell, I'll even settle for a nightmare!

Then there's a loud rapping on the door and my father's bellowing voice joins the *bawk, bawk, bawk*ing. "Bibi, I'm coming in!"

"Abbuuuuuuuu," I whine, glaring blearily between his still

hazy form and the antique alarm clock on my nightstand. "It's, like, the crack of dawn. What do you want?"

"It's time for work," he answers. "Get dressed."

"Work?" I parrot, wondering if my sleep-addled brain heard him right.

I'm still not quite sure this *isn't* a figment of my imagination, because the beady black eyes of a literal rooster are level with mine. When I lift a finger to poke its beak, it snaps at me, beginning to struggle in my father's grasp.

"BAWK-A-BAWK-BAWK-BAWK!"

"Holy crap!" I exclaim, wide-awake now and pressed against my headboard with my arm clutched to my chest. "Where the hell did you get that? Do the Rahmans know it's here?"

I'm sure the whole house can hear its mutinous squalling.

Abbu is unruffled, even with the furiously crowing and flapping rooster between his large palms. I eye the bird as he sets it down on the ground and gives it a pat on its tail feathers to send it speeding off through my open door. My ears keep ringing long after it's gone.

"When I was growing up, that used to be my alarm," he declares, ignoring my question altogether. "I thought it might be nice if it woke you up for work too."

I scowl, not sure he knows the meaning of the word "nice." If *that* dragged me out of my slumber every morning, I might make it my mission in life to fry up its family too.

But wait.

"What do you mean, 'work'?" I ask slowly, a sinking feeling in my stomach.

He crosses his now empty arms over yet another button-up. "You didn't think your grounding was over simply because we came to Bangladesh, did you?"

"Um, yes?" I respond. "How can I work at Royal Fried Chicken if there *is* no Royal Fried Chicken in Bangladesh?"

Unless . . . *Has* he expanded all the way out here?

"Oh, you won't be working at Royal," he says.

I follow his gaze toward the giant arched window in my bedroom. Through the panes an endless field of green unfurls. *Oh no.*

"You can't be serious." Horror pitches my voice into a shrill squeak. "The tea garden?"

"The tea garden," he confirms with a glint in his eyes that is nothing short of evil. "I spoke to the Rahmans, and they agreed that you could use a lesson about the value of hard work."

"Well, of course *they* did," I mutter. "Who says no to getting free labor?"

Abbu barrels right past my complaint. "If you remember, your grounding was for the entire summer. You'll learn the ropes at the tea garden while you're here, and we'll reevaluate at the end of the summer."

"B-but—" I sputter. "That wasn't my— That Sohel guy and his family are—"

He stops me with a raised palm. "No *but*s. Even after all your eye rolling and grumbling at RFC, I was hoping you learned something after prom night, when you nearly gave your mother and me a heart attack with your vanishing act. You knew how important yesterday's dinner was to your sister, and you still made it the Bibi Show."

"I didn't mean . . . The Rahmans were the ones who started it!" The excuses sound half-hearted and pathetic even to my own ears.

Abbu shakes his head, and his disappointment is somehow worse than any of the times he got mad at me. "You came late and picked a fight with Sunny's brother. That tells me you've learned nothing. This will be good for you."

I can only pout down at my hands, willing my bottom lip not to wobble. I thought after he stood up for me last night, we would be in a better place, but I can never do *anything* right in his eyes. It's been a long time since I was his little nugget, a chip off the old block. These days I'm more like a bone stuck in his throat. Arguing about the tea garden won't change his mind if he and Ammu have already decided I'll finish out my grounding here.

As if summoned by my thoughts, my mother swoops through the door and comes to stand beside Abbu, holding a thick tome in her arms—probably an employee handbook for the tea garden. "Bibi, you're not up yet? Your sister and Sunny Bhaiya are already waiting for you."

Oh, great. . . . So there will be witnesses to my disgrace.

"Haven't you told her the good news?" she asks Abbu when I make an unintelligible sound.

Abbu grimaces.

I shoot her a look of betrayal. "*Good news?* Ammu, you have to tell him I can't work here!" I hold up my perfectly manicured nails. "I—I just got these done again for the wedding. I can't get dirt under them!"

So much could go wrong! I could get twigs—or bugs—in my hair! A snake might bite me! A tiger might eat me! Isn't this exactly the sort of place where tiger attacks happen? They'd regret making me work at the tea garden then—probably—but I'd already be a cute little canapé for some wild beast, so what would the guilt trip matter?

Ammu must see the imminent freak-out in my eyes because she plops down next to me on the bed and runs a hand through my sleep-rumpled but pest-free hair. "Oh, Bibi, calm down. It won't be so bad. Your sister and Sunny Bhaiya will be there too."

"As if that's any better," I reply. "Halima Afu *hates* me now."

"She does not." Ammu tries to sound consoling, though she can't repress the hint of laughter in her voice. She sets the giant book between us. Technically, it's a binder, but it's so thick, I can't help thinking of it as a book. "Besides, there *is* good news. Your father and I came to an agreement."

"What kind of agreement?" I ask, eyes darting between the two of them and the quasi-book.

Abbu clears his throat, before gruffly explaining, "After careful consideration, we've decided we will let you go on some dates this summer."

"W-what?" My eyes become saucers. "You will?!"

"*Supervised* dates with a few of the boys from your thathu's biodata book," he clarifies, because of course he can't let me soar too high before popping my bubble. "Sunny has recommended a handful of young men from his family's circle as well. Don't even think of looking at anyone not in this book, bucho ni?"

Although I'd be willing to bet that the cardinal sin of being hot meant an immediate veto from my father, I never in a million years thought they would ever let me meet a boy, much less so many, chaperoned or not!

"Just to give you something to do," Ammu adds, even as Abbu interjects, "And to keep you out of trouble until the wedding is done."

Under his breath, I catch him muttering, "It's not like banning boys permanently has had the effect we hoped."

"It will be fun!" my mother chirps. "But if you want to prove to us that you're grown-up enough for it, you'll have to take your time at the tea garden seriously—starting now. Get dressed for your orientation."

I'm so stunned that I can't even muster up a protest when she manhandles me out of bed and gives me a light push toward my bathroom.

Huh.

How does a tea garden—er, farmer even dress?

CHAPTER SEVEN

Forty-five minutes later I'm finally ready for my hot-
farm-girl summer.

I settled on a pair of Miu Miu overalls, a white cotton tee from Lilysilk, and brown Jimmy Choo boots—farmer chic, *non?*—finishing off the look by tying my hair up into pigtails to keep it out of the way of any errant branches.

I wish I could FaceTime Nayelli and model for her, or flip through the Great Big Book of Biodatas together to decide who to swipe right on. But even if I somehow succeeded in stealing my phone back from my parents, it's probably impossible to get a bar of service on the tea estate. Every room comes equipped with a retro rotary phone that must have been among the first models out of Alexander Graham Bell's laboratory a bazillion years ago, and the TVs still operate with antennas. Some people would love the quaint allure of this place, but I wish the Rahmans would join the rest of us in the twenty-first century.

Another knock at the door forces me to abandon my antiquated but at least air-conditioned haven. When I open it,

Halima is standing outside in a simple but comfortable shalwar kameez. She immediately shoves a cup of lukewarm tea and a piece of toast—sweeter than the American kind—slathered with orange marmalade into my hands. It's freshly made and admittedly delicious, but her sour expression dims my mood.

"How much longer will you take?" she asks, crossing her arms over her chest.

I want to apologize for last night, but what comes out instead is a pithy "Perfection takes time, you know?" punctuated with a flip of one of my pigtails.

Normally my sister is reluctantly charmed by my antics, but her frown only deepens. "Are you going to take this seriously, Bibi? Because if not, I can tell Ammu and Abbu—"

"Okay, okay!" I turn back to my room to finish up. "Sheesh, you were always such a tattletale."

She glares but gives me another minute to shove the toast into my face and wash it down with the tea. I leave the cup behind on a table in my room and follow her down to the courtyard in front of the main mansion.

Sunny waves to us from the fountain at the heart of the plaza. I watch in bemusement as Halima goes to join him, sitting on the stone lip and dropping her hand into the basin. They smile at each other but don't strike up a conversation.

"Who are we waiting for?" I ask. "Mr. Rahman?"

"You can call me that if you'd like," a familiar, snidely posh voice chimes in.

I wheel around to find Sohel coming up the path—or, at

least, I think it's him. He's in a white full-body jumpsuit with a giant woven veiled hat, looking like an astronaut who crash-landed on Earth. "What the hell are you wearing?"

"You're one to talk." Sohel stares me down. Even with his features barely visible through the veil, I can tell he's skeptical of my carefully curated outfit.

"I'm the only one dressed appropriately," I insist, doing a little twirl.

"Do you make it a habit to make fun of people's fashion choices in their own homes?" he asks instead of disputing me. "You didn't get enough of insulting me last night?"

"God, are you *always* this dramatic?" I grumble.

"No." A smirk slowly begins to unfurl across his face. "But I don't think I'd want to piss off your new boss on your very first day."

"My new *what*?" I ask, jaw dropping.

Sohel sets his gloved hands on his hips. "Who do you think will be reporting back to your father about whether or not you've done well enough to go on your cute little dates? You're lucky I decided to take time out of my busy summer to do you a favor."

There's a vindictive twinkle in his eyes that renders me speechless. My mouth opens and closes at least three times before Sunny stands to meet us. "Thanks for doing this, Sohu."

Immediately it's as if someone has doused the light in Sohel's eyes. He frowns down at the ground as he plucks off the hat and gloves with more viciousness than strictly necessary and tosses them next to the fountain. "Don't patronize me. I'm not in the mood."

"I wasn't!" Sunny says, holding up his hands and looking genuinely baffled.

Halima clears her throat before Sohel can decide on his biting comeback. She gives him a saintly beam that would brighten up even a haunted house. "*Actually*, your brother was telling me you're the foremost expert when it comes to the garden and its history, Sohel. I look forward to learning from you and getting to know each other better!"

Sohel's eyes widen. Clearly caught off guard, he glances away and answers brusquely, "Well, I guess I can't deny that. Sunny Bhai has never cared much about this place."

Sunny reaches to ruffle his hair. "That's what I have you for, right? Ouch—" He gives up when his hand is smacked away.

Halima links arms with me as we tread carefully behind the brothers down a trimmed path into the gardens. I let her do it, stamping down my surprise. I may be a city girl, but my sister is a homebody through and through, perhaps even more afraid of nature than I am. I guess the prospect of planting face-first into the ground in front of her fiancé beats out being close to me—or maybe she doesn't want to be as obvious about her aggravation with me as Sohel is with Sunny. Either way, it's hard to picture her living in this place.

As we trek through the dense terraces of tea plants, I start to get a little lightheaded from the steep climb and the inkling of rain in the air. It dews on tea leaves and soaks into the earth. I almost wish it would rain again, because the only shelters from the blazing hot sun are the tall, thin trees that reach high above our heads and the occasional wooden pavilions. Then again, the ground would become even more difficult to walk on in that case.

"Rubber and agarwood trees," Sohel lectures, navigating through the slick earth with a nimbleness that makes me envious. "We also have orange, lemon, mango, banana, palm, and lime groves"—he points out the brightly colored fruits in the distance, then gestures even farther away—"as well as pineapple thickets separating the property from the nature preserve nearby. The prickly bushes and brambles are a natural deterrent to keep wild animals from wandering out of the forest and damaging the crops or hurting anyone."

"What kind of wild animals?" I ask, creeping closer to my sister.

"Elephants," Sohel says. "Monkeys."

"Oh . . . well, that's not so bad," Halima replies.

I nod weakly. "Those are cute, right?"

Except he's far from done. I almost whimper when he starts counting down on his long fingers. "Snakes, bears, birds of prey, foxes . . . tigers."

"Tigers?" I exclaim, loud enough that some of the employees glance toward us in concern.

"It's called a *Bengal* tiger for a reason," he answers snarkily. "They're endangered, so we do our part to keep them safe."

"What about *me*?" I don't bother holding back a distressed whine anymore. "Am I about to become an endangered species too?"

A wicked smile splits his lips as he says in an incongruously light tone, "Not if you can follow directions. I have a feeling that doesn't come easy for you."

"Sohel, don't scare them," Sunny intervenes with an uneasy chuckle. "Bibi, it's perfectly safe, so long as you don't wander too close to the perimeter. We have security to protect our staff, guests, and the animals around the clock."

Sohel snorts but doesn't deny this as he climbs even higher. Men stand with buckets beneath the spigots sticking out from tree trunks, collecting syrupy goo, while others are tasked with scraping off resin. Women tend to tea leaves, snipping them off with tiny scissors and dropping them into woven baskets it must take hours to fill. Transport vehicles arrive every hour to retrieve collected materials and take them to a refinery.

Even with so many people around, I get the impression that it would be easy to get lost here if the Rahman boys didn't stay within sight. I'm glad I opted for boots this time instead of heels, but the walk already has me huffing and puffing. My Jimmy Choos are caked with mud, the stylish tears in my overalls looking more *disastrous* than distressed after a run-in with a particularly pointy branch. My sister isn't faring much better but shushes me when I whisper a complaint, in spite of the fact that she's weighed down by a bag full of Bengali snacks and water bottles, the handle of an umbrella peeking out of it.

I'm halfway tempted to beg her to open it up over our heads to shield us from the scorching sun, when Sohel continues, "This land has been in my family since before the British introduced tea to it," spreading his arms open in front of him without a single bead of sweat on his brow from the trek up this latest hill.

"Oh?" Halima replies, hanging on to his every word like the big nerd she is, despite the debilitating heat. "That's fascinating. Were they farming before the East India Company made its way to Bangladesh?"

The avidness in her voice perks Sohel up, too, because he begins regaling us with a lively history lesson about how the plantation came to be, gesticulating all the while. "The East India Company repossessed—or, to be more frank, stole—this land from my great-great-great-grandfather, a zamindar, in the seventeenth century when the British discovered they could breed Chinese tea with the Assamese leaves on the hill tracts of the Sylhet–Assam border. Before that my ancestors were using the land for rice paddies."

"It's hard to believe. It feels like tea has always been a part of our culture," Halima says, shaking her head. "But it really only goes back a few hundred years."

"Indeed," Sohel answers, crossing his arms as he contemplates her words. "They razed many of our indigenous plants to begin tea production. Before that, under the

Mughals, coffee was actually the drink of choice throughout the subcontinent."

"I've never thought tea could have so much history," I confess.

The smile he flashes me seems like a genuine one. "It does. This place means so much to me, but it has a complicated colonial history tied to it. After local rebellions left them without cheap labor, the British brought in coolies from other parts of India, usually tribal laborers, often by force, whose descendants still live and work here to this day."

"I hate how unfair the world is," Halima says, "and how much something like the coincidence of someone's birth, where they're born, who their parents are, decides their fate before they even understand it."

An expression of discomfort pinches Sunny's face, and I realize he hasn't spoken a word since the orientation started. Maybe he just doesn't want to step on his brother's toes again.

Sohel nods. "I couldn't agree more. The people of the tribes lost their language, their culture, their rights—I have an obligation to keep fighting for better for them, better for this land that's become their home. It seems like the least I can do since I have the good fortune of being my father's son." He shoots his older brother a meaningful look. "Don't you think so?"

"Uh, o-of course I do," Sunny replies, rubbing the back of his neck. "Things have already been much better under Baba. I hope I can keep that going."

Sohel doesn't seem pleased by that answer, but before the brewing tension between the brothers can boil over like the tea in their veins, I pipe up, "Wow, my dad would die of joy if I cared about our family business half as much as you do."

"Oh?" Sohel lists his head to one side. "The chicken shop, right?"

"National fried-chicken chain, actually," I respond with a blasé shrug, buffing my nails on my overalls. "It's kind of a big deal."

"Is it?" he muses, as his eyes drag down my frame again. "Have you ever helped out? No offense, but I can't picture you breaking a nail, much less working at a takeaway."

"Why, thank you, Astronaut Boy," I quip with a winning smile, not bothering to correct him. "I'll take that as a compliment." That startles a laugh out of Sunny, which he's quick to turn into a cough.

"Astronaut?" Confusion scrunches Sohel's face. "Do you mean—It's a beekeeper's hat, bedisha."

"*That's* what it is?" I gasp and whip my head around in search of the bees in question, my skin crawling. There are already mosquito bites blooming up and down my arms and the beginnings of a sunburn on the back of my neck, in spite of all the sunscreen and bug spray I dabbed on before leaving. "Of course you'd be obsessed with bugs."

"I am not!" He glares daggers at me. "Bees help pollinate the crops, produce honey that can be sold in the gift shop, and increase repopulation efforts for endangered colonies—you

77

know what, I don't know why I'm bothering to explain this to you when you don't know the first thing about tea, Miss America."

I lift my chin, hands on my hips. "Well, that's not a very clever insult because Miss America is pretty. You're zero for two now."

He rolls his eyes. "Let's keep it moving, then, beauty queen."

THE GREAT BIG BOOK OF BIODATAS

 **Akash Mamun**
(WOW he's gorgeous)

DOB: 10-4-2005
(and our horoscopes are totally compatible!!!)

Address: Gulshan, Dhaka, Bangladesh

Height: 6'0"
(okaaaaay 🙄🙄)

Education: Eton College
(we're both private school kids!)

Career: Bowler, Bangladesh National Cricket Team
(that's kinda like baseball, isn't it?)

Father: Raju Mamun, Chairman of Mamun Petrol, Ltd.

Mother: Dolly Mamun, daughter of Osman Chowdhury,
Chairman of Chapati Foods, Inc.

(please, please, please do not be a catfish)

CHAPTER EIGHT

The following morning I officially start at the tea estate.

Thankfully, it's not my father or his demonic rooster that wakes me up, but another familiar face: the teenage girl who's been helping me in the mornings since I got here.

All I've been able to weasel out of her in that time is her name: Ireima.

My attempts to convince her she doesn't need to warm up my bathwater have only led to her pretending she doesn't understand English so she can keep doing it. I almost respect her stubbornness, to be honest.

Instead I've made a game out of trying to decipher what she thinks about my outfit choices from her reactions alone. If I ask directly, she claims everything is "very nice, miss," but even if Ireima didn't have such big, expressive doe eyes, she has a few other tells: her tendency to chew on her bottom lip, play with the tail of her braid, and crinkle her nose.

Today she carries a folded uniform in her arms.

"Ugh, a *uniform*?" I glance between it and her shifty eyes when a thought abruptly occurs to me. She nearly jumps out of her skin when I reach out to grab her shoulders, a Cheshire cat grin spreading across my face. "Does this mean we're working together, Ireima?"

"S-sorry, miss," she says, wincing.

"If we're going to be co-workers, you *can't* call me 'miss' anymore. We're officially friends now," I declare, then frown at her, hands moving to my hips. "I'm not your boss. If anything, you've got seniority."

"Oh." Her eyes go round.

"You *have* to call me Bibi, okay?"

She swallows but ultimately relents. "Okay . . . Bibi . . . Afa."

I sigh. I guess being called "big sis" is better than the alternative. She hands the emerald-green polo to me. I hold it aloft, letting the sunlight streaming through my giant window glint across the gold leaf pattern on the pocket and the elaborate buttons.

"Back in a snap," I tell her. "You don't have to help!"

Halima is already there when we make it to the courtyard, chatting among a gaggle of other uniformed staff members. She perks up and waves when she sees me. "Bibi, come meet the rest of our group!"

I flash her a strained smile, hyperaware of the sweat-stache beading on my upper lip. Even though I lathered on more bug

81

spray and SPF 70, the brisk walk over to the fountain already has me feeling like I'll melt into a puddle before my shift even starts. For some reason this only attracts more mosquitoes, as if I'm their personal Bella Swan. Ireima keeps casting sidelong glances at me as I use one hand to fan my reddening face and the other to swat at the cloud of bugs buzzing around my head.

"Hi, everyone. I'm Bibi," I muster.

A chorus of hellos and salaams greets me.

"This is Khoibi."

My sister indicates a girl older than me with a mane of curly hair tamed into a messy ponytail and a freer smile than bashful Ireima's. I nod and wave as Halima goes through the rest of the introductions, internally musing that most of the names are pretty uncommon.

Other than Jui and Parek from Abbu's village below the cliff, there's a guy a few years older than me named Taamba, a bubbly teenage girl named Yumjao who is Ireima's younger sister, and a girl about Halima's age called Nganu whose five-year-old daughter clings to her leg.

All in all, nine of us. A few key faces are missing, though.

"Where's Sunny?" I ask my sister.

She frowns down at her phone. "He hasn't replied to my messages yet, but I'm sure he and Sohel will be here soon."

As if summoned by his name, the younger Rahman brother lopes up the pathway, one hand in his pocket, the other raised in a curt wave. "Right. Sorry I'm late."

Taamba moves to fling an arm around him straightaway.

I'm surprised when Sohel doesn't bristle like a wet cat the way he does with his own brother. There's even a hint of a smile on his face as he and Taamba exchange words in Bengali too fast for me to translate. Yumjao giggles and whispers something to Ireima, who blushes and quickly shushes her.

Oh?

"That's weird, right?" I ask Ireima. "Him being all smiley?"

She only blinks, which gives my suspicions credibility. Sohel doesn't seem like the smiley type. He must be plotting something.

"Um, Sohel." Halima's tentative voice draws my attention back to her. "Where's your brother?"

The smile slips off Sohel's lips as his eyes sweep from her apprehensive face to the nervous way she plays with the tassels at the end of her urna. "He didn't tell you? He and Baba went down to Dhaka for business. They probably won't be back until late tonight."

"Oh, I see. . . ." She can't seem to meet his gaze.

Sohel combs his fingers through his hair, a furrow creasing his forehead. "My father probably sprung it on him last minute."

People pleaser that she is, my sister waves both hands in the air. "N-no, it's fine! It's better that he learns everything he needs to know."

"I suppose," Sohel concedes, but he doesn't sound like he agrees.

Khoibi must sense the tension, because she catches Halima's hand in hers and gently pats her knuckles. "You will be fine. We will show you everything, won't we?"

A flurry of agreement ripples through the small group.

My sister fishes out a brighter smile. "Thank you. Should we get going, then?"

The question startles Sohel out of some moody reverie. He nods and clears his throat, retrieving a small notepad from his pocket. "Right. Shall we start with the fields?"

I soon learn that a thousand-acre estate needs *a lot* of upkeep.

I can't quash my sigh of relief when Sohel says, "I won't make you pick the tea leaves *this time*"—the emphasis kills me—"but we need someone to go around collecting the baskets and bringing them to the factory for refinement."

"I can do that," Taamba volunteers. "Spent plenty of time in those fields."

"Bhai, ami shaad deetham ni?" Nganu offers.

Sohel shakes his head and points his pen at Parek instead. "The baskets can get pretty heavy. Can you operate a CNG?" At Parek's nod, he checks something off. "All right, you and Taamba take care of that, then."

"Aye aye, sir," Taamba replies. Sohel rolls his eyes.

Nganu stares after the two boys as they wander off into the green, then asks in broken English, "I do . . . what, bhai?"

I catch a glimpse of Sohel's warm, disarming smile before his back is to me. Nganu's shoulders relax.

Next to me, Yumjao whispers, "Poor Nganu Afu. When she received a proposal, her parents took her out of school to marry. That's why her English is not so good. This is her first time doing anything but picking tea."

Finally someone who jumps right to workplace gossip! Ireima gives her a subtle shake of the head, frowning, but her younger sister takes no notice. I watch as Sohel kneels in front of Nganu's daughter and sets a hand on her head, conspiratorially stage-whispering something about the kitchen staff and sweets that makes her flash a gap-toothed grin.

"Sohel Bhaiya wants us all to learn more of the easy hospitality work instead of the farming," Yumjao continues. "There are better opportunities, but you need to have English and education." She hooks our arms together and gazes at me with bright, hopeful eyes. "Can I practice English with you, Afu?"

"You need to *know* English," I correct gently.

"Know English," Yumjao repeats with a smile.

"Yumjao, enough." Ireima's eyes narrow at her sister. "She's also a guest."

I shake my head with a snort. "Yeesh, you two are just like me and Halima. Ireima, I seriously don't mind. You two can come chill with me after work anytime, okay? This place is waaaaay too boring otherwise."

"Anytime?" Ireima parrots, sounding aghast.

Yumjao, on the other hand, radiates delight. "Chill? What is 'chill'?"

"It means 'hang out,'" explains Jui, who's been eavesdropping. "Like, spending time with friends. I watch a lot of American TV. Can I come too?"

Before I can nod, Halima shushes us.

Just for that, she's totally not invited to my slumber party.

Sohel returns to the fountain, notepad and serious expression back in place. Nganu and her daughter disappear in the direction of the main house. He doesn't look at them as he examines his list.

"Now for the guesthouse—"

I raise my hand up high and wave it in the air. "Me! Me! I volunteer as tribute!" At his dubiously arched brow, I try to look as earnest as possible. "I will pass out clean towels and do laundry or whatever other task you need of me, O Fearless Leader."

Anything to get out of this wretched heat and back into the AC.

He scoffs at my sucking-up but doesn't object. "Fine, just for today. Ireima, can you and Yumjao keep an eye on her?"

Ireima bobs her head in agreement so fast, my own neck almost gets whiplash in her place, while her sister jumps up and down clapping. I nudge the older of the two with my elbow and whisper, "What'd I tell you? Seniority."

I *think* this gets a smile out of her, but Sohel is already moving along, and Ireima's eyes glue right back onto him. Hmm, if I didn't know better, I'd think Ireima had a crush on our tetchy boss. She hangs on his every word like it's gospel as he explains, "Since the teahouse is closed for the time being, we only need a few extra hands at outdoor guest facilities like the pool."

"How's that sound, Miss Halima?" Khoibi, who's been sitting next to my sister on the lip of the fountain, asks her.

Halima considers this momentarily. Her face is as flushed as mine from the hundred-degree heat, for once not as put together as I'm used to seeing her. If anything, she's even less suited for manual labor than me—for the last decade, she kept her nose buried in textbooks.

Before I can suggest she join me inside the guesthouse for today, she says, "I can do that. But, Sohel? I'd like to see how everything else works as well, if it's okay? I want to learn everything about how this place runs."

"Afu!" I protest. "I somehow doubt Mrs. Rahman is going around cleaning pools."

Halima fires a warning glare my way. "I'll be fine, Bibi. You behave too."

"If you're sure . . . ," Sohel answers, looking as doubtful as I feel. "Once you're done at the pool, the others can take you around."

I glower after her over my crossed arms as she and Khoibi, with Jui in tow, march off toward the pool.

"Come on, Afu!"

Yumjao's peppy voice—and her surprisingly strong grip on my arm—drags me out of my bad mood and toward the guesthouse, Ireima falling into step beside us.

Inside, the sisters inform me which of the rooms are mine to dress down, then leave me to my own devices. Once they're gone, I dart over to one of the bay windows in the winding hallway, overlooking the pool where my sister toils away. I can see her struggling with a net to get out clumps of leaves blown into it by the last storm.

I sigh, then leap about a foot into the air when a teasing voice asks, "Nature not really your thing, Miss America?" from right behind me.

Of *course* Sohel had to follow me into the guesthouse.

"What gave it away?" I snap without turning. "All these bug bites up and down my arms"—not to mention the unmentionable ones that snuck under my *clothes* somehow— "or is it that my face is redder than a Valentino dress?"

When he doesn't answer, I pivot to face him, hands on my hips. He looks annoyingly perfect, not a single strand of hair out of place, but his full lips are twisted into a thoughtful frown.

"I apologize, I shouldn't make fun of you," he says. "It's not easy working in a place like this if you're not used to it. You can take a break. I won't tell your father."

"No, no, it's not that!" I reply, waving away his concern. "I mean, sure, it's hotter than the sauna at the SoJo Spa right now, and the bugs aren't great, but . . ."

When I catch my bottom lip between my teeth, his eyes dart to it. "But?"

"It's my sister," I confess, nodding toward the window. Sohel comes to stand beside me, observing Halima through it too. "She hasn't been acting like herself. Ever since she was a little girl, she's had all these dreams. Become a lawyer, help people."

"I didn't know that," Sohel murmurs.

"Yeah, well, it's true," I say with more edge than I mean. "I know you see it too. My sister's not a screwup like me."

"I—I don't think you're a screwup," he answers, though his averted gaze and cracking voice say otherwise. At my disbelieving bark of laughter, he coughs into a fist, growing as red as me. "All right, fine, I've been an arse. But I get it. What it's like to be the disappointing spare."

I roll my eyes. This is false modesty at best. If his aunts were anything to go by at the disaster dinner, their darling nephew can do no wrong. His family clearly trusts him to have the run of this place, to help Sunny with it someday, while Abbu never once let me out of his sight during my stint at Royal Fried Chicken.

We're far from the same.

But Sohel's brown eyes are unwavering, pinning me in place like a butterfly on a board. He genuinely believes what he's saying.

I clear my throat. "That's not the point. *I* am perfectly happy not being a people pleaser, while Halima is now giving everything up for Sunny, and . . . no offense, but your family kind of sucks and your brother is totally AWOL."

Sohel raises his eyebrows. "None taken?"

"Sorry, but it's true," I huff with an unapologetic shrug. "I feel like Halima might be rushing into things."

Sohel's frown etches deeper as we both watch my sister accidentally drop a tray filled with dirty glasses that were left behind by the last guests at the pool. Khoibi rushes in to help her sweep before she can cut her fingers on the glass.

He's quiet for so long, I tense, wondering if I've gone too far. Then he says, "No, you're right. Sunny should be here." A bitter smile quirks his lips. "It wouldn't be the first time he's been a no-show when someone needed him, though." I can tell he speaks from personal experience. He pauses. "I was surprised when I heard about the engagement. She might not be the only one in over her head."

"Right?" I exclaim. "Oh, thank God, you see it too! She's not the 'rushing into it' type at all, but everyone else is acting like it's completely normal."

Sohel hums absent-mindedly. "It's not like there's much we can do but watch the train wreck from afar, is there?"

For a moment I'm lost in thought, deliberating over his words, and then it hits me. When I whirl on him, he retreats from the wild gleam in my eyes. "What if . . . if we can't make them listen . . . we *show* them they need to pump the brakes?"

"Show them?" he echoes, puzzled. "What does that mean? Your father warned me not to get caught up in your tricks to get out of work."

"It's not a ploy!" I glare daggers at him, then try to school my expression into a friendlier one. "Look, I know we don't like each other, but we *both* know this wedding is a bad idea."

A gamut of emotions runs across his face, the cogs turning in his head, but he can't disagree with me. "Let's say I was willing to entertain one of your ridiculous propositions. How exactly do you suggest we deal with this problem, Miss America?"

A sly grin possesses my lips. "What do you say we team up?"

It wouldn't be very difficult at all. The way things stand, our families get along about as well as Louboutin and Saint Laurent, and I've got just the pair of red bottoms to kick off a Shakespearean-level feud. Like my sister said, I only ever have to be a bit too *Bibi* for it all to come tumbling down. With a Rahman helping to sow the seeds of doubt from the other side, it would be even simpler.

"Team up?" Sohel continues to look skeptical, but leans in closer and listens intently despite his doubts as I lay out my plan of attack. By the time I'm done, he blows out a long breath. "That might just be mad enough to work."

I stick out my hand.

He eyes it for no more than a second, before clasping it in his own. I try not to notice the way his willowy fingers wrap all the way around mine, how warm and faintly callused they are. My own hand is still horribly clammy from the heat, but none of that matters because . . .

Operation Breakup is a go.

CHAPTER NINE

A week later I'm finally lounging by the pool in the sundress, straw hat, and sunglasses I wanted to wear to Cape May with Enzo once upon a time, enjoying a much-deserved day off. I try to ignore the fact that my body is now covered in itchy welts from pesky mosquitoes and that my manicured nails have several chips. This is the first moment that has felt like summer vacation since we arrived, and boy, is it sweet.

With the hat tipped lazily over my eyes, I can scarcely make out the shadow of Taamba approaching to take my next drink order. I shake the mostly empty glass of fizzy pink mocktail I'm holding till the melting ice clinks. "Mmm, this grapefruit one is tasty, but I think I'll try that mango drink you recommended next."

A whistle drags my eyes up to the person looming over me. It's not Taamba.

Sohel smirks. "You've adapted back to the finer things in life rather quickly, haven't you, Miss America?"

"It's my day off," I grumble, throwing my legs over the side of the lounger and stretching my arms above my head. The slit on the side of the skirt exposes a glimpse of brown at the motion. "Let me enjoy having cute cabana boys wait on me for once. I'm sick of picking and pouring tea for your—"

Sohel's loud clearing of the throat cuts me off. When I frown up at him, I notice he's looking anywhere but at me, a flush across the bridge of his nose that I'd attribute to the heat if he hadn't been immune to it during every other one of our grueling shifts this week.

I'm about to comment on it when he extends a familiar book toward me. "Lose something?"

My eyes bulge out. For a few seconds I gape at him and the book—which feels lighter than I remember when I finally accept it. "Where did you get this?"

"You left it in the tea gardens the other day," he reveals with a shrug.

I snatch it back and clutch it against my chest, an accusation in my glare. "I've been turning my room inside out trying to find it for *days*. You could've given it back before!"

Okay, so maybe I shouldn't have taken the Great Big Book of Biodatas with me to work when I knew Abbu would tear me a new one if he found out, but there are *so many* boys inside to investigate, and I have so little time in Bangladesh to meet them all before the summer ends—especially if Halima returns to her senses sooner rather than later.

"I made a few notes," Sohel answers cryptically. "You're welcome."

When my brain catches up at last, I cry out, "What does *that* mean?" before hurrying off the lounger and setting the book down on top of it to crack it wide open. As I flip through page after page, I groan at his handiwork. "*Why* do you insist on making me miserable?"

Sohel has completely vandalized the Great Big Book of Biodatas. Virtually every page is filled with his scrawled commentary and doodles. What's worse—the petty jerk has cruelly disfigured the hottest guys the most.

Stroking the photo of some poor handsome soul defaced with devil horns and a goatee, I scowl at Sohel's choked-off laugh. He coughs into his fist and, without so much as an apology, begins to head back over to the guesthouse, but hesitates at the poolside entrance. "You know . . . not all of my notes are bad. Maybe they'll help you narrow down who you want to . . ." I might have bought his faux-concerned act, if not for the taunting kiss he blows at me, before turning and sauntering through the door.

"Ugh, as if!" I toss an errant pool floatie after him, but he's already gone.

A few hours later Halima and I are standing on a platform in front of a circle of mirrors and an even bigger circle of aunties who are cooing over my sister's every move.

We're at a boutique in Moulvibazar getting our sharis for

the wedding. I resist the urge to twirl, especially since there's currently a seamstress with a death grip on my waist holding a needle perilously close to my skin.

"Akash *Mamum*?" someone asks.

I nod while glancing around the glitzy boutique. I've just made the mistake of mentioning my need for new date outfits to our seamstress, and now the Biodata Boys—especially one in particular—are all anyone can talk about. "Uh-huh. Do you know him?"

"Do I know him? Do I know him?!" she repeats in a frenzied, hushed voice, eyes skittering in the direction of Sunny's family. "Akash Mamun is the only son of *Raju* Mamun, a cousin of Anwarul Rahman's with a fortune rumored to be in the . . ." She lowers her tone to a whisper. "Billions. They run Bangladesh's largest oil company."

I almost snort out the complimentary water I took a sip of, ignoring the disgusted way Sunny's aunts stick up their own noses. "Seriously?"

Another one nods. "Akash has been a favorite for Bangladesh's national cricket team since he debuted and will probably be one of the youngest millionaires in the country soon."

"You two sure are so lucky," one of my cousins sighs.

My stomach does a tiny flip. I was already excited about my first-ever date, but now I'm doubly so. I'm sort of surprised he wants to meet me. Surely a guy with money and connections doesn't need to be set up by his family. What's the catch?

Halima, who's been listening quietly, finally reacts with a small smile and a gesture toward the swell of my cousin's belly, barely hidden by the meticulous draping of her shari. "Afu, aren't you already married?"

My cousin brushes the idea away with a flap of her hand. "Yes, yes, and your thulabhai is perfectly fine, but *he* didn't send me to Shundori Boutique with a titanium card during *our* wedding planning, Lima."

My sister's lips tighten, but before I can step in, Sunny's mom tells us we have to hurry since there are approximately eleventy billion outfits to get through for each of the ceremonies.

Soon I find myself shuttled to a new dais while a tailor works on hemming the ankles of the wide-legged shalwar that my sinifaan outfit comes with. I'm surrounded by other women in similar states of undress. The entire boutique has been booked by the Rahmans for the day, but my date with Akash seems to be all anyone cares about. At least the boutique is big enough that the Rahmans are on one side and my family is on the other, hopefully with enough distance between us that they can't eavesdrop.

"Akash Mamun is *so* dreamy," a younger cousin assures me. "If he was old enough, he'd probably be in *Vogue India*'s list of Asia's most eligible bachelors or something. I didn't realize he was already so serious about marriage."

Neither did I. . . .

"Uh, well, I don't know about all *that*." I rub the back of my neck. The ornate necklace that has been tied around it with a heavy gold rope makes my nape feel scratchy and uncomfortable, catching the hairs there—but the conversation certainly doesn't help. "Maybe he's ready, but I'm definitely too young to be a bride."

One of my aunts wags a finger at me. "Astagfirullah, Bibi! You shouldn't be meeting with any boys if you're not sure about a commitment, like your sister is. I can't believe your ma and baba would let you act this way. Have some haya!"

Oof, here come the comparisons again.

Before I can help myself, I fling back, "If I were like my sister, I wouldn't even bother with this matchmaking nonsense. Halima found Sunny *all* on her own."

"What do you mean?" my aunt demands, as others start tittering and shaking their heads. Her voice is so loud, even some of Sunny's family takes notice. "Your sister wouldn't strut around with boys. Astagfirullah!"

Oh, crap.

I clap a hand over my open mouth. Despite my scheming with Sohel, I didn't mean to blurt out my sister's business like that. Falling in love with Sunny was probably an accident. Halima doesn't have a sneaky bone in her body.

But a vivid imagination is like Miracle-Gro for the auntie grapevine. It won't take much for them to latch on to my slip of the tongue, craft it into a juicier rumor, and spread it far and wide like a viral WhatsApp copypasta. Halima and Ammu are too far away to have caught my screwup, Sunny's aunts nitpicking every thread on the bridal shari she poses in, but my grandmother, who's been nursing a cup of tea on a nearby couch, rises creakily.

"Now, now, Suleka," Thathu chides, coming to stand beside me, "if I recall correctly, *your* baba complained endlessly about all the boys you'd meet when you were supposed to be in class. The poor man went gray so quickly."

I pivot toward my aunt with a gasp. "No way!"

Her face turns an unflattering shade of purple, and she makes a hasty excuse to go inspect Halima's brocade with Ammu.

Thathu and I are left mostly alone. We burst into giggles, until the tailor accidentally pricks me. I do my best to stand still after that, though a grin stretches my cheeks so wide, they hurt. "Thanks for rescuing me, Thathu."

"No need to thank me," she replies, grinning back. "Your aunts forget what it was like to be a girl. It's normal for a young lady to have a great love or two throughout her life. Just don't go telling anyone else, eh?"

I raise my hand to grasp hers where it rests on my shoulder. "Like you and Thatha?"

Thathu winks at me. "Who says I meant your grandfather?"

"What?!"

Ammu beckons her over before she can elaborate, and I'm left gawking after her. Could she really have meant . . . ? There's no way . . . right?

One way or another, I'm going to get her to tell me *this* story.

THE GREAT BIG BOOK OF BIODATAS

MD Aabid Kazi

DOB: 01-08-2005
(S: bit old, innit?)
(B: it's not THAT much of a difference)
(S: yes it is . . .)

Address: Habiganj, Sylhet

Height: 5'6"
(S: at least his stature suits you)
(B: short jokes, REAL mature 😠)

Education: Shahjalal University of Science and Technology

Career: Student in the field of programming

Father: MD Badrul Kazi, farmer

Mother: Bushra Kazi Begum, homemaker

Grandfather: The late MD Hasnat Kazi, farmer
(B: Why do people list their entire families, anyway?
I don't care about this dude's grandpa. . . .)

(S: don't you know that your family matters more
than who YOU are here?)
(B: . . . for real?)
(S: you've got a lot to learn about Bangladesh,
Miss America. . . .)

CHAPTER TEN

On the day of my first-ever date, I contemplate my reflection in the full-length mirror. The royal purple dress I've chosen—a Hamza Adhikari original by one of my favorite up-and-coming designers—accentuates my figure.

Thanks to the heavily embroidered pearl collar, I don't even have to accessorize, besides matching earrings and bangles. The dramatic slit down the front of the skirt shows off the cinched shimmering lavender pants that make me look a little taller, especially in white heels. A plaited braid crown completes the ensemble, creating a fairy-princess effect.

It's not quite what I envisioned wearing whenever I fantasized about my first proper date—it's better! I always assumed I'd be going mini golfing or something else passé, not meeting with a billionaire's son . . . who is also a professional athlete . . . rolling in more dough than the loaded Rahmans. . . . What would a date with someone like that look like?

A knock at the door sounds just as I'm spritzing watermelon-scented setting spray onto my face. It must be Sunny, who agreed to chaperone with Halima so I wouldn't have to have my Dad eyeing my and my date's every move like a hungry jackal.

I gesture for Ammu and Halima to remain seated. "I'll get it, I'm already up!" I open the door with "Sunny Bhaiya" on the tip of my tongue, only to end up sputtering, "Y-y-you!"

"Me," Sohel replies, at once smarmy and indifferent.

He's leaning against the wall directly parallel to my room with practiced, casual boredom, arching a brow at me like I'm the one who barged into *his* private sanctum.

My fingers tighten on the doorframe as he sizes me up. I tell myself I'm not disappointed when he does nothing but make a scoffing sound in the back of his throat. After all, what right does *he* have to judge my fashion sense when he wears the tea garden uniform so often, you'd think it was stitched to him like Peter Pan's shadow?

"What are you doing here? Where's Sunny Bhaiya? He's the one who's supposed to—"

Sohel swats away my concerns like they're pesky flies buzzing around his head. "Baba took him to Dhaka for the day."

"Again?" Halima joins us, an edge creeping into her voice.

Sohel gives her a sympathetic look. "When my father sets his mind on something, he can't be talked out of it. That, or my blockhead brother forgot. Amma made—er, requested that I keep you company in his place today."

"Great." I turn my head heavenward as I bite back a groan. "Just what I needed."

Sohel quirks another infuriating brow as he swans into my

room without waiting for permission, scanning it with a critical eye. "It's your first date, Miss America? I'd have thought you'd have someone pining for you stateside already."

Ammu rises to step between us, inclining her head at him. "Yes, it is. That's why I'm so grateful to you for taking the time to accompany her and Halima, Sohel. I'm sure you must have had other things to do."

"N-no, please, it's fine, ma'am," Sohel replies, cheeks tinting darker. The blush rises all the way up to the tips of his ears when Halima joins Ammu in thanking him effusively. "Afa, Auntie, it's n-nothing at all. I'm happy to do it."

It takes me a minute to extricate myself from the bear hug an emotional Ammu yanks me into, but when I manage to stage my escape into the hall, I ask, "Where are we going?"

"Abbu didn't want us to leave the estate," Halima answers, with a note of apology in her tone, "but we haven't had a chance to visit the resort's Michelin-starred teahouse. I thought it might be a good opportunity to try the desserts they're catering for the wedding."

I stifle a sigh. "Of course."

It's too pretty a day to take a baby taxi, so we trail our temperamental escort down a picturesque path lined on both sides with lemon trees, over to a glass building with a wooden sign that reads JANNAT TEAHOUSE in English and Bangla—a paradise in a dream.

A gasp escapes me, all else forgotten the instant we step inside. It's a converted greenhouse, abloom with a hundred different kinds of fragrant exotic plants. Butterflies in every color you can imagine flutter throughout the length of the building, separated from the guests by a netted gate overrun with vines. Fairy lights and metal hurricane lanterns hang from the rafters, too high to pose a threat to the jewel-like insects, but they're unnecessary, with so much sunlight streaming through the large glass panes.

After speaking with the host, Sohel leads us over to a gazebo at the very heart of the restaurant, strewn with flowering vines. My eyes practically pop out of my head at the lushness all around us. I have to stop in my tracks to keep from bumping into him when he makes a sweeping motion toward the steps.

As if it pains him to ask, he grits out, "Do you need help?"

With a *hmph*, I bat his hand aside, lift my skirts, and carefully climb the wooden steps to the gazebo. Halima doesn't accompany me, instead taking a seat with Sohel at the table right next to the gazebo stairs. It's the best possible scenario I could have asked for, but I start to wonder if I accidentally swallowed a few butterflies, because my stomach flutters.

It hits me all at once that I'm actually on a date.

Did the walk over frizz up my hair? Am I sweating?

I'm more and more convinced of this when the scheduled time to meet my date comes and goes. As the minutes tick by, I squirm in my seat, wishing I had my phone. Halima and even Sohel cast pitying looks at me when they think I'm not paying attention.

Where is my date?

Did he realize how ridiculous this whole concept is and back out? Did he not spare me a second thought?

I'm so lost in my doom spiral that I pay no mind to the quiet footsteps, creak of wheels spinning closer, or tinkling ceramic that fill the greenhouse. Halima and Sohel must have gotten tired of waiting to order—not that I blame them.

Just as I scoot my chair back to abscond to the restroom for the second time, it bumps into something. A clay cup and a matching dish swoop down in front of me, both with painted leaves swirling around the hand-crafted red earth.

Sohel hovers over my left shoulder.

"Tea?" he asks with a practiced customer service voice.

My face flares hotter than the spiced tea in the clay pot he grasps. "What?"

He begins to speak slowly, like I'm five. "I thought I'd do you the honor of serving you your first well-made cup of tea, Miss America."

My ears are aflame, now from the urge to tell him where he can shove his cup. The humidity within the greenhouse isn't helping, but the thought of sitting here by myself like a pathetic loser for another minute longer doesn't seem appetizing—at least, not as much as the sweets I spot on the tea cart in front of the gazebo steps.

"Okay. . . ."

Sohel smiles. I catch myself watching his long, deft fingers as he lifts the teapot high and somehow manages to keep the scalding hot fluid flowing perfectly into my cup. He returns to the cart, and with more grace than I could ever manage, carries platters of freshly baked treats back up the steps—orange scones, lemon tarts, mango and banana custards, pineapple upside-down cake, and two more pastries iced with masala chai and matcha glaze, piped with beautifully Instagrammable flowers and leaves. I find myself missing my phone for an entirely different reason now.

The tea is brewed more strongly than I prefer, but bursts with enough flavor on my tongue that my eyes drift shut and I emit a little sigh, my nerves no longer on edge. When I open them again, Sohel is staring at me from the seat meant for my date, with his head in both hands, clearly pleased with himself. Even when I drop a few—or five—sugar cubes into my cup, he rolls his eyes but doesn't comment.

"If your cousin's not coming, you and Afu may as well get up here," I tell him.

The tiny smile vanishes. "My . . . cousin?"

Before I can confirm that yes, the guy standing me up is another jerk from the Rahman bloodline, a breathless new voice exclaims, "Hey! Sorry I'm late! I forgot how terrible traffic could be in Bangladesh."

Sohel blanches so white, it's a good thing it isn't Labor Day yet. "*You're* her date? But I told Sunny—"

I spring to my feet before he can say something that ruins this for me. "Hi!"

"Hi," Akash replies, an unassuming smile brightening his face.

He's somehow even more gorgeous in real life, one hand in the pocket of his black slacks, a matching jacket slung over his shoulder. Piercing gray eyes flicker between Sohel and me as he runs a large hand over his buzzed scalp.

"Sohel, would you be a good boy and get me a cuppa too?" Before his cousin can do more than bristle, he returns the full force of his attention to me and inclines his head with a hand on his chest. "Salaams. I know I had no business keeping such a pretty girl waiting. I hope you'll forgive me."

Warmth blossoms from the tips of my toes to the tips of my ears, but I manage to splutter, "Um, wa alaikum salam— but you don't need to be—um—"

Sohel scoffs behind me, but Halima thankfully intervenes, leaving her seat to greet Akash. "It's okay! We're getting used to the traffic ourselves. I'm Halima Hossain, Bibi's big sister. Sohel and I will be chaperoning today, but please, pretend we're not even here."

"Thank you," Akash responds. "I hope it isn't too much trouble for you to spend your day here, Afa. You must have a lot left to do before your wedding."

"Please, it's no bother," Halima replies sheepishly. "Besides, our mothers seem to have a firm handle on wedding planning."

Akash smiles with teeth that glint like a Colgate model's. "Sunny Bhai is lucky to have so many beautiful women joining his family."

"You and Sunny certainly share the sweet-talking genes, don't you?" Halima asks with a laugh, cutting off Sohel before he can vocalize the snide comment he was undoubtedly gearing up to share. "We'll be over here, then! Good luck, you two!"

She motions for Sohel to return with her to her table, close enough that they can eavesdrop and step in if the need arises. I can't help wondering if she might be the one who needs rescuing from her surly brother-in-law-to-be. When I glance back at my date, I notice he's surveying me with an amused expression.

"S-sorry, I was just . . ." How can I explain, though? I swallow and finish faintly, "Nervous. This is my first date."

Akash's heavy brows draw together. "I find that hard to believe."

"Why does everyone say that?" I retort, recalling Sohel's doubtfulness earlier.

Akash shakes his head. "No offense meant. It's just a surprise you don't have boys asking you out all the time, that's all."

Normally such a cheesy line would make me laugh in his face, but his gaze is so intent that heat courses through me again. A smile spreads across my red lips. This boy has game, and I'm not mad about it. Not one bit.

"*Actually*, my father didn't let me date until now, so consider yourself lucky that he changed his mind." I cock my head to one side in a way I hope makes me look coy.

"The luckiest," Akash agrees with a twinkle in his eye.

This is going to be fun.

We both sit, and I pour him a cup of tea from the pot Sohel set on the table.

Akash inspects me for a second longer, before rumbling an infectious laugh. "Sunny Bhai was right about you."

"He was?" I ask. "What did he say?"

Since arriving in Bangladesh, I've barely seen my future brother-in-law, so I'm not sure what he could possibly have to say about me.

"That you were a cute, adventurous girl from a good family," my date replies, leaning closer to me. "He also mentioned the infamous first dinner."

I shrug. "In my defense, Sohel had it coming."

"I have no doubt," Akash concurs with a chuckle. He glances in his cousin's direction, before adding, "Sohel has always been a bit holier-than-thou. I'm sure you only livened up the place."

"You're telling me! Thank God someone understands." I shoot a victorious smirk toward the boy in question, who sinks into his chair with his arms crossed, as Halima attempts to coax him into tasting desserts with her.

That reminds me to push the tea service tray in Akash's direction. As he accepts a scone, our fingertips brush, sending an electric thrill through me. His voice is too soft for anyone else to hear. "I'm glad I listened to Sunny."

His smile makes the butterflies in my belly do somersaults, but I huff, "All right, Romeo, why don't you tell me about yourself?" I motion toward him, letting him know the floor is his.

Akash shakes his head, gray eyes dancing with amusement. "Well, please don't think I'm a bad Bangladeshi son, but I just took a gap year to take part in cricket tourneys."

He pauses, as if bracing for impact, then visibly lets out a breath when I squeal, "Oh my God, I've been thinking about taking a gap year too."

"Really?" he asks. "You're not just saying that to soothe my bruised ego?"

"No way," I insist. "It's just, like, there's an entire world out there. Why not see a little bit of it while we're still young and—"

"Exactly! The chance to see more of the world, play while I'm in the prime of my youth, stand on that pitch with the cheers of my fans reverberating into my very bones. . . ." The wistfulness in his voice sends a pang through my chest. I cup my cheek in one hand and sigh at his dreamy expression. "There will be plenty of time later to put on a tie and become the son my parents want, but like you said, we're young. What's the harm in having a bit of fun before settling down?"

"The way you talk about it makes me want to watch cricket," I tell him with a giggle. "It's not really a thing in the US. Maybe you can bring me to a match one day?" It's only when Akash's eyes widen that I realize how bold that was and hurry to add, "I mean, if you want to, of course! I didn't mean to force your hand or anything—"

"No, please," he interrupts. "It's refreshing how candid you are. I don't have any test matches for a while, but I'd love to make that happen, Bibi."

I award him a playful grin, even though my heart is

thundering in my chest. "That's okay. I can stomach a few unrelated dates with you first."

"You can, can you?" he teases.

"You're not that bad to look at," I divulge.

He dimples again. "Well, now you're flattering me."

We lose track of time. Although I know nothing about cricket, I could listen to Akash talk about his adventures on the pitch for hours. I learn that he used to attend the same boarding school as Sohel in the UK, until Sohel transferred to a school back home. Akash was accepted at Cambridge but recently deferred for a gap year to hone his skills as a bowler.

"I want to be the next Shakib Al Hasan," he says. "Scandals off the pitch aside, he's one of the best all-rounders Bangladesh has ever produced, perhaps even one of the best of all time."

I nod as if I know what the heck he's talking about. "I bet your family is super proud."

Akash's eyes grow dull. "I wouldn't say that."

"Seriously?" I gape at him. "What more do they want? You're good-looking, talented, have a backup plan at one of the most prestigious universities in the world. . . . If they're not satisfied with you, I'm not sure people like me have a hope in the world."

"Let's just say they're used to making decisions for me," he admits with a self-effacing smile. "Cricket is the first thing I've chosen for myself. I'm sure I sound pathetic."

I shake my head. "No! I get that. My father is the king of fried chicken—a self-made man living the American dream—

which basically means my entire life has to be *perfect* or it won't measure up."

Akash lets out a breath, sounding almost sad. "I don't meet many girls like you, Bibi Hossain."

The butterflies in my belly do an encore beneath the intensity of his gaze. I watch his hand creep across the table, stopping just behind the teapot. If I move mine forward an inch or two, they'll be touching. I can almost feel the electric charge between us.

Then his phone pings.

Akash frowns at whatever message pops up. "Is it this late already? I'm sorry, but I have to go. There's an appointment I can't miss."

"It's cool, no worries." Before I can talk myself out of it, I hold out my hand. "Can I see your phone for a sec before you go?"

Akash's brows rise to meet his hairline, but he unlocks it and sets the device in my palm. Ignoring all the text message notifications on the bottom of the screen—and there are *so many* that at least a few, statistically, have to be from girls—I diligently open the contacts page, switch the font to English, and tap the details of my own number into it. Abbu still has my phone, but maybe I can sweet-talk him into giving it back because of these dates. *He* vetted the Biodata Boys, after all.

Sliding his phone back across the table to him, I declare, "There! Now you can text me anytime."

"That I can." He grins at me.

After stepping out of the gazebo first, he holds out his hand to help me down the stairs. I accept it without hesitation, and can't help marveling at how much bigger it is than mine. His warm hand encases mine so carefully that I feel like a princess while descending.

He releases me quickly—probably sensing my chaperones' disapproving stares boring into his back. I ball my fingers at my side, suddenly bereft, until he plucks a small, trumpet-shaped orange flower from one of the vines growing around the gazebo and presents it to me between his thumb and forefinger.

I cradle it in both hands. "Th-thanks."

A certain someone makes a retching sound, but I don't hear it over the good-byes and good nights I exchange with Akash.

My eyes follow him out of the teahouse until he's no longer in view.

Back at the guest house, I throw myself onto the bed between Ammu and Abbu, ignoring their synchronized *Oomph!* to declare, "I have to hand it to you two—I didn't think you could do it, but Akash is everything I ever imagined and more!"

Nayelli is going to flip out when she hears that my first *real* date was with a billionaire athlete straight out of the romance novels she loves. Eat your heart out, Enzo Romano!

Abbu sets down the Bangla patrika he's been reading to inspect me for boy-inflected contagions, before he says, "A good fisherman will release a hundred shorputi before he reels in a single shol."

"What does that mean?" I exclaim, glancing at Ammu to translate.

"It means," he answers sternly, "don't count your chickens before they're hatched—which is why I've arranged a series of other dates for you this coming week."

I can't help feeling a stab of disappointment at his lackluster response. It seems like even when I try to do everything by the book, he still takes issue with how I'm proceeding.

"I'm glad you liked him, moyna," Ammu adds, "but your father is right."

Grabbing one of their spare pillows, I hug it to my chest and muffle a "Whatever" into the pillowcase, but their apathy can't dull the twinge of excitement I feel at the prospect of meeting with Akash again.

Who knows?

Maybe they're right and he's only the first in a parade of drool-worthy boys?

A girl can dream.

CHAPTER ELEVEN

The days between the dates are *agonizing*.

I keep pestering my parents to ask if Akash has texted, until Abbu gets so fed up that he decides to give me an hour to check my phone every night. But Akash never does, even though he regularly posts story updates on Instagram. I'm mildly embarrassed to cyber-stalk him, since he has more than a hundred thousand followers. I'm as invisible as any one of the thousands of screaming fans in the stands of his cricket matches.

If I spend a bit too long studying the videos of his shirtless workout routines during my pitiful phone time, it's only because I'm reading the comments to see how many girls are there.

The answer: a lot.

At least today Abbu has given me the day off from the tea gardens to visit Thathu's village with her. When we arrive, I take some time to greet relatives—and Thathu's goats and chickens, who bray and squawk at us while running around our legs.

Thathu chuckles as she watches a baby goat chew on my skirt. He's so cute that I don't mind him ruining my Akris Punto midi. It's from three seasons ago, anyway. "What name have you given this little one, Bibi zaan?"

I eye him for a second, scratching under his scraggly chin. "Pine." I've been giving all of Thathu's farm animals names ever since I found out she never bothered to. The goats seem to like me best. Maybe the chickens can sense how many of their friends I've fried.

"Pine?"

I nod. "After Chris Pine's salt-and-pepper beard. He's my favorite Hollywood Chris."

Thathu gives me a confused look before slapping her knee. "You really are boy-crazy, Bibi, but I can see why they'd like you, too. My happy, funny girl."

"Well, that's not true," I reply, cheeks burning. "The boy from the other day . . . I *thought* he liked me, but he hasn't texted me at all." My bottom lip juts out. "I don't think I'll ever understand boys."

Thathu's eyebrow ticks higher. "Hasn't it only been a few days?"

"I—I guess," I sputter. The second brow joins the first. "But that's basically weeks in texting etiquette. Maybe even months!"

She snorts and beckons me inside. "Today you're with me. Perhaps he could sense you didn't need a distraction. Let your grandmother make you something to eat."

Despite my protests that she doesn't need to bother, she whips up a whole feast of snacks, plenty to sate the aunts, uncles, and cousins who stream in and out to chat with us.

It's only after they're gone and we've retreated to her bedroom that I tell her everything that went down on my date, flipping through a family album I found on top of her wardrobe. I finish by informing her of what Abbu told me about not getting my hopes up about Akash.

"Your father is one to talk about love at first sight," she replies with a soft laugh.

Not bothering to correct her that I'm far from in *love*, I glower down at a photo of Abbu at nineteen or twenty when he first arrived in America, dressed in the white shirt and black pants of a waiter. "Because of Ammu?"

I've heard the story before, of course, but tilt closer to Thathu nevertheless. She sets down the shari she's been folding into an open bag next to me and shakes her head, her smile fond and faraway. "I still remember when he met her. He called me that very night to tell me the woman he wanted to marry had walked into his restaurant that day."

I knew it all moved fast, but not *that* fast. "For real? How did you react?"

"The same way he did with you, I suppose," she reveals, rubbing her chin. "I told him he hadn't been there very long and was too young to think about marriage while he was getting settled, but he was always like you. Adamant. He said he would regret it if he didn't at least try to see where things went with her. You won't believe how long I spent praying that she would only come back to see him if she was good for your father—and Alhamdulillah, she was."

I flip to the middle of the album. A photo of my first birthday appears. Abbu is holding me aloft with his hands under my fat baby arms like I'm Simba while Ammu stuffs a spoonful of cake into my eager mouth, my chubby cheeks smeared with pink frosting. Halima hovers next to her, sporting a bowl cut and a secretive, smug smile—probably because she blew out my candle. I wonder what she wished for back then?

"We're nothing alike anymore," I mutter as I start smoothing out the creased corner of the photo. Something sticks out from behind it, making the plastic sleeve containing the photo lumpy. I really should help Thathu digitize these at some point. "*You* trusted him to come to America on his own, to be with who he wanted." The words catch in my throat. "Abbu doesn't trust me at all. Not like he trusts Halima Afu."

It hurts a bit whenever I remember how close we used to be. When I was little, we were inseparable. We used to have flour fights while he showed me how to prepare Royal Fried Chicken's secret seasoning and sauce. He'd tell me stories before bedtime and drive me to school before opening up the restaurant every day. He'd wake me up on Sundays, surprising me with daddy-daughter dates to places like the Paterson waterfall or a little tea shop in town called Chai Ho. We used to talk for hours.

Things are different now. He's always disappointed in me.

And every time he gets disappointed, he adds a new rule to the list of things I'm prohibited from doing, until they pile together like bricks in a wall meant to keep us apart.

Thathu tuts and shakes her head. "He's proud of you *both*." Before I can dispute this, she continues, "But it's hard for him to forget the baby girl in that photo, I suppose."

I wrinkle my nose, allergic to the idea of being babied when my seventeenth birthday is, like, a month away. That's an adult in a bunch of different countries!

In my frustration I peel back the plastic sleeve to try to fix my birthday photo. At least one version of our family should remain blissfully unaware of these troubles, after all. But the creased corner refuses to smooth out again because of whatever is behind it.

I pull out the glossy wedge enough to realize it's a second photo, a date and something in Bengali scrawled in Thathu's neat script in one corner: *1971* is all I can read. That was before she was married, before Abbu was born.

My grandmother's hands fall still when she notices what I've found, but she doesn't ask me to stop. My pupils flick between the album and her nostalgic expression. Suddenly I'm reminded of what she told me when we were getting fitted at the boutique.

"The other day you said it's normal for a girl to have a few great loves, isn't it?" I decide to carefully approach the topic I've been dying to ask her about. "Was Thatha . . . No . . . Thatha wasn't your first love, was he?"

To my surprise, a sad smile alights across her face. "Can you pass me that album, Bibi zaan?"

I slide it over to her at once. My heart begins to pound in anticipation as Thathu peels open the plastic and removes my birthday photo entirely. A Polaroid sticks to the page beneath. She sets aside the first and gently extricates the Polaroid. It's a sepia photo of a young man—handsome, even with rust-colored stains on the gloss, dressed in a simple pale button-up and darker pants. He holds a musket in his arms, but it's the young woman standing beside him who shocks me.

"Th-Thathu, is that you?" I ask, even though I intrinsically know it is.

The girl has the same mischievous smile, the same clever dark eyes, and parts her braided hair the same way Thathu does to this day, a plait she taught me. She's wearing a white shari and has a musket strapped to her own back, looking like a certified badass, but a deep crinkle has formed on the photo between her and the boy.

Thathu nods. "This was taken in Dhaka during the Liberation War, when Bangladesh was still East Pakistan. We were both juniors at the university. Students were often at the forefront of the conflict, fighting for the right to speak Bangla, fighting for our nation's independence."

Emotion clogs her voice, but her eyes are latched to his face.

I don't know what to think.

Ammu and Abbu were born after the war, so they rarely

talk about it. I never thought about how my grandmother is older than the country she calls home.

"You loved him," I whisper, without even meaning to.

Thathu meets my gaze at last, something like shame in hers. "I did. Perhaps a part of me never stopped."

"What happened? Did he . . . ?" I can't bear to finish the sentence.

Thathu swallows. "I don't know. When the war began to pick up, it became dangerous to remain in Dhaka, especially as a young woman. Pakistani soldiers were doing unspeakable things to captured girls back then. My family decided it would be safer for us to relocate to Sylhet. I didn't want to leave before graduation, leave my friends, to leave my . . . to leave him."

I can fill in the blanks thanks to the tender way she traces a finger over the photograph. I set my own hand on top of hers.

"In the end, *he* was the one who begged me to go," she confides. "I asked him to come with me, to marry me, but he said he wanted to protect the country *for* me. Of course, war pursued us even into Sylhet eventually. Soldiers razed the very gardens we're staying at, and his letters stopped coming."

I pull her hand against my chest between both of mine, tears springing into my eyes. "Thathu, I'm so sorry."

Here I was, whining about Akash not texting for a few days, when Thathu has been pining after the one that got away for more than fifty years.

She gives a melancholy shake of her head. "So many died then that there isn't even a national record. They didn't always get formal burials. Because of that, I might never know what happened to him . . . but I like to think he's out there somewhere, still writing the beautiful poems that made me fall for him in the first place."

I squeeze her hand and nod. "I'm sure he is. What was his name?"

"Mohammed Ahmed," she answers with a sigh. "And before you start—I'm afraid even your Google can't help me." She winks at me, and we both pretend not to notice the teardrop that slips out. Even now, she can read my mind. "That's why I can't quite fault you for your adventures, moyna. Falling in love with Mohammed may not have been proper. When I told my parents about him, they urged me to let him go. But I never regretted my time with him either. That is the only photo of the two of us together, but I still kept his letters. Even when love ends in heartache, it's a blessing to briefly know it when so many people never do."

My heart clenches at the sadness and yearning in her voice. It's too bad "Mohammed Ahmed" is the Bangladeshi equivalent of "John Smith," less a needle in a haystack than a needle in a mountainous pile of a bazillion more needles.

It'd be easier to track down a collector willing to part with their spring 2004 dark turquoise Balenciaga bag, but just because it's challenging doesn't mean it's impossible, right? These days there are people who can pinpoint any place on earth using nothing but a tiny landmark in a picture or the location of the sun or something.

My cyber-stalking skills are nowhere near *that* level of creepy, but I've sniffed out more than one cheating boyfriend's finsta for my friends. I was the reason Nayelli finally saw the light and dumped her loser ex Hunter freshmen year. Since then she and her boyfriend of two years, Anton, have been attached at the lips. Their lovey-doveyness and constant canoodling would make me gag if I wasn't the one who hooked them up in the first place.

I can do this if I try hard enough.

Thathu carefully tucks the photo into the album and changes the subject back to her packing, but I can't put what I've learned out of my mind. She's been so lonely since Thatha died and all her kids moved away, and she's so stubborn, she won't move in with us, won't leave her home. Tracking down Mohammed could give her a second chance at a happily-ever-after—or at least bring her some well-deserved closure after all this time. She wouldn't even have to know if I failed. Maybe it's a lofty goal, but I want to find him for her.

"Thathu . . . would it be okay if I saw your friend's letters?"

THE GREAT BIG BOOK OF BIODATAS

Haidur Alam Haque

Age: 17
(B: oh yay just like me!)
(S: Thought you were 16?)
(B: I'm almost 17! it counts!)

Address: Sylhet City

Height: 5'7"
(S: That's not so bad . . .
you won't hurt your neck trying to kiss him)
(B: . . . please remember I am the perfect
height to stab you with a fork)
(S: ooh, hot . . . are guys usually into threats, Miss America?)
(B: ➤━ u)

Education: Sylhet Cadet College
(B: Cadet? Does that mean he's a soldier?)
(S: Trying to be. That's a military school.)
(B: hmmm idk, I want a lover not a fighter.)

Complexion: Fosha
(B: why do I need to know this?)
(S: Doesn't him being pale make you want to go running into

his arms?)
(B: yuck as if)
(S: I'm sure he'll be surprised)

Career: Please see attached.
(B: he wrote me a note?? that's kind of sweet!)
(S: Oh?)

Father: Saidur Alam Haque, Commodore of the Bangladeshi Navy, Gulaful Zamindar Bari

Mother: Eshita Hassan Haque of Futul Zamindar Bari

The Personal Statement of Haidur Alam Haque

Dearest Habiba,

(S: Your name is Habiba?) (B: do NOT call me that!)

Before you make a decision, I would like to inform you that I am a feminist.
(B: o . . . kay???) (S: Dying to see where THIS is going. . . .)

You will not find many enlightened men like me in Bangladesh who accept a woman's ambitions and equal right to have a career.
(B: is that true?!) (S: . . . I mean, there's always room for improvement, but they're hardly unicorns. Several of our PMs were women.)

Although I am aware I do not have much to offer at present, I believe you will not regret marrying me and bringing me to America, where I hope to earn my medical license and use my hands for healing rather than hurting. I am handsome, smart, and will pass on good genes to our children. In fact, I have better breeding than your sister's husband, since both

sides of my family are zamindars.
(S: quite confident, isn't he?) (B: he's quite
SOMETHING, all right)

If you support me, you will be a doctor's
wife someday.
(B: every teen girl's dream!)

Even so, I'm sure you'll agree that women
have had it easy for this long.
(B: will I!?)

It's about time they returned the favor and
supported their husbands for once. Especially
since you come from an affluent family, I
believe Allah SWT will bless you for your
generosity if you take a chance on me. I look
forward to hearing from you.

Yours,

H. A. H.
(B: hah)
(S: . . . do you need me to tell you NOT to
meet this guy?)
(B: no . . . I'll tell my dad to banish him
back to Reddit. . . .)

CHAPTER TWELVE

I fight to keep my yawn in check as we all huddle around Sohel and his clipboard. "Most of you will be in the gardens this time." He looks at me head-on. "It's time our friend Bibi here gets to appreciate the full tea garden experience."

"It's so beautiful here that I appreciate everything just as much through through the windows of the mansion, I swear!"

The wonderful *temperature-controlled* mansion.

He gives me a dubious once-over above crossed arms—some teammate he is, doubting me like that!—but Yumjao crooks her elbow into mine before I can defend myself. "Come on, Bibi Afa, it will be fun! Maybe we can play some music again while we work."

"We will look after you and Jui," Ireima volunteers, destroying the remainder of my protests about how I don't even have my phone. "It's not so bad."

Jui comes up on my other side with a blindingly bright smile, and I cautiously smile back. Last night after work all of the girls and I piled into my room so we could blast my dance playlist and do each other's nails. Even Halima and Khoibi joined us. After, the tea garden girls taught me a few moves from their traditional dance style, called Raas Leela. Although I miss Nayelli and my American friends, the company here has been surprisingly nice.

Maybe, just maybe, I'll survive my first day picking tea after all.

As if reading my mind, Sohel the Menace says, "If that's settled, we do need a few other hands on deck at the guesthouse—Halima Afa, I'd like you to take that on."

A gasp wrenches out of me. "You're taking my emotional support sister away *again*?"

"Bibi, you'll be fine without me," Halima promises, dodging my attempt to lunge into her arms. She frowns at Sohel. "But you're not giving me the easy work just because I'm marrying Sunny, are you?"

He looks her dead in the eye. "I can assure you, I would never do that. The manager of pool services requested you back."

Between his stern gaze and voice, she wavers. "O-okay. I'll do my best."

"Afuuuuuu . . ." My arm stretches out toward her receding back, but I quickly replace my mournful expression with a glare when Sohel sidles up beside me. "Why'd you do that?" I hiss at him. "Wouldn't she be more likely to hate it here if you stuck her in the hot sun with the rest of us peons?"

"Pipe down," he returns with another roll of his eyes.

"Trust me when I say she'll be wishing she was with you soon enough."

My brows knit together warily. "Why am I scared of you right now?"

A sinister smile possesses his full lips as he explains, "I have it on good authority that my aunts are visiting the pool today."

This time my eyebrows shoot up. *Aah*. Operation Breakup is in full swing, and my partner in crime is taking more initiative than I imagined. Before I can wheedle any deets out of him, he prods me toward the other girls. "Carry on, Miss America. You're wasting daylight."

"How can you stand listening to that uptight nepo baby all day?" I ask once Sohel stalks off from the field. I'm kneeling in front of my woven basket, which currently has two freshly plucked tea leaves inside. It will take forever to fill up.

"You shouldn't mouth badly about Sohel Bhaiya in front of Ireima Afu," Yumjao whispers, a grin that promises trouble unfurling across her round face.

"You mean 'bad-mouth,'" Ireima grits out, jabbing an elbow toward the giggly girl with more viciousness than necessary. "Focus on your studies, Yumi, not chitchat."

While Yumjao wiggles out of reach, Jui and I exchange loaded looks, which we refocus on Ireima, the growing tea all but forgotten for a tastier kind. A tomato-red blush rises from her collar all the way to her hairline, but she continues to diligently ignore us in favor of yanking leaves off their stems with her gloved fingers.

"Ireima . . ." A giddy, bubbly feeling fizzes in my chest. "Do you . . . like Sohel?"

She ducks her head, bangs hiding her face, but chokes out, "I—I do not dislike Sohel Bhaiya. I think he's kinder than you think."

Hmm. I'm not so sure about that, since he seemed to take so much delight in sending Halima off to her doom at the hands of his aunties. And he certainly takes a sick pleasure in making me sit in dirt and touch leaves that bugs may have peed on too. But I know all too well how a crush can blind you to a beautiful boy's flaws.

"So many of the girls here are in love with Sohel Bhaiya," Yumjao confides. "I think he's handsome too, but"—she pouts—"he treats me like a tiny child because I'm one of the youngest. Is four years apart so bad?" At her sister's mutinous look, she scrambles to tack on, "Not that I'd ever thief him away from Afa anyway."

"I get it," Jui says with a dreamy sigh. "Sohel is hot. So much hotter than the boys down in the village, who are so immature. Did you know my cousin Parek stole a banana right out of my tiffin on the drive here this morning? Then he ate it in front of me!"

"Guys like Sohel are only attractive if you're into the broody type that takes himself too seriously," I gripe, even as I reach into the brush in front of me and stroke one of the velvety leaves. No beetles or ants bite my fingers, which is sort of progress. "I'm not. Bo-ring!"

"The serious type doesn't have to be so bad," Ireima argues without much heat, her own basket already lined with a layer of the leaves.

Yumjao grabs her by the sleeve and pleads, "Afa, can you please tell them the story of when you fell for him?"

When Ireima shakes her sister off and reddens further, Jui and I join in on the mantra of "Please, please, please, pretty please, tell us!" until her willpower crumbles.

"I didn't fall for him," she grumbles. "I—I fell down a hill and twisted my ankle on the way back home when no one else was around, so he . . ."

"So he?" we all chant.

She removes her gloves to bury her crimson face in her palms, the next sentence coming out jumbled. "Hegavemeapiggybackride."

"He did what?" I exclaim, so loud that several others—including a befuddled Sohel—cast alarmed glances at us. Colorful birds and an orange mama macaque on the tree behind us are also startled by my cry. While the birds scatter, the monkey scrabbles onto a higher branch with her baby in her arms, then waves a fist and chitters at me. I press my hands together in apology. "S-sorry, cuties!"

Jui has the sense to be more subtle. "It's like something out of a romance movie!"

"Right?" Yumjao nods at her furtive excitement.

To me Ireima says, "Sohel cares about everyone here the way no one else does. Ever since he returned from England, he's pushed for us to get better schooling and safety practices, more opportunities to do hospitality work, even better pay than every other tea garden in the country."

"He's done all that?" I reply, craning my neck to seek him out.

Luckily, he's gone off to talk to a different set of employees, nodding at something they show him on a clipboard, but I can't help seeing him in a—slightly—better light.

Parek, on the other hand, is sneaking peeks our way, perhaps wondering what gossip we're so heatedly engaged in, but when his gaze snags mine—having lingered a few meaningful seconds too long on Ireima—he flushes and returns to his work, Taamba chuckling beside him.

Huh.

"Mm-hmm," Ireima replies. "I've only been working here two years, and Yumi started not long before you, since she's fourteen now, but our baba told us before Sohel Bhaiya came back, the daily wage in the gardens for farmers was about three hundred taka." At my blank look, she clarifies, "Er, three US dollars, I think?"

"Th-three dollars?" I cry out, gesticulating in front of me with my already achy, sweaty arms. "For a whole day of this?"

"And that is almost three times what the others pay," her sister adds with a frank shrug, as if it's no big deal that they were basically being paid slave wages.

Jui's shoulders slump. "I never knew it used to be so little.

Most people in the village are employed by the tea estate, but we've always been paid more."

"That's because you are considered a real Bangladeshi," Yumjao explains to her gently.

"It's better these days." Ireima musters up a comforting smile. "Sohel Bhaiya has been convincing his father to raise our pay enough to match the minimum wage of other industries. He told Mr. Rahman that since the new policies meant more of us would have opportunities to go to college and explore different careers, the wage should appeal to outsiders, too, so someday the tea garden won't have to rely on tribal labor alone. We're the one tea estate in the country that does that."

A breathless "Wow" escapes me.

The conversation dwindles soon after that when Sohel makes his patrols, handing out bottles of cold water and fresh fruits for us. Once my snack is finished, I decide I'm going to take my task seriously from now on. I tug my gloves back on, lower my head, and do my best not to look at my basket until Sohel returns yet again to declare, "Why don't we take a lunch break?"

"Yay!" I proclaim. "I'm starving!"

Sohel snorts before squinting at my basket. I do the same, ready to crow in triumph at my accomplishment, but it's not even a quarter full. Although he wisely refrains from commenting, I can't help feeling a surge of disappointment as I inspect the other girls' baskets and realize they have way more inside.

We all pile into baby taxis and head to a small village on the outskirts of the estate, surrounded by some of the tallest trees on the property.

Ireima, Yumjao, and Taamba live here. In a language I learn is called Meitei, the latter shouts something that must mean "We're back," because others wave and line up to greet us.

Hundreds of wooden shanties cluster close together, separated by nothing but vibrant, partially woven tapestries on looms. Some adults sit at these looms, while others work pottery into various shapes or stoke the fires of earthen stoves, singing the whole time. The roads here are unpaved, the ground covered in a blanket of grass, the trees making a home for themselves between each of the shacks, the sound of a running river a backdrop to all of the voices within.

"The longest buildings," Yumjao points out to me, perhaps to return the favor for me helping her practice English, "are the school bari and the clinic."

A gaggle of kids are kicking a ball around the open area in the center. When Taamba spots them, he says, "Ey, they're playing footie! Sohel, Parek, should we join?"

Parek nods at once, but Sohel hesitates. "I don't know, mate. My father doesn't exactly like me coming here at all."

"Oh, come on!" The bigger boy thumps him on the back with enough force to almost send him toppling. "It's because I handed you your skinny behind last time, isn't it?"

A ruthless gleam enters Sohel's eyes. "You're on. Don't come crying to me later about your back hurting, old man."

The other girls and I watch in amusement as the boys run off, until some of the women of the village shepherd us away to sit on the porch of the empty schoolhouse so we can spectate without standing. An equally awed Jui beside me, I gape at all the food that soon follows on handmade clay dishes. Yumjao informs me about each delicacy, with her sister occasionally jumping in to clarify if she gets a detail wrong.

My favorite ends up being a pancake steamed inside a banana leaf, a paaknam, which is rich with fresh herbs, spices like chilies, a pungent fermented fish, and veggies. I wash it down with a tea that tastes sweet and gingery, different from the ones served in the guesthouse.

"I'm surprised you like it so much," Jui comments, nibbling on a kabok, which is a kind of Manipuri Rice Krispies Treat sweetened with honey and molasses—also delicious. "My American cousins don't even like hutki. They say it's too stinky."

"I'm not in the habit of eating much hutki," I confess. "It tastes good sometimes, don't get me wrong, but letting my clothes smell like cured fish would probably get me an automatic rejection from FIT."

"Launderettes exist in the wilds of New Jersey, do they not?" Sohel interrupts, plopping down onto the veranda beside me and stealing a pancake from my personal banana leaf. He ignores my glower to stuff his face with it.

"Yes," I retort, feeling more generous now that my stomach

is full. "We even have a washing machine in our house."

"Then, what's the problem?" he asks with his mouth full.

Before I can explain the intricacies of not washing delicate designer clothes too often, or how most are dry clean only, another baby taxi trundles into the village. My sister practically collapses into a human puddle outside it.

I run to her side before she can. "What happened, Afu? Are you okay?"

"I'm fine," she murmurs, although her rumpled scarf and uniform tell a different story. "Just tired. So tired."

Khoibi and Nganu help me get her over to the schoolhouse, where the others clear some space for the new arrivals. Once she's had some of the pancakes and a vegetable stew called chamthong, Halima is ultimately ready to tell us what went down at the pool.

Her fingers tighten around the clay cup in her hands. "Today we really just took care of Sunny's aunts, and . . ."

"And?" I broach gently, hoping I don't sound too eager.

"Bibi, they were so mean," she replies, chin quivering. "Sometimes they would talk about me as if I wasn't there. Other times they would tell me to my face. That I'm not good enough for their nephew. That they don't want any more 'rabble' dirtying the family. I thought the looks I got from people when I started to wear the hijab in America were bad, but . . . I've never felt so low in my life."

I pull her into my arms while some of the others nod,

commiserating. When I shift my curious look to her, Ireima releases her bottom lip to mumble, "Some of the Rahmans can be crueler than any of our other guests."

"Guests like to take pictures," Yumjao agrees. "Sometimes, when they tour our village and the gardens, they treat us like we are . . . I don't know, zoo animals?"

"But the Rahmans treat us as less than that," Taamba offers, scratching his chin. His eyes flick to Sohel, who hasn't said a word. "Some Rahmans."

"I had no idea Sunny's family could be that way. Why didn't he warn me?" my sister whispers as she dries her eyes with a handkerchief Nganu proffers to her, before also remembering the presence of her brother-in-law-to-be. "N-no offense, Sohel! Your aunties being like that doesn't mean I think you or Sunny are! Your brother has always been sweet to everyone—that's one reason I love him."

Sohel smiles tightly. "Believe me, I know we have a lot of prejudices to overcome." He swallows, gazing off into the distance. "I'm sorry."

Although feeding Halima to the wolves was his plan in the first place, he sounds genuinely remorseful—enough that my sister shakes her head and smiles. "It's fine. I'd rather hear all about this place instead, if that's okay with everyone."

Upon extracting a promise that we'll visit again soon, the villagers send us back an hour later with pretty woven stoles to wear in the sun and trinkets made of pottery to keep as souvenirs, both of which I can't stop staring at as I try to fall asleep later in my room.

The day was far from easy, and life in the tea garden is so different from what I'm used to, but I can't help thinking it wasn't all terrible. While I hate the way Ireima and the others are treated, they are so welcoming in the face of that ugliness. How is a teenager like Sohel supposed to change hundreds of years of that sort of discrimination all alone? If I let myself think about it for too long, I'll probably become as gloomy as him.

CHAPTER THIRTEEN

An entire week has gone by without so much as a text from Akash. He's all I can think about as I suffer through a series of speed dates organized by my father over the weekend.

Sunny is—once again—a no-show, but Sohel does an admirable job of eyeballing the first man who shuffles through the door of the teahouse, decked out in a gray pin-striped three-piece suit with sweat stains already seeping through the heavy material. "Are you actually nineteen or did you lie on your biodata?"

"Y-yes." The man glances past Sohel's shoulder to where I'm sitting at the gazebo. When he turns back to Sohel, he puffs out his chest and hardens his gaze, but it doesn't make much of an impact when he's a good half foot shorter. "I am. I take offense at your implication."

An unspoken "young man" hangs in the air between them.

"You're a year older than me?" Sohel emphasizes each word with the slow rise of his eyebrows. "Is that honestly the story you want to go with here? Because *she's* only sixteen."

Halima flings a warning glance from the chaperone table that makes me clam right up before I can chime that I'm almost seventeen. She knows my bad habits well.

"Look," my personal bouncer continues over crossed arms, "I'm trying to give you an out here, man. If her father saw you . . ."

My date pales at the way Sohel drags a thumb across his own neck, a universal gesture. The not-nineteen-year-old taps agitated fingers against the glass face of his worn leather wristwatch. "A-actually, would you look at the time. . . . I—I forgot I have another meeting. . . ."

"With your boss?" Sohel suggests helpfully.

"Ye—no, my professor," sputters my date. "I'll have to reschedule with Lukman Mama."

"You do that." Sohel's smile is all teeth but not very friendly.

In his haste to escape, my no-longer-date stumbles over his own feet and hurriedly reaches to right the skewed toupee on his head. Sohel stares after him with a curled upper lip, but softens when Halima beckons him back over to their table.

"Thanks for handling that, Sohel." My sister frowns down at her bowl of mango mousse. "I knew some might exaggerate, but . . ."

"You didn't expect a pensioner?" he offers, reclining in his chair. "I almost understand the desperation. Opportunities can be scarce here if your family doesn't come from money. A marriage with a foreigner is like a golden ticket."

The iced seven-color tea I've been sipping curdles in my belly. "I don't want to waste my time here if all these guys are just after a green card marriage," I complain to my sister. "I don't even want a *marriage* right now."

Sohel parts his lips, but Halima intervenes before he can ream me out about how naïve I was to expect anything else, her smile sympathetic. "He's only the first one, Bibi. Let's meet a few more, okay? Someone might surprise you."

"Okay," I whisper as the host announces my next date.

This one isn't nineteen going on ninety, but all of our jaws drop to the floor when he struts in wearing a ten-gallon hat, boots with spurs on the heels, a fringed vest over a star-spangled red-white-and-blue shirt, and actual cowhide *chaps* on the crotch of his jeans. Ew.

"Howdy, ma'am!" he bellows, tipping the hat at me.

It's the first time I've ever heard a thick Banglish accent trying to masquerade as a Southern twang. I'm so stunned, I don't even remember to stand, but that doesn't stop him from maneuvering himself into the seat opposite me once he manages to steer his enormous hat past the low-hanging roof of the gazebo. "Um, howdy? You're . . . Mikael, right?"

"I prefer Michael," he answers. "Or Mike. Mikey's fine too."

I force a nod, ignoring the muffled grunt below. Halima must have kicked Sohel under the table to quell one of his snarky comments, but I almost wish she'd let him scare off this date, too. "Uh, right. That's cool! Bibi is also a nickname."

Give him a chance, Bibi. Give him a chance, I tell myself over and over.

"I plan to legally change my name to Michael as soon as

I permanently settle in America," Cowboy Mike informs me, straightening his fringed shoulders with pride.

In spite of how strange the date has been so far, I perk up, hoping we'll manage to find some sort of common ground. "Oh yeah, I saw something about you living in America for a few months. Did you like it?"

Big mistake.

Cowboy Mike yaps my ear off for nearly an hour about the Holy Land that is the Lone Star State, the American dream, and how much time he spent at the shooting range during his last visit to Texas. He barely asks anything about me. At some point I zone out and mechanically nod every few minutes. Not that he notices.

I don't even realize he's waiting for me to say something until Halima clears her throat loudly, which forces me to meet Cowboy Mike's expectant gaze.

"Um, sorry? What was that?"

"I *said*," he huffs, crossing his thick arms, "you don't have to dress so traditional next time. Ever heard of a Southern belle? You'd be even prettier in one of the sweet, simple dresses they wear. Those girls are mighty classy."

My fake smile stiffens as my grip tightens around my glass. It's one thing for him to come dressed like he's an extra from Wild West City, but taking a crack at *my* Falguni Shane gown is a step too far. Before I can decide whether to dump my tea over his big, goofy hat or challenge him to a shoot-out, Sohel is there, ushering the bigger boy out of the gazebo.

"Right," he says with his patented customer service smile. "About next time. We'll have our people call your people, all right, mate? Or is it, er, 'partner'?" As he herds Cowboy Mike out of there, I hear the vague beginnings of a lecture on American geography that starts with "And are you aware that all of America isn't Texas? You'd think an Americanophile would know that. That *is* what you lot are called, isn't it?"

I can't help myself: I dissolve into a fit of giggles and don't spare a thought as to whether Cowboy Mike can hear me. Instead of shushing me, my sister joins in. A notch forms between Sohel's eyebrows when he returns to find us bent over our tables, pounding our fists into the wood, but I don't think I imagine the twitch of his lips.

If the rest of the weekend was spent eating cakes with him and Halima, I wouldn't mind. Ever since the two of us sort of bonded over our siblings' relationship woes, Sohel has been far from the worst part of my time here—even if he does rudely swipe the Great Big Book of Biodatas out of my reach whenever the opportunity strikes so he can leave it riddled with more notes and doodles. I absolutely do not bring it to work just to give him the chance.

But, quelle tragique, my dating nightmare is far from over.

The next day, after the fifth of a series of excruciating dates, I throw myself into a chair across from Halima and Sohel at the teahouse and hide my head in my arms. "Kill me."

"That bad, huh?" my sister asks, grimacing.

I turn my head just enough to nod at them with kicked-puppy eyes. "I can't decide who's worse—the mama's boy in the anime shirt who let Ammu dearest do all the talking while he played his Switch or the one who said he only came to meet me because he thought I'd be like *you*. Pretty sure he implied before he left that I'd go to hell for not veiling."

"Who does he think he is, to speak to you that way?" An uncharacteristically incensed expression pinches my sister's pretty face. "We sent along your biodata and photo before he agreed to meet. Why is he pretending he was taken advantage of?"

"It's okay!" I try to assure her. "Everybody has preferences. I wouldn't be compatible with a guy like that anyway. It's whatever, no hard feelings, yadda yadda."

"Well, I'd *prefer* to give him a piece of my mind," she grouches, folding her arms over her chest with one last harrumph.

I grin. When she gets like this, it's easy to see why guys go gaga over a chance with her, even from a continent away. They don't realize she'd be more of a handful than she looks, at least when it comes to defending me. If only she could stand up for herself, too.

Before she can make up her mind about chasing after him to give him a dressing down, Sohel taps the side of a glass of water and says, "Personally, my vote's on the mama's boy. We serve everything you can imagine here, but she kept trying to foist that mysterious liquid onto you. You didn't drink it, did you, Miss America?" I shake my head, shuddering at the memory. "Good, because I wouldn't put it past her to do black magic. She had menacing eyes." He wriggles his long fingers in the air.

"Oh, shut up! You're just trying to scare me!" I laugh, kicking at his ankle beneath the table. "She said it was for my *skin*, actually. So I could have a 'brighter' complexion to match her beautiful boy. Her own DIY Fair & Lovely recipe."

Sohel's nose crinkles. "I can truly say I might prefer a love potion."

Having gotten over her ire, my ever-the-optimist sister marshals the subject to less turbulent waters. "Surely there's at least one you'd like to meet again?"

I release a long-suffering sigh.

There is.

The tiny orange flower Akash gave me springs to mind. Without its stem, in spite of my best efforts to give it water and sunshine the way I've seen Ammu do in her garden, it pretty quickly began to wilt. In that time, Akash never texted.

I pressed it into the pages of a book of Bengali fables I found in one of the drawers of my room and stuffed it under some clothes in my luggage. The entire time, I felt like the world's biggest loser, because clearly he wasn't thinking about me half as much if he couldn't take two seconds to reply to the pitiful Wyd?◗◗ I sent him after three days of silence, but . . .

It's the first time a guy who wasn't my dad has given me a flower.

I shake my head at Halima. "No." There may have been a

few that were . . . okay. Boring and forgettable but at least not total perverts or control freaks.

But now that I've gone through this seemingly endless parade of guys, I'm left grappling with the revelation that all of them came to meet me because they're ready for marriage.

I'm not.

So much for my fun summer fling.

On Monday morning during breakfast, Abbu slides my phone past a plate of eggs over to me. "You can have this back for now, but *only* if you keep taking your tea garden punishment seriously, or I'll confiscate it again. Bucho?"

"I promise," I squeal, clutching it against my chest in delight and rising to smack wet kisses onto both of my parents' cheeks. "Thank you, thank you, thank you! You won't regret it!"

I can't help scrolling through it on the walk up to the staff cabin with Halima. Now that she and I have settled into our roles at the tea estate, we no longer meet Sohel in the courtyard but check in at the main office to get our assignments for the day. Unfortunately, it takes us through the scenic route, up a winding, overgrown hill behind the guest house and Rahman manor, humming with mosquitoes, dragonflies, and other creepy-crawlies.

Plenty of new messages distract me from my wheezing lungs on the uphill climb.

Nayelli has sent me over a hundred Snaps of her beach adventure. As I swipe away pathetic attempts to flirt from a few of the Biodata Boys—"howdy" is never going to work on me, Cowboy Mike—I make a note to send her some pics from my own trip at last. This place may be a pain in the butt to work in, but I can't deny it's uniquely beautiful.

Drama aficionado that she is, Nayelli will eat up everything that has happened to me—my suspicions about Sunny, tentative truce with Sohel, Abbu allowing me to date, Akash vibing with me before his vanishing act—like a tub of artisanal ice cream from Applegate Farms on a hot summer day. That would almost make the agony worth it.

Texts from friends.

Dance practice reminders for the fall.

Pet sitter check-ins with adorable photos of Rosho Gulla attached.

More half-baked come-ons, from Hillam boys this time.

But no matter how long I scroll, one name never pops up. Just outside the rickety log cabin that is the staff building, I groan and stamp my foot. "Whyyyy isn't Akash caaaaalling me?"

"Are you still going on about that?" my sister snaps.

I blink, taken aback by the razor edge in her voice. "Yeesh, who pissed in your cereal this morning, Afu?"

She *was* especially glum at breakfast, looking back, but I don't know how we went from giggling together over the weekend to her biting my head off now. Her withering gaze locks on to my mystified one before she deflates and lowers herself into a bench in front of the cabin. "Can we talk for a minute?"

I take a seat beside her. "What's up?"

"I think," she begins carefully, fiddling with her scarf, "you should be careful with Akash. Don't you think you're getting your hopes up too much after one date?"

"What?" I recoil, not having expected her to come right out and tell me how ridiculous I've been acting. When her hand inches toward my knee, I vault to my feet, bracing for the conversation that's been lodged in my throat since we got to the tea estate. "Yeah, well . . ." My voice sounds bitter to my own ears. "Maybe we're more alike than we think."

My sister is silent for a long moment, then whispers, "What is that supposed to mean?"

"What do you think?" I demand, rounding so fast to face her that she shrinks into the bench. "Akash isn't the only ghost, is he? Where the hell is your fiancé, Halima?"

All the color drains from her face. "Bibi, you know that's not the same. Sunny went to Dhaka for business. He *had* to leave. It's his job."

"Did he?" I press, setting my hands on my hips. "Can you honestly tell me this is what you thought you signed up for? That he's the same Sunny you fell in love with at Princeton? Or did you pine after him like a good little wife while he disappeared for days on end back then, too? 'Cause I find it hard to believe you'd be the type to fall for him just because his family has some money, but maybe I don't know you as well as I thought."

She gasps, eyes glossy. "How could you ever believe that's

the reason? Sunny's money isn't . . . It's only ever been . . . I'm *not* that person, Bibi."

"What else am I supposed to think?" I counter, throwing my hands up into the air in exasperation. "It's not like you ever talk to me these days. I haven't seen proof of anything you told me on the plane, because I never see Sunny at all, and neither do you!"

As my voice escalates in pitch, a few people poke their heads out of the cabin to determine the source of the commotion, Sohel among them. He chews the inside of his cheek as he considers our shifty-eyed, guilty faces, then asks, "Everything okay?"

"Peachy," I mutter before glowering down at my sister. "Maybe you should worry about yourself, Afu. That's all I'm saying. Sunny—"

"Please," she hisses. "Drop it. Now."

My teeth clack together. In the silence that follows, the whispers around us are clamorous and growing. Now that my head has begun to clear, I swallow, noticing my sister's blanched knuckles and the way her chin trembles as she does her best to keep her lips pressed into a tight line. "Afu, I didn't mean—"

"Sohel," she cuts in. "I'm sorry we're late. I'll head inside and get my assignment now."

The other girls from our group are hot on Halima's heels, already tutting words of comfort, but Sohel lingers behind. "You all right?"

"Ugh, don't feel sorry for me," I reply, collapsing onto the bench again. "I was acting like a bitch." When he doesn't disagree, I heave a sigh. "As much as I hate when she's right, maybe I *should* give up on Akash."

"Hate to break it to you," he deadpans, "but this is one of those times."

I brandish my baleful pout at him. "You don't sound very sorry. Why doesn't your cousin text? I thought we clicked."

I've had plenty of time to wonder. Maybe he only met me as a favor to Sunny. Maybe he goes around flirting with anything on two legs. Maybe I scared him off with my impulsive overeagerness for a second date.

"This is all my brother's fault," Sohel mutters under his breath, pinching the bridge of his nose. "He never should have introduced you to that prat."

I study him accusingly. "Did *you* sabotage it?"

"What? No!" He scowls at me like I've besmirched his honor. "You know, I have better things to do than meddle in your affairs, Miss America. This job, for one. My cousin doesn't *do* second dates, and that's nothing to do with me."

"Oh."

It's not like I hadn't figured as much. Why would there be a shortage of girls interested in a tall, handsome, rich athlete like him? There are plenty propositioning him in his social media comments alone. When I looked up videos of his games, he had entire fan clubs screaming his name from the stands while he played.

"Look." Sohel clears his throat until I lift my despondent

gaze to his. "I know Akash. More than my brother does. You're honestly better off if he doesn't get in touch. Trust me."

"If you say so," I mumble.

"Don't give up," he continues, rubbing the back of his neck. "The—what did you call it? Big Book of Biodata?" I nod. That name is more accurate, anyway, since the book isn't half as great as I thought. "It has plenty of options left if you keep an open mind."

As if he hasn't been viciously mocking everyone inside.

Just then my phone vibrates in my pocket. I've spent so long without it that I jump half a foot into the air, grasping at my chest. My heart is still working overtime when I retrieve it, only to do a double take at the name on the screen. "Oh my God—you manifested him! It's Akash!"

Sohel narrows his gaze. "It is?"

I ignore his leeriness to read his cousin's message: Bibi, so sorry for vanishing on you. I had to make an impromptu trip to Singapore for a last minute interview, but I RSVP'd to your sister's sinifaan next week. Can't wait to see you again.

Holding my phone out for Sohel, I smirk, butterflies aflutter in my belly.

"He doesn't do second dates, huh?"

It's not a cricket match but I guess it'll have to do, I text back. I expect you to make it up to me. 😉

CHAPTER FOURTEEN

I daydream about seeing Akash again the whole time we prepare for the sinifaan—aka Halima and Sunny's engagement party. Technically it's the first formal event of the wedding, since most of our closest friends and family have flown in to attend it, with the main ceremony mere weeks away.

While the majority of the estate staff—me included—string up lights throughout the entire courtyard in front of the manor, the teahouse bakes delectable treats to accompany mishtis catered by a premium sweet shop all the way in Dhaka's swankiest neighborhood, Gulshan.

There's kalajam, roshomalai, roshogulla (my cat's namesake), zilafi—all the classic Bengali desserts. But it's the teahouse's specialties that have me swooning: intricate leaf-shaped pastries piled onto the banana leaves lining every table, veins etched with gold icing and bursting with lemon, pineapple, mango, and banana curd.

"Are these tea leaves?" I ask Ireima as she stacks some into a precarious pyramid. It takes every ounce of my willpower not to steal one.

She offers me a blank look, then casts her gaze somewhere over my shoulder. I don't need to turn to know who will be standing there.

Sohel kisses his teeth. "You have no idea what 'sinifaan' means, do you?"

"Let's agree I don't," I rejoin, "since you're clearly *dying* to tell me, smart-ass."

He rolls his eyes. "Sini. Faan. Sound it out. It's a simple concept, Miss America. You at least know what each individual word means, don't you?"

Although I don't want to give him the satisfaction of being right, the second I consider it that way, it makes perfect sense. "Sini" means "sugar," and "faan" is . . . well, faan. It's a leaf that older people like my grandma like to chew with various fillings. There are separate tables arranged around the courtyard with carefully wrapped parcels of faan and shubari: betel leaves with chopped areca nuts and other delicacies inside, such as slaked lime, aniseed, and cardamom, sometimes even tobacco. It's not as popular with younger people because it can give you a serious case of gum disease.

Sohel eyes me expectantly. Rather than inflate the air in his already ginormous head, I turn back to Ireima and her sister as they continue creating pastry towers to declare, "Khub shundor! Good job!" and clap with a wide smile across my face.

Yumjao claps back, while Ireima returns my smile with a

hint of pride. Jui and the sisters are starting to get used to my Bibi-ness at last. I wish they could attend the party as guests and not waitstaff, but since Halima and I haven't been on the best terms since my blowup at her, I didn't have a chance to propose the idea.

Without bothering to glance back at my know-it-all shadow, I continue, "I'd better go get dressed now. See ya later." The girls wave, but I'm sure Sohel must be fuming, which is more than enough of a victory.

Halima is sequestered in her room. Even though it's huge, I suspect it won't accommodate all of the nosy relatives from both sides who'll be popping in nonstop to give her their unasked-for opinions about everything. It's too bad, because I'm dying to see her in her engagement dress, but not enough to brave the vultures. She and Sunny have decided to take a Western angle for their sinifaan, since they want the mehndi and shaadi itself to be traditional, and I just know they're getting a dressing down over it.

While humming under my breath, I put on silver crescent-shaped chandbali earrings, opting against a necklace. A matching tikka glistens like the sun on my brow instead. The V-neck of my midnight-blue sharara suit accentuates my collarbones. The wide, flowy, paler blue pants flutter like a billowing skirt so that the shorter, actual skirt of the kameez above them forms an elaborate second layer. A gauzy silver urna and shimmery makeup complete the ensemble, matching the starry sequins of the dress.

I twirl one last time in front of the mirror before making my way out of my room. Abbu is waiting for me in the hall, dressed in an Armani suit I picked out for him back home, smoking against a windowsill. The second he spots me, he snubs out the butt of the cigarette against the frame of the window, then pitches it into a trash can.

"Ugh, Abbu, gross," I complain, running back into my room to snatch up a vial of my Miss Dior perfume. "You know that stuff will kill you, *and* it stinks."

He coughs when I spritz the perfume around him. "You might just kill me first, Bibi zaan."

"Oh, I bet Ammu would get there before me," I quip, but don't press the matter.

He all but gave up the habit when I was a baby but occasionally takes it up again when he's nervous. I suppose a day like today, his oldest daughter's engagement party, is one of those times. Maybe nerves are also why his face darkens when he notices the way my urna has slipped off my shoulder. "Is that what you're wearing?"

"Why?" I bristle. "I think it's pretty."

"It's a beautiful dress," he relents, "but isn't that gauzy sleeve a bit too much? What did Sunny even pay those tailors at that blasted boutique to do? Shouldn't he know how his family gets? Did your mother—"

"Why are you here?" I grind out, as I pick up my skirts and make to hurry past him. "*No one* will be looking at me tonight. It's Halima Afu's big day."

156

Well. That's not strictly true.

Akash and I exchanged a few more messages since his return from Singapore, but if Abbu knew I'd be seeing him tonight, he'd frog-march me right back to my room and force me to change into something frumpy that would make Akash ghost me for real.

I grimace when I hear my father's footsteps, but he drops the subject of my dress. "I thought since your mother and grandmother are with your sister, I might escort you down to the party."

I don't answer, but don't refuse his help into the baby taxi outside the guest house, if only because the pencil heels on my Miu Miu slingbacks make it tricky to hold my skirt and climb at the same time.

We can already hear drums and singing from the courtyard, and arrive to find guests beginning to flow in from both the guest house and elsewhere. They stand around the plaza, chatting with one another. It isn't long before my sociable father finds a familiar face.

I slip away without him noticing and wander off on my own, making a beeline for the desserts I haven't been able to stop thinking about since this morning. They're separated into piles based on filling, so of course I grab a mango. A single bite has me moaning with pleasure at the subtle combination of bitterness from the matcha used to dye the pastry green and the sweetness of the fruit. It's so fresh. No wonder the teahouse has a Michelin star.

"That's my favorite too," a voice chimes behind me.

Pivoting on my heel, I catch Akash smiling at me. He looks impossibly suave in a deep indigo fanjabi with a silver chain sewn in an arc around the breast pocket. A heavy stole hangs off one arm, decorated in shimmering geometric patterns.

"You're early!" I blurt before slamming a hand over my mouth to keep crumbs from flying out. *So* not sexy.

"I couldn't wait another minute to see you," he replies. "The whole time I was in Singapore, I could only think about how much more fun it would be in the right company."

"And whose fault was that?" I tease, trying not to let on the way his words get my pulse racing. "Do phones not work there?"

He holds up his hands. "Guilty. Sorry, Beebs. My manager takes my phone to make sure I'm avoiding my vices."

My smile fades as I recall what Sohel told me about Akash being a player, but I shake the concerns out of my head. Sohel may have known his cousin longer, but he's clearly biased. "Do you want one of these cakes? They're delicious!"

His eyes stray to my lips. A rush of embarrassment burns my cheeks when I slip my tongue out to catch a fat glob of mango in the corner, but it changes to an entirely different kind of heat when he murmurs, "Tempting, but I'd rather spend some time alone with you."

Something about the intensity of his words makes me accidentally squeeze my pastry too hard. Mango curd spills onto my fingers. I yelp, and Akash leaps into action, grabbing an emerald cloth napkin and wrapping it under my hand between both of his own. His touch sends an electric charge through me, even through the napkin.

"Th-thanks."

His cheeks dimple. "Anytime. How about we go sit by the fountain?"

Just then a wave of excitement ripples through the crowd. We turn to observe Sunny and Halima's entrance, followed by an entourage of parents and grandparents. My breath catches in my throat at the sight of my sister, who shines like a dove against the twilight in her opalescent gown. The balloon skirt pinches at her waist and pools onto the ground like a train, the entire silhouette embroidered with intricate zardozi work in rose gold. Rather than a veil, there's a sheer urna pinned carefully into her hair by a tikka, the chiffon material trailing to the floor.

Sunny looks incredibly handsome at her side, decked out in a Jodhpuri suit—cut in a way that emulates the length of a western suit jacket, but with a silken gloss to the material, jeweled buttons, and embossed gold threadwork in the pattern of elegant vines winding down half of his torso. Black velvet pants tailored close to his tree-trunk legs complement his livery, his hair slicked into a dignified man bun.

My doubts aside, they might just be the most gorgeous couple I've ever laid my eyes on. Their enamored audience appears to be in agreement. Although I want to tell my sister as much in person as a peace offering, they are soon swarmed by their new fan club. The entire party is now warbling with curiosity, wondering where Sunny found such an enchanting wife, and musing over how adorable their future children will be. Not even Sunny's grandfather's complaints about too many immodestly dressed women can deter them.

I hesitate for only a second, remembering my sister's warning, before I tell Akash, "Yeah, let's go sit by the fountain."

He offers his hand, eyes twinkling. It would be such an innocent gesture back home, but in Bangladesh, where PDA can get you a hefty fine, around so many ogling eyes, the mere thought of lacing our fingers together sends a thrill through me.

When he looks at me like this, it's easy to give in to the temptation and place my own hand in his. I take a few less than subtle peeks around us, but no one is paying attention, with Sunny and Halima at the center of the universe.

I wonder what they'd think of Akash and me. Whether they'd think we suit each other too. Because I feel so comfortable at his side.

The fountain is teeming with other guests when we arrive, but Akash manages to find space for us beneath the arc of a leaping koi, its stone scales visible even in the falling dusk. There are living koi swimming around in the algae-green water beneath, lit from below by the lights built into the fountain to brighten every square foot of the courtyard.

"I've been here hundreds of times before, but tonight is really beautiful," I whisper, trailing a hand in the water and creating a ripple that the fish first dart away from, then flock around, ticklish against my fingertips.

"It is," Akash murmurs.

When I glance up to meet his gaze, I find that he's watching me already, his face so close that I could bridge the distance between us if I leaned forward a few inches.

My heart pounds hard in my chest like there's a bird beating its wings against the bars of a cage inside. I want to set it free. I want to forget about everything else and take the risk with this boy, who looks at me like he's never seen anything so wondrous.

Instead I confess, "I know this is only our second time seeing each other, but being around you makes me . . ."

Happy? Nervous? Excited?

"I know," he answers with a smile. "You—you're not like any girl I've ever met, Bibi."

Heat blazes on my cheeks.

It's silly, the sort of pickup line my friends and I have snickered at while watching cheesy nineties rom-coms. A voice that sounds remarkably like Sohel's reminds me that the chances of him meaning it are almost negligible, given how popular he is, but . . .

I want him to be my first kiss.

It could never happen here when we're surrounded by so many people, but before I can so much as fantasize about pressing my lips to his, a shadow falls over the two of us.

I jolt so much at its abrupt appearance that I might have

tumbled backward into the fountain, if not for Akash reaching to steady me with an arm around my waist.

"Fancy meeting you here." The bane of my existence greets us with a smirk.

"What. Are. You. Doing. Here?" I demand.

His forehead furrows in faux confusion. "I take my chaperoning duties pretty seriously, yet here you are . . . chaperoneless. I can't just ignore that, can I?"

"Yes, you can," I hiss back, even as my eyes scream for him to take the hint and have mercy on me for once. "Please, if you've even sort of started to consider me a friend, go away."

He does not.

Instead he wedges himself against my other side, trapping me between both boys on the fountain. He then shoves Akash's arm off my back and taps one of the AirPods poking out of his ears. "Just pretend I'm not even here. I've been meaning to listen to this podcast I downloaded about getting rid of stubborn, invasive pests without using harmful pesticides, so I won't hear a thing."

I drop my face into my hands to smother a wail. My neck snaps up only when Akash says, "Bibi, I think I should go," ice in his voice.

"What?" I exclaim. "No, you don't have to!"

"No." He levels Sohel with a cool look and gets an equally frosty glare back. "I'm afraid if I don't go now, I'll ruin your sister's night."

"Big talk," Sohel replies, all traces of amusement gone. "The way I remember it, you're not the type to get your hands dirty off the pitch."

A sneer twists Akash's handsome face. "Well, I prefer to leave that to you."

"Oh yeah?" Sohel challenges. I can practically see little bolts of electricity zapping between them. "How's that hamstring injury, mate?"

"Okay, okay, enough!" I say placatingly, voice rising in pitch. A few people look our way with disapproval. More quietly I repeat myself. "*Enough.* Save whatever this is for some other day."

This snaps the boys out of their standoff.

Akash stands, offering me his hand again. I take it and let him tug me to my feet, heart still pounding from the proximity to him . . . and the uncomfortable tension between the cousins that felt like it could escalate any second.

Eyes might still be boring into us from every angle— one pair certainly burns a hole through my back—but when Akash leans to breathe against my ear, it's as if we're the only two people in the world. "I'll call you later. I mean it this time."

"O-okay," I stammer, too flustered to think of a clever comeback.

I track him until he disappears into the crowd, then whirl toward Sohel. "What was *that*? Were you actually about to hit him?"

"What do you mean?" He gives me a blank look, cocking his head. It's the same exact mask he wore that first night when he pretended not to know me, except after weeks of being forced together, I can see right through his act. "I was only making sure you didn't get in trouble for sneaking around without a chaperone. If I noticed you, your parents or another busybody would have soon enough. So, you're welcome."

"Oh, you are *so* full of it," I grind out. "Are you not going to tell me? Seriously?"

He hesitates, and for a second I think he might change his mind, but then he shrugs dismissively. "Anyway, now that he's gone, should we discuss Operation Breakup? They're engaged now, so our timeline is shrinking, but it wouldn't take much to rile up my grandfather and aunts."

I stare at him for several long seconds. If breaking up our siblings was his priority, wouldn't it have been better to let me get caught with Akash? It would have ruined my chances of seeing him again, but I doubt Sohel cares about that. Unless he wanted to make a scene with his cousin on purpose?

"I can't do this right now," I mutter. "I'm going to go find my family." I shove my way through the crowd without a second glance. "Do. Not. Follow."

Thankfully, he avoids me for the rest of the night as prayers are recited and Sunny and Halima exchange engagement rings, promising to love each other forever.

I'm not sure why *that* sours my mood more.

CHAPTER FIFTEEN

My fears that Sohel has scared away Akash are proven unfounded when the latter texts me the morning after the engagement party to request another date.

Chaperoned this time, of course, he adds cheekily. You haven't had much time to play tourist and I'd love to rectify that.

I hug my phone to my chest and roll around in my bed, squealing.

I wish we'd gotten to kiss last night. I wish I'd at least taken a picture with him to show my friends. Sohel ruined all that, but I won't let him mess anything else up.

Tomorrow? I reply to Akash. Where are we going?

It's a surprise, he responds right away. I'll pick you up after breakfast. Wear something outdoorsy.

Outdoorsy?

I almost trip over my own feet in my excitement to tear apart my closet for the perfect outfit, racking my brain for what the hell *outdoorsy* people wear. When I tell my family at breakfast, Ammu and Thathu give me a *That's nice, sweetie* look while Abbu, ever the stickler, says, "As long as your sister and Sunny are with you."

"I know, Abbu," I huff in return.

But neither Sunny, who has joined us for breakfast for the first time in ages, nor my sister looks particularly enthused. Halima has dark bags beneath her eyes, while her fiancé yawns every few minutes, already pouring himself a second cup of tea.

"Tomorrow morning?" he asks. "I wish I knew earlier, Beebs. I'm leaving tonight with my father for Chittagong. We'll be back in three days."

"Three *days*?" I cry.

"We have to visit a warehouse there," he explains sorrowfully. "I can't put it off."

"I get it," I mumble, trying not to betray how disappointed I am.

"But," he continues, "Sohel can go in my place?"

I stiffen in my chair and notice that Halima does the same. Sohel has done 99 percent of the chaperoning for his brother, and on top of me not being her favorite person right now, I'm sure my sister has grown tired of his company. *I* certainly have after we *just* had yet another falling-out. Over Akash of all things. Bringing him on our date might be asking for more trouble.

"Your mother and I can come along instead," Abbu proposes when my silence drags on long enough to become awkward.

Oh, great. Now I have to choose between cutting off my leg above or below the knee. In that case, the younger Rahman is the lesser of two evils.

My sweet shemai and forota suddenly taste like ash in my mouth as I force myself to say, "Sunny Bhaiya, will you please ask him for me?"

"No need to ask," Sunny responds with an oblivious smile. "He volunteered."

Of course he did.

The Mamuns' personal driver arrives bright and early to pick us up, but after second-guessing what to wear for the dozenth time since Akash's text, *I'm* late.

Halima's text forces my hand: Akash is already here. Where are you?

Tossing aside one of my dance practice tracksuits, I throw on the Barbie pink tennis set I bought from Lululemon last summer, when Nayelli invited me to be her doubles partner at the country club against her brother and one of his football buddies. Although I quickly learned that I was not built for projectiles flying at my face, I sensed Enzo and his friend checking me out enough to know I looked cute as hell shrieking and running.

Finishing off the look with black tights, pink-and-white Nikes, and a bow tying back my bouncy ponytail, I blow a kiss at my reflection and hurry outside.

My sister's reaction is more doubtful, but she doesn't

comment on my attire. Sohel hasn't yet arrived from the main house, so Halima moves to stand under a palm tree some distance away, affording me a few precious minutes of privacy with my date.

Akash's eyes darken as he takes in my outfit before a self-deprecating smile sweeps across his full lips. "I have to admit, I've been tossing and turning all night, Bibi."

"Oh?" I tilt my head. "Why? Dreaming about me already?"

"Of course." He rumbles a chuckle that does something funny to my stomach. "A nightmare, actually. About you sending me on my way after hearing where I plan to take you. Not many girls are interested in trekking through wetlands."

Wet . . . lands? What are those?

Trying not to let my ignorance show on my face, I utter an easy, breezy laugh and lightly bat his shoulder. "No way! I am *such* a nature girlie!"

When I hear a loud snort behind me, I immediately recognize the culprit but do not turn around to face him. His presence, however, doesn't help with my nervous babbling habit. "Camping, hiking, er, tree . . . climbing. Sign me up for it all!"

Even the arrival of his archnemesis doesn't dampen Akash's dimpled grin. "Great! You'll love the Baikka Beel Sanctuary, then. They're one of the premier tourist spots in Sreemangal."

I nod eagerly on my way to his Range Rover. Just as Akash helps me inside, Sohel leans down to whisper, "Forget to bring your racket, Miss America?" I take great satisfaction in his *oomph* when I *accidentally* jab my elbow into his ribs.

Half an hour through the Bangladeshi countryside later, we are welcomed by an impossible expanse of water at our destination, glinting silver and green as far as the eye can see.

Breathless with anticipation, I flit every which way as we cross a long, wooden bridge with metal railings over to a lookout tower, where a man sells Akash four tickets. While he's busy with that, I eavesdrop on Sohel and Halima blathering about, of all things, *diseases*, like dengue and malaria, that come from mosquito bites.

"Don't worry," my sister is reassuring him. "We got all the required vaccines."

He nods in that usual, serious way of his. "My mother lost one of her brothers to it as a child. Luckily, we've made a lot of medical advancements since then."

I repress a shudder, the phantom sting of shots and healing bug bites coursing up my exposed arms. Seriously, does he have to be such a killjoy *all* the time?

Before I can rethink this date idea, Akash appears beside me and suggests, "Shall we go see it from higher up?"

I nod and follow him up the wooden stairs of the tower, wishing I could grab his swinging arm. When we reach the top, however, I'm so awestruck by the view that I almost forget how enticingly close we are, standing side by side, our hands touching on the railing as we stare out at the wetlands.

They're magical.

More water, broken only by the striking, sprawling green

of a half-sunken forest, lotus and lily pads, and wooden canoes. There are colorful birds soaring high above, but also roosting in the peaceful ebb and flow, dipping their beaks in to catch fish.

"There's over a hundred fish and bird species alone," Halima explains, reading off a pamphlet provided by the front desk.

Sohel indicates a telescope. "You can have a look, if you'd like. Baikka Beel hosts many protected species of wildlife you might not see anywhere else in the world."

He and Akash hang back while my sister and I take turns at the telescope, pointing out birds we find on the pamphlet to each other when we spot them.

I tear myself away from the telescope and turn to the boys. "Don't you want to look?"

Sohel removes binoculars from his bag. "I brought my own."

"That checks out." I roll my eyes. "You definitely get the Most Prepared badge."

He pulls a face, but I'm soon distracted by Akash dropping his chin onto my shoulder in order to peer through the telescope, hands on my waist. His voice is a breathy tickle against my cheek as he whispers, "Forget about him. Let's take a boat—see it up close."

"We're going out on *that*?" I exclaim, gesticulating toward the enormous body of water, with a dizzying mixture of excitement and fear.

Akash grins at my enthusiasm and guides me toward the other side of the tower, which opens onto a beach where rows of canoes and sailors wait. We carefully make our way onto two boats, Akash and me on one, Halima and Sohel on the other.

No one protests when Akash gives me a hand onto the teetering canoe. We're in close quarters inside it as the ferryman uses an oar to push us out into the serene waters of the mammoth lake. When we make it far enough, thousands of lotuses and lilies materialize through the wispy mist, glowing pink and white on the smooth, glasslike surface of the wetlands.

It's like a dream.

On an adjacent canoe, Sohel has an umbrella open over his and Halima's heads—what looks like the same umbrella from our first meeting—as he identifies a roosting crane for her, his binoculars in her grasp while she eagerly nods.

I feel a momentary pang, wishing I could hear their conversation, until Akash's hand reaches for mine. My date's eyes are also huge with amazement. I realize they're precisely the same shade of steely gray as the water beneath us. My breath hitches when they rise to meet mine.

"I forgot how amazing this place could be," he admits.

I grin at him mischievously. "I'm glad I could remind you."

"You do have a flair for that," he agrees with an easy laugh. "When you spend as much time out of the country as me, it's easy to forget the . . . charms of home."

The insinuation in his gaze makes my pulse quicken, but I do my best to sound unaffected as I continue, "I'm jealous. Not only am I a complete coconut, but my family doesn't actually *do* much travel. Not the way you do."

Heavy is the head that wears the Chicken King crown, so Abbu rarely has time for family vacations, even to come back to Bangladesh. Aside from brief trips here and to England, where I have family, and a class trip that rushed us through Europe faster than I could say "bon voyage," I've never left America. Only Halima's engagement triggered him to act.

"Checking up on me, have you?" Akash remarks, brow ticking higher.

"Oh, shut up!" I splash him with some water from my side of the canoe, giggling when he flicks some back at me. "I maaaay have googled you, hotshot. Did you really film a sports drink ad in Dubai?" At his humble one-shoulder shrug, I whistle. "Swanky."

"It's true, the rumors about Dubai's swankiness are not exaggerated," he says, turning his head to survey the water, "but my favorite thing to do anywhere I go is to give my entourage the slip and disappear among the locals. Wandering the souks in Marrakesh and Tunisia, snapping photographs on safari through the Maasai Mara in Kenya, even just taking a stroll through Singapore's Gardens by the Bay. I have to admit, it's hard for me to stay put when there's so much of the world out there to see and experience."

I cup my chin in both hands, sighing at the picture he paints of his globe-trotting. How is he only two years older? "You make it sound soooo dreamy. The FOMO might kill me. Even when my friends invite me on vacation with their families, my parents don't allow me to go farther than driving distance. They keep saying I can travel to my heart's content . . . with my future husband."

The second I say it, I curse my big, fat mouth. Akash blinks, clearly taken aback, but the sight of his dimples sets me at ease. "They might have a point. Even the greatest adventure can be improved by having the right person along on the journey. I don't know if I'm ready for a *wife*, but traveling with my teammates isn't exactly what it's cut out to be."

I tap my chin and list my head in fake concern. "Don't tell me the bromance is dead? Your fans will be heartbroken."

"It certainly *smells* that way at times, stuck in hotels with a bunch of sweaty cricketers." He exchanges his roguish grin for a languid smile, eyes hooded and pinning me in place again. They'd be as easy to drown in as the beel itself. "You're far more pleasant company."

"Y-you too," I manage to squeak out.

When we make it to the beach on the opposite shore, we're greeted by fishermen who cast wide nets into the water, standing nearby on a makeshift pier cobbled together with bamboo sticks. They present the opportunity for us to fish, with the vow that we can keep anything we catch.

"Sorry, mate," Akash laments, eyeing their rickety setup dubiously. "Whole fit's paid for by sponsorships. Can't afford to get on their bad side by ruining it."

"For an athlete you're a lot more clean-cut than I would have expected." Despite my ribbing, I can't blame him. He looks *good* in the motorsport jacket and shorts he wears, the sneakers also featuring the brand's logo.

"I reserve all my roughhousing for the pitch," Akash retorts with an apologetic shrug. "Never developed much of a taste for getting muddy off it."

"How about for fish?" Sohel cuts in before I can answer. "You haven't grown so used to the sludge they fed us in the refectory that you'd turn down a proper Bengali dinner, have you?"

I giggle at Akash. "I hope not!"

Like my parents always say, "Maaseh baathe Bangali!" You can't be a real Bengali if you're not cramming fish and rice into your mouth like it's the solution to all of life's woes.

When his cousin merely shakes his head, Sohel raises his hand to shade his eyes from the sun, and I studiously ignore the way they shine like amber beneath the gleam. "Well, ladies? Don't tell me you're afraid of a little water too?"

Halima takes a step back, all too eager to accept defeat. The temporary pier is so wobbly that I'm tempted to do the same. The deck is made up of a few long, horizontal bamboo sticks that stretch over the water, held in place on either side by a series of other bamboo sticks, this time vertical and stuck in the sediment of the beel. The fishermen walk across the flimsy deck as if it's a tightrope. You have to hold on to the sticks if you don't want to fall so you can make it to the slightly sturdier bamboo ledge at the end, where multiple fishermen can stand, and even that requires putting a lot of faith in the ropes that bind all the bamboo together.

My eyes narrow. I'm not about to let Sohel call me scared. Besides, when in Rome . . . ?

Sucking in a deep breath, I spare a glance down at my outfit and the once again pristine manicure I got redone at a parlor in Moulvibazar before the engagement party, say a quick prayer for both, and join Sohel among the throng of fishermen in front of the pier. "Let's catch some dinner!"

His eyebrows shoot up when I kick off my sneakers, but the second I tip my chin at him defiantly, he moves to do the same. With a smile across his face that, dare I say it, borders on impressed, he rolls up the sleeves of his loose white shirt and the ankles of his black pants.

My boldness evaporates the instant he starts climbing onto the shaky bamboo deck, gripping one of the vertical poles that comprise the improvised railing to keep himself steady. He slings a daring grin over his shoulder. "What's the matter, Miss America? Thought you weren't scared?"

"I'm not," I lie, eyeing the murky green depths of the beel. It's hard to see what lurks below the algae and floating lily pads.

There might be snakes, right? Crocodiles? At the very least, fish that bite?

He tsks and extends his free hand. "C'mon. I'd never let you fall."

His gaze is steadfast and sincere when I meet it. I dawdle for one more minute, gulp, and let him twine our fingers together, testing my foot on a bamboo pole. With one hand in his and the other moving from pole to pole, the two of us clamber our way to the fishermen on the ledge, who are trying not to look too amused by our clumsy approach.

The end of the pier is sturdy enough that Sohel releases my hand. It feels empty without his in it, but I try to refocus on the fishermen as they half explain, half pantomime the process of catching fish in the nets. Since I've never seen normal fishing poles—and never took interest in the activity before—I have reservations.

Sohel, on the other hand, accepts a mesh net without hesitation. He proffers the other end to me, then grips one of the vertical poles as he slowly lowers himself waist-deep into the water and wades a few steps forward. The gentle tugging sensation doesn't give me much of a chance to second-guess. Mimicking what he did, I bite back a gasp at the sudden rush of cold. It soaks into the material of my tights at once, making everything heavier. A breathy laugh escapes me at the ticklish sensation of tiny fish around my ankles.

"See?" Sohel's avid grin is brighter than any I've ever seen on his usually doleful face. Droplets already shimmer in his hair and dew across his golden skin. "Not so bad, is it?"

I shake my head wordlessly, tongue too thick to function. Grasping the net together, I follow his lead and lift part of it above our heads, then pitch it as far as we can away from us, until only a thick rope remains. This we hold on to for dear life, his fingers once again mere inches from mine.

"Are you sure this will work?" I whisper to him.

"Just watch," he replies. "I used to do this with my nana all the time."

I track his gaze over to the fishermen, who've cast a larger net into the water. Another gasp fills my lungs when fish begin to shimmy inside it, glistening like an entire jewelry box's worth of silver and scattered gemstones. Hundreds of them.

Our own net, by comparison, has sunk like a stone beneath the tranquil waters. A minute goes by. Three. Five. I feel a minute tug and tighten my fingers around the rope in time with Sohel's. More and more tugs join the first, then grow into full-on violent splashing. From the distant shore Halima whoops and cheers.

"I think it's a big one," Sohel declares, clearly delighted.

A hard wrench almost pitches me face-first into the beel. I yelp, but manage to dig the soles of my bare feet into the sand underwater in time. All at once I realize this might have been a bad idea, but it's not like I can leave Sohel high and dry *now*.

Without a word he releases his pole to maneuver himself forward until he's in front of me. With his body between me and what's possibly the scariest tug-of-war opponent ever, I let out the breath I was holding, feeling more grounded.

Sohel releases a hiss between his teeth. "Let go, Miss America."

Before I can ask him why, the rope grows taut in my grasp,

burning the skin of my palm. That's all the warning I get before a mighty yank reverberates through the length of it.

"Bibi, let go!" someone else shouts from shore.

Mind growing blank with panic, I do, nearly pinwheeling backward. Only my other hand around a bamboo pole saves me.

One minute, Sohel is in front of me. The next, he plunges into the water, a wave crashing against my torso from the impact of his body meeting it. The surface remains so dark that I can't tell if the thrashing beneath is him or the fish when I lower my arms.

"Sohel!" I scream after him.

For what feels like the longest thirty seconds of my life, there's no response. Then the surface breaks as he bursts through it with a sputtering intake of breath, tossing back his head to dispel droplets of water from the inky strands. Before I know it, I'm closing the distance between us, gripping him by the shoulders and checking him over.

"Worried about me?" He has the audacity to smirk. "This end is waist-deep."

My mouth falls open, but I snap it shut, aggravation in my eyes. "You want me to shove you right back in?"

"Wait! Before you do . . ." He hefts the net in his arms for me to see. The mass of mesh squirms weakly. "We did it, Miss America. We caught a fish."

"We . . . did?"

I squint at the net. Silver scales glint inside.

Soon we're surrounded by the fishermen, who clap Sohel on the back and tousle his sopping-wet hair, plucking strings of seaweed out of it and off his clothes. Now that I know the insensitive asshole is unharmed, I allow myself to return to the pier, raking my eyes over his drenched frame from afar. His soaked white shirt clings to his body, all but see-through now. As he jokes around with the fishermen, he absent-mindedly grabs the hem and lifts it to wipe away the rivulets sluicing down his sharp jawline.

His efforts are futile, of course. My throat parches as I watch the journey of that stubborn bead down the vee collar of his shirt, all the way to the lean, toned lines of his stomach. It's clear that while he might not work out in the traditional sense like his brother, Sohel's romps through the tea garden have kept him *plenty* fit.

Halima's voice shatters my trance. "Come back to shore and dry off, you two!"

"Shall we?" Sohel asks, breaking away from his new friends. At my nod, he helps me tiptoe my way across the pier again. When Halima rushes to meet us, he holds aloft our catch for her to inspect. "This could feed us for at least a couple days."

"Where would we cook, though?" she wonders aloud. "Make a fire?"

Sohel starts to pull out the site map, but it's all but

disintegrating after his dip into the marsh. "There's a bonfire not too far from us on the beach."

Something soft and warm drapes across my shoulders, the divine aroma of vanilla enveloping me. I blink up at Akash, who is shaking his head at his cousin. "I rented out a private bungalow for the day. It's a good thing I did. Bibi needs to dry off before she contracts some illness. You shouldn't have dragged her into your stunt."

A muscle jumps in Sohel's jaw, but his voice remains level when he says, "She was perfectly safe the entire time. If you cared so much, why didn't *you* stop her, Mr. White Knight? Or better yet, go along?"

"I'm okay," I try to persuade them both before another argument can break out. "Fishing wasn't as bad as I thought." Akash's frown wanes when I add, "Are you sure about giving me this, though? I thought you didn't want to ruin it."

Without a moment of hesitation, he replies, "For you, it's worth it.".

"Oh, um, th-thanks!" My mouth starts to flap like the fish Sohel is still cradling, but nothing more intelligible comes out. The smell of Akash's expensive cologne engulfs me, making my head go distractingly fuzzy.

I'm grateful when my normally reserved sister saves me from another bout of nervous babbling by blurting out, "Alhamdulillah! I need the ladies' room stat."

We all burst out laughing.

"You really thought of everything," I tell my date as we

plod over to the bungalow. It's taking every ounce of willpower for me not to sniff his jacket anytime he looks away.

"Only the best for you, Bibi," he answers, his dimples performing an encore. My heart almost stages a revolt right then and there, but I succeed in keeping it inside my ribs.

After toweling off and grilling up the fish, we follow a private tour guide through the half-submerged forest. If anyone notices my proximity to Akash, or the way his hand comes to rest at the small of my back, they don't bring attention to it, because the forest floor is so slippery that we almost have to lean on each other to keep from falling.

We get back to the observation tower where we first embarked, with burning thighs and glistening foreheads, but I can't remember the last time I had this much fun. Maybe Akash is going to make a nature girlie out of me after all. While we wait for our driver to pull around, a child comes by selling lotus blossoms, and Akash ends up buying me the entire basket.

I smile and stroke the silky pink petals all the way home.

CHAPTER SIXTEEN

The morning Sunny returns from Chittagong, my parents take Thathu to see my mom's side of the family, leaving me at the breakfast table with my sister and her fiancé. It's the perfect opening to ask him a burning question.

"Bhaiya . . ."

He slows midchew. "Hm?"

"Do you think you can help me find someone?" I reply, pulling out my phone.

"Another of the Biodata Boys?" Halima asks from beside him.

I pinch my lips together and shake my head.

I have enough of my own boy drama at the moment.

"Actually . . ." I scroll through my camera roll until I find a picture of Thathu's mystery man. I slide my phone across the table to show Sunny. "I want to find this man. He's probably in his seventies now, but he was a student at Dhaka University when the picture was taken."

Sunny picks up my phone in his meaty hand and squints

down at the screen, making room for Halima to inspect it alongside him. I hold my breath for a few seconds, even though I expect his ultimate response: "I don't recognize him. Sorry."

"I didn't think you would," I say, waving my hand in the air. "I was hoping you could help me find out who could. Is there . . . some sort of historical record?"

"I'm not the best person to help you with that," Sunny admits. "I haven't lived in Bangladesh for decades now. Even when I did, I was never much of a history buff. Sorry, kiddo."

"I had to tutor him in our historical analysis class," Halima confirms before zooming the picture out. "That—that girl next to him is Thathu, isn't she?"

I nod. "We found the photo while cleaning up at her house. She told me she's always wanted to know what happened to him after he disappeared."

Halima mulls this over, then meets my gaze with determination in her own. "Sunny and I have three separate dawaths with his aunts today, but, you know, if there's anyone who can help you with this, Bibi—"

"It's Sohel," I finish with a long-suffering sigh.

Because Sohel *never* makes anything easy for me, he's not in the guesthouse or manor. I have to ask no less than three people where to find him in the tea garden.

Finally it's Jui who says, "He's with Ireima and Yumjao at the orchards."

When I'm unable to bite back a groan at the prospect of

trawling a thousand acres on a debilitating hundred-and-ten-degree day to find him, Parek takes pity on me and offers to ferry me over to the fruit groves on the border of the estate by baby taxi—although he might have his own ulterior motive, to catch a glimpse of a certain someone.

There are so many orchards with fruits and flowers in so many bright colors that I don't automatically spot Sohel among all the people woven to fill up woven baskets under the trees. The scent of citrus suffuses the entire thicket.

Luckily, he generally stands a head taller than most people, so after several minutes I pinpoint him at last beneath a lemon tree. As always, he looks terribly broody, arms crossed and a frown marring his face.

I quickly thank Parek for the ride, snatch up one of the water bottles stored in the baby taxi, and vault out of the car before it's fully stopped, hoping to offer the water up as a bribe.

Sohel's no-nonsense Bangla floats over to me, but he hasn't noticed my presence yet. He's speaking to a vaguely familiar, sweating, red-faced older woman in a washed-out orange shari who is sitting with her back against the tree. She must be one of the people who works directly in the farm, since the hospitality staff all wear uniforms. Kneeling beside her is Ireima, eyes huge with worry as she gives the woman sips of water and fans her face with a hand.

"Is she okay?" I exclaim.

Sohel and Ireima turn toward me in tandem, but the woman seems so out of it that she doesn't hear me. Frown deepening, Sohel drops into a squat in front of her to peer into her bleary eyes, arms splayed over his knees.

"Khala . . ." I watch as he points at an upended basket of lemons, at himself, and then motions into the distance. When the woman begins to protest weakly, he shakes his head with a small smile, tapping his own chest again. His tone is so light, you'd think I imagined the tension earlier. She dithers for a moment longer, until Ireima whispers something to her. To the girl, Sohel says in English, "Can you bring your mother back to a medical cabin? Take a CNG."

"Achaa, bhaiya," she agrees at once.

I step aside as she and a loitering Parek help the woman into a different baby taxi. Then I ask Sohel, "That's her mom? We met in their village, I think."

"Mmm, yeah," he answers without looking up from the scattered lemons. I stoop to help him gather the rest and toss them into the basket. Once it's filled again, he lifts it up and cocks a brow at me. "What're you doing all the way out here on your day off, Miss America? Not that I don't appreciate the help."

"You definitely need to work on your thank-yous," I grumble, falling into step next to him on the path over to the closest wooden pavilion and ignoring the way the muscles in his arms bulge from the exertion.

He chuckles. "All right, thank you, O Generous One."

"You're welcome!" I beam angelically. "Was that so hard?"

He rolls his eyes. "*Now* will you tell me what you're doing here?"

"I was looking for you—"

Before I can finish, we're greeted by more staff at the pavilion, who accept the basket from him with disapproving expressions. There's a pavilion every few miles, so workers can take a break from the heat and turn in whatever they've collected. I understand enough to know they're telling him off about working in the heat. He waves away their fussing, instructing them to go around with more water bottles and wrap up early.

I eye him in my peripheral vision on the walk back to the groves where we can flag another baby taxi. Perspiration glistens in his hair. He tugs at the collar of his shirt and dabs at his flushed cheeks, ever so slightly lifting the hem.

Clearing my throat, I look away from that glimpse of sweaty golden skin and shove the water bottle at him. "Why'd you tell them you weren't hot when you clearly are?"

He takes a long swig from the bottle as he considers my question, Adam's apple bobbing. A few droplets trickle down his chin and follow the jut of his collarbone into his shirt, but he doesn't appear to mind. Once the bottle is empty and crumpled up, he shrugs. "The only difference between Ireima and me is our parents. If I can do at least this much to help her family and everyone else here, I want to."

For a few seconds I can only stare, taken aback as always by how passionate he is. Then he snaps his fingers in my face, and I tell myself to get a grip. There's a reason I sought him out in the first place, and it wasn't to swoon over his farm-boy-with-a-heart-of-gold schtick.

"If you're not busy," I hedge, "I was hoping you could help me with something."

It's my first time asking for his help instead of having it foisted on me. A trench forms between Sohel's eyebrows, but he listens intently as I explain everything I know about the letters and photo I discovered at Thathu's house, as well as my plan to find out what happened to my grandmother's lost first love.

I hand over my phone and once again wait with bated breath for his reaction. He presses a thumb against his plush bottom lip as he pores over the pictures I snapped of the Polaroid and Mohammed's letters once I got my phone back. His jet-black lashes dust ever so slightly over the curves of his high cheekbones.

A rebellious fist closes around my heart.

Why does he have to be so unfairly pretty?

My shoulders sag when he ultimately shakes his head, breaking the spell. "He signed every letter 'Mohammed Z. Ahmed.' Do you know how common both his first and last name are in Bangladesh alone? 'Mohammed' is now one of the top five most popular names worldwide."

"I know," I whine. "Believe me, I know."

"Not only that," Sohel adds, "but the war . . . Pakistan has never claimed responsibility for what happened. Even our government doesn't know exactly how many people were displaced or killed. The numbers range anywhere from three hundred thousand to three *million*. Do you get what a huge difference that is?"

I fiddle with the edges of my shirt, peering at him through

my eyelashes and willing my voice not to break. "Does that mean you can't help?"

Sohel frowns at the photo of Thathu and Mohammed for a long stretch before he says, "It means . . . I make no promises, but . . . I'll try."

"Really?" I exclaim. "Oh, I could just hug you!"

"Uh, please don't," he replies, returning my phone without meeting my eyes. "If you actually want to do this, go get ready. We're going to have to go to Dhaka."

"That's pretty far, isn't it?" I mentally calculate the distance and grimace. "I guess if everyone else is preoccupied today, we may as well take advantage. But you know you'll have to be alone with me, right?"

"Oh, because you're so traditional now?" he challenges, arms crossed.

I grin. "Touché."

He rubs his chin, ignoring my leer. "It will take about three hours by car, which doesn't give us much time to get there, research the information we need, and come back without anyone kicking up a fuss. If you're serious—"

"I'm serious! Thanks again for this, Sohel!"

I'm already dashing away before he can change his mind.

"Bibi, we're here."

A soft voice lures me out of a dream sometime later, close enough to overtake the incessant din of beeping cars and conversations all around us.

I realize, as I squeeze my eyelids tighter and inhale sharply through my nose, that it's gotten chilly because of the AC. One side of me is warmer than the other, the scent of tea and citrus invading all my senses. I'm loath to release whatever I'm snuggled up against until I feel it move, and I snap my eyes open.

Only then do I, red-faced, scoot away from Sohel, whose shoulder I hijacked. There's drool drying in the corner of my mouth—probably on *his sleeve*, too—and my eyes feel crusty when I blink. "W-what time is it?"

"Almost one," he replies while stretching his arms until they crack.

I wince, wondering if he had to sit in place for long because of me. Then the truth sinks in like a stone. "Wait! You mean you let me use you as a pillow for over an hour? Why the hell didn't you wake me up sooner?" If you'd ever told me this would happen before today, I'd have laughed you out of the country.

"Maybe I liked the silence," he responds with a shrug, smirking at my resulting scowl. Turning his attention to Ekhlas, the driver, he says, "Thanks, Sasa. I'll be in touch when we need a pickup."

I continue glaring daggers at his back while forcing my sleeping legs to follow him out of the car. They tingle with pins and needles even after I use one of our water bottles to spritz myself, scrubbing my knuckles against my hair, chin, and eyes to remove all evidence of looking like a bridge troll. At least the excursion hasn't wrinkled my cotton candy–pink Dior shirtdress too much.

We stand out of the way of the busy street, with thousands of bodies and vehicles milling about. A park is in front of us, with murals painted on the fences that separate it from crowded Dhaka city, depicting what look like historical events from the Independence War. There's a grander mural at the very center of the red cobblestone path, a large flower with multicolored petals, but the monument at the far end steals my gaze.

"Where are we?"

"The Shohid Minar," Sohel says. "It was erected to honor the students who lost their lives during protests against the Pakistani government."

"There's one in Paterson back home," I tell him, though I only saw it a few times while going to Bangla Melas with my mother. "This is *much* cooler, though."

There's something about Old Dhaka that's like a museum in city form. I can almost imagine Thathu as a girl my own age, slipping through the crowds on her way to class. Did she used to stop and get street food along the way? Did she have secret rendezvous with her lost boy? How much has changed these past fifty years and how much has stayed the same?

Sohel nods. "The Dhaka University campus is over there, not far from my boarding school. Our best bet is to check student records from around the time your grandmother and this mystery man attended. We can cross-check our findings at the National Archives, but all we know about Mohammed Z. Ahmed right now is his name and that he was a student at DU."

"That makes sense." I twiddle the half-empty bottle between

my hands. "Sohel . . . thanks for coming all this way with me."

When he doesn't acknowledge me right away, I suspect he's about to take a jab at my Americanness again, but instead he says, "I think it's . . . nice, what you're trying to do for your grandmother." A teasing grin overtakes his contemplative features. "Maybe not the smartest or most logical gesture—"

"Hey!"

"*But*," he continues, "it's nice that you're close with your grandparents." A note of envy bleeds into his voice as he smiles ruefully down at the flower mural beneath our feet.

"You're not close with yours? You live with your grandpa!"

"Don't remind me," he mutters, scrunching up his face. "He was a nightmare to grow up with, if I'm honest. Always on me about something. And my nana and nani . . . We don't have enough time to open *that* can of worms. Ready to go?"

Although I want to know more Sohel lore, I make myself nod, and hurry to keep pace with him as we enter the city square. There's endless traffic between the colorful Jenga towers of skyscrapers, unobstructed by the flashing traffic lights. Painted buses, cars, taxis, rickshaws, and more whir by. Other pedestrians cross the onslaught without a care in the world. The sidewalks, if you can even call them that, are humming with life, vendors shouting their wares.

My head swivels every which way during the short expedition to the Dhaka University campus. I've gone on a few campus tours, but this campus doesn't resemble any I've seen before.

You can tell the campus is *old*.

There's history in every direction. The main building looks like an ancient palace out of a fairy tale, a brilliant red against the gray-blue of the afternoon sky, composed of dozens of arched windows and doors with patterned frames, trellises, and a crown of turrets.

We head to a newer building, the office of the registrar. Sohel strides in like he owns the place and marches up to the desk, smiling at the man reading a magazine behind it, who regards us both with apathy. "Apnake shaijo korte pari?"

That's my cue to hang back.

Sohel deliberates over the matter with the receptionist, who shakes his head. Although I get a pit in my stomach at the prospect of us coming all this way for nothing, my partner in crime doesn't let that dissuade him. He soldiers on more urgently, gesticulating his arms, until the two men reach an impasse. Removing his leather wallet from his bag, Sohel slides a wad of violet bills over to the man. The guy pauses, then sneakily pockets them and hands over a key chain.

I suppress a gasp. Sohel nods at whatever his extorter says for several more minutes before returning to my side and guiding me out of the building.

"Did you just bribe him?" I giggle, hardly able to believe what I saw.

He winks at me. "Money opens doors." I do a double take, trying to find words for my surprise. A foxlike grin possesses his lips. "Still think I'm so stuffy and traditional?"

"Far from it," I counter with a shake of my head, sounding breathless to my own ears.

Sohel clears his throat. "The receptionist told me they're in the process of digitizing their pre-independence records, but the university library has access to those digital records, their older paper files, *and* books about the war and its aftermath. He couldn't guarantee we'd find exactly what we need. But if it exists, it's here."

I whistle, impressed. "You are something else."

He takes a half bow, the keys swinging from his fingers. "I know."

We don't stop laughing until we reach the university library, a relatively recently remodeled building where a librarian shushes us at the door. We clam up but keep smirking behind her back until she's out of sight.

Although it's summer, the main library area is a maze of long and round tables with textbooks, laptops, and notebooks scattered across them. None of the students pay us any mind as we make our way through this labyrinth, too caught up in their own woes.

I trail Sohel up red stairs onto a mezzanine floor packed with yet more bookshelves. He makes for a door with a sign I can't read but assume says DO NOT ENTER or EMPLOYEES ONLY, if the all caps and red underline are to be believed.

Using the key, he unlocks the door and holds it open for me, then lets it shut behind us so we're the only two people in the long, cramped room of dusty shelves.

"These are the nondigitized student records."

I crane my neck and take it all in, wide-eyed. "There's a lot."

"What did you expect?" He's already brushing past me with purpose. His sharp eyes scan the shelves beneath the dingy lights hanging above, until reaching one in particular. "If they arrange their records by last name, these three shelves, from here to there"—he indicates two specific points—"contain all the students with *A* surnames. Here's where 'Ahmed' begins. Unfortunately, they only use initials for first names, so we'll have to dig."

It's still a lot, but slightly more practical. "I can't read Bengali, but I can bring you the files if I know what to look for. I have Google Lens on my phone!"

"Remind me after this to start teaching you," he murmurs distractedly, which makes me blush for some reason, my imagination running wild with images of the two of us, our heads bent together, studying like the students we just passed.

I shake the fantasy from my treacherous brain. Thankfully, Sohel's too busy to notice, grabbing an armful of *Ahmed, M.* files and bringing them over to the nearest table.

He starts sifting through the files, neatly setting aside any that are *not* Mohammed. I carry over more and more for him, replacing the ones he discards back on the shelves as carefully as possible to avoid getting in trouble with the university registrar.

About an hour in, we've retrieved all of the *Ahmed, M.* files. There are no windows in the musty room and only two thirds of the lights are working, the rest either flickering or already dead, but since I don't read Bangla, there's little else to do besides exploring the planes of Sohel's face.

He has a habit of chewing on his thumbnail while concentrating, something that draws my gaze to the bow of his upper lip, a stark contrast to his fuller bottom lip. A persistent, wavy lock droops into his face whenever he lowers his head too much, prompting him to wrinkle his nose and puff to blow it out of his eyes.

There's something about Sohel that is entirely fascinating and completely unlike any of the other boys I've ever met. He's so focused and so . . . intense. Whenever his attention is on you, it feels like nothing else in the world exists.

In the end we find three Mohammed Ahmeds and one Mohammed Z. Ahmed who would have attended the University of Dhaka around the time that ours did. While Sohel takes pictures of their transcripts on his phone, I dance back over to the shelves with the leftover folders in my arms, ecstatic that we've managed to accomplish so much.

My glee is cut short by . . . well, my own lack of height.

I gripe under my breath as I stand as tall as I possibly can on my tiptoes, trying to return the final few files to a shelf looming above my head. A second later I sense Sohel approaching behind me. His fingertips graze mine as he takes the files from me and places them where they belong.

I turn around in the cage of his arms and gape up at him, my eyes wide, my face ablaze. His throat is inches away, close enough for me to hear his nervous swallow. If I stand up on my tiptoes again, I could . . .

I could . . .

He steps away and coughs into his fist. "Would it kill you to ask for help?"

"Th-thanks," I murmur, rooted to the same spot, my hand pressed against my rapidly beating heart. We both avoid eye contact as we hurry to leave.

Outside, we find our driver waiting for us. It's late, but the summer sun still lingers over the horizon, haloing the world in a sleepy, muzzy rose gold. For a while the AC is the only sound in the van as Ekhlas weaves through Dhaka traffic.

"Thanks again for today, Sohel," I say quietly. "I owe you a favor—maybe multiple for all that chaperoning you've done . . . so ask and ye shall receive."

"Buy me dinner?" he proposes.

I blink. "That's all?" When he nods, my stomach growls loudly in response. We both laugh. I suddenly realize we haven't eaten a real meal since breakfast. "Okay, what do you want? I'm sure Uncle Ekhlas and a handy-dandy Google search can find us a good pit stop."

Sohel taps his chin. "How about fried chicken?"

I grin. "Now we're speaking the same language."

CHAPTER SEVENTEEN

I don't have much time to fill my sister in on everything that transpired in Dhaka, because the next morning her friends—who landed from the states not long ago and have been taking tours ever since—corner me while I'm cleaning the pool after breakfast.

"Is it true you can dance?" her best friend, Tameka, asks, while her former roommate and the final member of their Princeton Brown Girl Gang, Aracely, hovers behind her.

"Not well enough to win the state dance championships," I joke, "but sure, I'm vice captain of the squad."

It's a little deeper than that, but they don't need to know. Back in New Jersey, my friends and I frequently pile into one of our rooms after school and dance along to K-pop idols, pop stars, and Bollywood movies until we collapse into a sweaty heap. I love dance so much that I don't get sick of it, even after long practices.

"Don't be so humble," Aracely insists. "Halima showed

us your team's performance from last year. You won second place, right?"

I nod, surprised my sister shared that with them. Even if she wasn't a hijabi, dancing is one of those things she wouldn't get caught dead doing, too meek to ever want to be the center of attention that way, so I didn't think she brought it up to her Princeton friends.

"Her gaye holud is in a couple nights," Tameka continues, enunciating the words carefully. "We know it's short notice, but we've been watching some videos of ceremonies on YouTube—"

"So, we thought we could do a small introduction dance for her," Aracely finishes. "Nothing complicated! Some simple choreo for the three of us and any of your cousins who are interested as she makes an entrance at the ceremony? Maybe a blend of Bollywood-type stuff and some US styles, since she's both American and Desi? If you think she'd like it, that is."

A light bulb flickers to life above my head.

A gaye holud is a party where turmeric is applied to the happy couple as an ancient skin care remedy so the bride in particular glows on her wedding night. It'd be one thing if it were at a party with only women in attendance, but Sunny and Halima have decided to celebrate together. After everything Sohel's shared about his curmudgeon of a grandfather, prudish parents, and judgy aunts, the vision of his family clutching their pearls in shock almost makes me cackle right then and there.

"She'd love it," I answer with a cherubic smile.

Over the next couple of days, I spend every waking minute practicing with Halima's bridal party. I even rope in Ireima and Yumjao to help teach the choreography, since Sohel graciously offered to cover for us all so none of the adults find out. Before we know it, the night of the gaye holud has arrived. This time the entire bridal party wears coordinating orange sharis with red and white roses weaving through our extravagant buns and gauzy golden shawls.

My sister, meanwhile, dons a bright yellow shari with a crown of yellow and orange marigolds across her brow. I climb into one of several waiting baby taxis meant for her, our parents, and our three grandparents, every inch adorned in matching marigolds, which slowly roll over to the main house while the rest of the bridal party follows all around the taxis, tossing petals.

We can hear music long before we've arrived. At the gate, members of the groomsmen, including Sohel and Akash—whom I haven't seen since our Baikka Beel date—greet us with more flower petals, tiny trinkets, and candy wrapped in shiny metallic foil.

The dining hall is similarly decorated, transformed beyond recognition with the table replaced for the night by many smaller ones filled with thals of traditional sweets and a menagerie of beautifully carved fruits. A raised dais sits at the far end, a curtain made up of intricately arranged rose and marigold garlands behind it. Sunny waits there for Halima.

Ammu and Abbu stand on either side of her, grandparents just behind them, me preceding everyone. While our cousins not involved in the dance lift a long veil above Halima's head for her to walk beneath, I take a step into the room and lift an arm high above my head, stretching out the other behind my back—a signal for the rest of our impromptu dance troupe.

Right away they jeté over to join me, "Oo Antava Oo Oo Antava" streaming from the speakers around the room thanks to a surreptitious click of Sohel's phone.

We turn in one fluid movement to smile at my shell-shocked sister before pirouetting on a single foot, spinning back around to the room, and flicking our wrists in time with the music. Many of the guests gasp, whistle, and cheer, but I can't help seeking out a few in particular. My own parents only glance at each other in surprise, probably wondering if they should have been aware that this was coming, but Sunny's have gone bone-pale, stunned into silence. His aunts and grandparents, on the other hand, have erupted into fierce whispers, the old man's fists trembling while his sagging face goes purple in apoplectic rage.

"What is the meaning of this?" he wheezes. "Kheh khoiseh beshorom naas khorthai?"

The crescendo of the music drowns out his furious questions, but I'm far from finished. When I crook my finger in the direction of the entranced groomsmen, while Akash watches me with his mouth wide open, Sohel smoothly transitions the song from the classic Tollywood number into a

sexier beat that pumps a funky bass through the entire room—
"Pony" by Ginuwine, an idea I borrowed from *Magic Mike*,
toning it down just enough to avoid getting grounded for the
rest of our lives while testing the limits of auntie-network
infamy.

A growing clamor ripples through the audience as my
crew collects chairs for all of us to lift a leg onto, hips already
gyrating suggestively to metaphors only the most adept English
speakers understand. The ones that do catch our drift collapse
into their own chairs at the double entendres about horseback
riding. We sink ourselves more dexterously into our own chairs
with our hands braced on top and knees on either side, flipping
our hair round and round, then strip off our golden shawls and
pitch them into the crowd.

"Wow," Akash mouths at me, catching mine.

I wink in his direction as we complete the dance by
twirling away from our chairs and crumpling into a bow that
leaves all of us scattered on the ground in front of my sister
like fallen blossoms, the pleated hems of our sharis splayed
around our legs. As a final touch, Sohel pops off a multicolored
smoke bomb that curls up around our feet. Although the acrid
odor makes my eyes water, I can't stop smiling at the raucous
applause that breaks out, interspersed with coughs and shouts.

Halima breaks character to hurry to me as fast as her
clicking heels allow. She yanks me up, her face more crimson
than the blush painted on her cheeks. "Bibi, what was that?"

"Did you like it?" I ask her, plastering an expression of

breathless anticipation onto my face, the other dancers circling us with excited hurrahs and hollers—and more than a few requests for numbers from handsome groomsmen. "We wanted to do something special for you."

She pauses as she takes in all of our hopeful expressions—some more genuine than others. *I* might not hear the end of it when she catches me alone later, but even if she wanted to string me up by my heels, she can't cause a scene about a gesture from her best friends in front of all these guests. It would make a bad situation worse.

"I . . . loved it," she lies, "but I don't think Sunny's family did. You couldn't have at least chosen a less, I don't know, racy song?"

As if on cue, a commotion draws our attention to the grand entrance of the dining room. Sunny's grandfather is storming toward the door as fast as his cane will allow, Sunny's mother and father at his heels. The groom simply goggles at them.

"Abba, ekhta minute ubao," Mr. Rahman pleads with his father.

"Baba, buuche naah tharah," his wife adds. "Maaf khoree lao."

But the obstinate old man shudders in revulsion. "Zotho theen ami baasya asi . . . History will *not* repeat itself under my watch!"

The resounding slam of the doors even makes me flinch. My sister's face blanches when Sunny rushes past her to check on his family instead of waiting out the storm alongside her.

Her friends offer her comfort on the way up to the now-empty dais, assuring her that nothing matters more than what she wants, as the bride, on her wedding day.

If only they knew the half of it.

Before I can follow them up there, I'm accosted by my parents.

"Habiba Hossain," my mother hisses, "why did you do such a thing?"

I blink up at her innocently. "What do you mean? It was a surprise. We did something similar for Bishty Afa's wedding. Lopa Afa's too. No one made such a big deal about it then."

"The Rahmans aren't like us," Abbu thunders from behind her. "They didn't need one more reason to look down on your sister—and what were you thinking with those godforsaken lyrics? This is a gaye holud, not a bachelor party in Las Vegas!"

I cross my arms and frown up at them. "Isn't that the issue? Why should we keep trying to kiss up to them when they treat Halima like—"

"*Enough*, Bibi!"

My mother's searing gaze shuts me right up. I sputter as she and Abbu dash toward the stage to run interference between Halima and all the nosy guests looking to get their gossip fix. They drop themselves on either side of my sister, who has her face buried in her hands, her shoulders quivering.

The sight twists a blade of guilt into my chest.

Sohel and I were supposed to be the ones to accompany her and Sunny up there. We were supposed to mix turmeric with milk across from one another with a mortar and pestle. The guests would then have flocked the stage—the women on Halima's side, the men on Sunny's—brushing yellow fingertips across the couple's radiant faces, until they were both dripping liquid gold.

Not sobbing.

But it's *not* my fault. If Sunny was good for her, he'd tell off his family for making a big deal about some little dance. He'd always be there for her. He'd *stay* by her side no matter what.

That's what my sister deserves.

Someday she'll realize that herself, but until she does, it's up to me to save her from making the biggest mistake of her life, even if it means she might hate me for it.

I suck in a deep breath, blink at the bright overhead lights until my eyes water, paste a mask of confused remorse onto my face, and steel myself to go up onstage.

Pretending to be sorry comes easier than I thought it would.

CHAPTER EIGHTEEN

Hours after the party I sit in front of my vanity, combing errant petals out of my freshly washed hair.

Eventually Sunny returned, noticeably lacking his parents and grandfather. Neither he nor Halima had their heart in it as the rest of the guests painted them with holdi and fed them little treats on toothpicks.

And then there's Akash. . . .

I didn't get much time to talk to him during the gaye holud but haven't been able to stop thinking about the way our eyes locked across the room.

About that single whispered "wow."

I touch my fingers to my lips as I imagine what it might be like to kiss him, then squeak when I hear the pit-pat of something against the window.

Frowning, I grab the closest potential weapon, my hair dryer, with both hands and cautiously make my way over to the sill, only to almost drop it on my foot when I spot the person who waits below the trellis with pebbles in his palm.

"A-Akash?" I stammer. "What are you doing here?"

"I couldn't go without getting to talk to you," he replies, his gray eyes longing.

My heart beats wildly in my chest.

"Please . . ." Akash's call is plaintive. "I—I have to leave again soon, but I didn't want to do it without seeing you first."

The desperation in his voice makes my decision for me. "Okay."

Now that the guesthouse is packed to the brim with family members from both sides, it will be impossible to sneak out without getting cornered by some auntie having a midnight snack. Although I've climbed down the elm tree in our backyard in New Jersey a few times, the trellises and vines outside my window here are a different story.

After slipping on a pair of sneakers and a light cashmere cardigan I "borrowed" from my sister and never returned, I carefully pick my way down until I'm close enough to the ground that Akash says, "Let go!"

"A-are you sure?" I fret, since the only thing worse than getting caught would be doing it after breaking my neck. "I might be heavier than you think."

"I can catch you," he promises.

And he does.

I let out an *oomph* when I land in his arms, my own instinctively winding around the back of his neck, then find myself staring deep into his gray eyes. They are a different kind of beautiful under the stars.

"Should we take a moonlit stroll through the tea garden?" he asks, setting me back down on my feet.

"Okay," I whisper back, hardly hearing myself over my thrumming pulse.

He takes my hand at once, ushering me away from the house and down the path leading into the gardens. My heart is drumming so hard in my chest, I worry he must hear it, but I'm not sure whether it's solely nerves or Sohel's voice in my head, warning me that there are wild animals—even the occasional tiger—that sometimes stray into the estate at night.

I gaze up at Akash's face and find his brows drawn together, his eyes far away. We haven't known each other long, but he's never been this nervous with me before.

"What's wrong?" I ask, giving his hand a squeeze.

His laugh sounds brittle. "I was just thinking how much I've wanted to kiss you since we met, Bibi."

"Oh." The word is no more than a breath.

"Do you want to kiss me?" The query hangs between us. "Or should I never have brought it up?"

I shake my head, swallow, and murmur, "I . . . would. Like to kiss you, that is."

A smile dawns across his face and his cheeks dimple. I no longer fight the desire to raise my hands and cradle them as I stand on my tiptoes and tip my chin up, my thumbs resting in the little dips that I haven't stopped thinking about since I first saw his dimples.

Akash lowers his head.

His lips brush against mine gently, one of his large hands finding my hip, the other lifting to cup the back of my head. My skin burns pleasantly wherever he touches, and I gasp into his mouth, eliciting a smile against my own.

My first-ever kiss!

He pulls away too soon. "Thank you, Bibi."

For some reason that embarrasses me. "Don't—don't thank me. That makes it weird. I wanted to kiss you too."

"You really are so special, you know that?" he replies. "Most girls aren't honest about the things they want. Even your sister—it's hard to believe you're from the same family."

I frown, not sure why the mention of Halima bothers me. Not sure why he has to bring her up in the first place. "What's up with you tonight?" Akash freezes. The expression on his face puts me on high alert at once. "What? Is this— Does this have something to do with that trip you have to take?"

"You must have heard that . . ." He stops and seems to turn the words over in his mind. "There's been some pressure on me to find a wife for a while now."

"W-what?" My heart begins to palpitate anew, my mouth so dry, I barely manage to croak out, "So soon?"

Akash frowns over at a tree in the distance. "I know it must not make sense to an American girl like you, but families like mine enter into marriages for business. That's what my mother and father did."

I frown and nod. Love marriages are still a somewhat recent concept, but does this mean Akash is about to propose to *me*? My throat feels constricted and my brain can't think, even though my mind is tripping over itself trying to process everything.

How the hell would marrying me be advantageous to the Mamuns? Are they trying to expand into the fast-food industry? To break ground in America?

Unless . . .

My heart begins to creep toward the ground as I whisper, "Akash . . . what exactly are you trying to tell me right now?"

"I wanted you to be the first to know. . . ." Guilt thickens his voice and weighs down his shoulders. "Tomorrow my family will be announcing my engagement to Yashma Baig, of the Baig hotelier family in England."

I stare at him blankly, not registering his words for several seconds. "W-what?"

"Bibi, I never meant to hurt you," he continues with urgency. "When Sunny Bhaiya mentioned you, nothing was arranged yet, talks were very, very early, and I thought—I would meet you and see how I felt. I never expected that I would like you so much."

"Do you—do you love her?" I ask. "I mean, do you like her more than me?"

Perhaps that's an unfair question to ask.

After all, Akash and I have only had two official dates. I don't love him, either, and I suppose I've also been meeting with other people like he has, but I foolishly began to think that there was a spark between us that might be possible to nurture.

Now I know there's always been someone else.

He *kissed* me after getting *engaged* to someone else.

"It's not so simple as that," he explains, running a frustrated hand over his buzzed scalp. "I had the most incredible time with you, Bibi, and—perhaps nothing has to change?" I purse my lips together, unable to even give voice to the disgust that rises like vomit in my throat, until he grimaces and starts to ramble. "Yashma isn't from Bangladesh. She doesn't have to know. It'll be a while before anything happens between us, months or even years, and—you're leaving soon too. Before you go, I can show you the cricket pitch like I—"

A resounding slap echoes through the silent tea garden. Akash lifts shaky fingers to his reddening cheek while I ball my own stinging hand into a fist at my side, tears streaming down my face at last as I glare up at him.

"I *never* want to see you again," I whisper heatedly.

If he calls after me, I don't know, because I run back to the guesthouse as fast as my legs will carry me, no longer caring if I'm spotted along the way.

(B: terrible, horrible, no good, very bad)

THE GREAT BIG BOOK OF BIODATAS

(S: What did he do?!)
(B: it's not him, it's ALL OF YOU 😣))
(S: Good luck, mate . . .)

Muaz Torafdar

DOB: 09-09
(B: what year??)

Address: Sylhet
(B: . . . where in Sylhet??)

Height: The Bangladeshi average
(B: and WHAT is that?)
(S: Taller than you if it helps)
(B: it does NOT, jerk)

Education: Vocational diploma
(B: from?? I feel like I'm losing my mind here. . . .)
(S: Who vetted this guy? My brother?)

Career: Engineering
(B: I'm just gonna stop asking. . . .)

Father: Akhtarul Torafdar Sheikh

Mother: Fathema Bibi

Grandfather: Joynul Torafdar Sheikh
(S: All these names and not a detail among them. . . .
I think you're better off tearing out any pages my
brother put in here, Miss America)
(B: I think I'm better off throwing the whole book
away or maybe setting it ON FIRE 🙁)
(S: . . . You good?)
(B: NO!)

CHAPTER NINETEEN

I sleep in the next morning.

None of my family tries to rouse me, perhaps assuming I'm tired from the gaye holud, but my eyes are still puffy from crying when I eventually drag myself out of bed—so much so, even my hundred-dollar Chanel concealer barely makes a dent in the circles.

When my sister and I end up alone at the breakfast table, I'm not sure whether to be relieved or on guard, since I'm not in the mood for a tongue-lashing after what happened last night. I hold my breath and pray she'll give me the cold shoulder.

Instead she says, "I came looking for you last night."

"Y-you did?" In my effort to come across as casual, I prop my face up in one hand, internally wincing when I remember I drizzled my chithol fita with thick honey that's now tacky against my skin. My elbow almost knocks over a teapot. "Why? If it's about the gaye holud, I already said I was sorry, I never thought the Rahmans would flip—"

"Bibi . . ." She stops my babbling short with a shrewd look

that seems to smolder a hole through me. I sink into my chair, gulping. "You weren't there when I came the first time, even though it was midnight."

"I was taking a stroll?" I attempt.

Halima's eyes narrow. "I see. What about when I came back an hour later? I thought I heard you crying."

Her tone is cynical, not sympathetic, as if she knows I was up to no good. Fresh tears well in my eyes. I catch my wobbling lip between my teeth and blink them away, then bite out, "Well, I felt bad for ruining your party. Isn't that what you *want* from me?"

She sucks in a sharp breath but doesn't immediately respond. Fisting my hands into the material of my jeans, I glower down at my plate, unable to meet her gaze. The sound of her chair scraping across the floor makes me wince. I wait for the slam of the door to follow.

Can I even blame her?

After all, I was the reason for *her* tears last night.

But it never comes.

I almost recoil when a hand half-heartedly drops onto my shoulder. Then I collapse against her, clinging to the soft silk of her blouse. She tenses against me as I blubber, "I'm sorry. I'm really sorry, Afu." Her arm wraps stiffly around me, and she pats my back in awkward intervals, but at least she doesn't push me away.

"What are you sorry for?" she asks, gripping my shoulders, when I've cried myself out at last. "Bibi, where did you go after the party?"

"Promise you won't get mad," I whisper, feeling like I'm all of five and have to own up to breaking her science project again.

Her lips thin into a firm line. "Tell me."

The words tumble out of me like quarters in an upturned Telfar bag. I confess to sneaking out with Akash, to kissing him. I tell her about his engagement. Everything short of divulging that I've been plotting to break her and Sunny up, because as I watch disappointment pucker her face, I admit to myself that I can't bear to see it transform into something worse.

I selfishly want my big sister to tell me everything will be okay.

She exhales a weary breath, using the fringes of her hijab to wipe the tears from my face without speaking. I bite my lip as I will her to say something, anything . . . though I don't know what. Yell at me? Forgive me? Hug me harder?

"It was a very dangerous thing you did, Bibi," she responds instead. "We were told not to wander through the tea gardens by ourselves, especially at night, and you went with a boy you barely know? *Anything* could have happened to you, and no one would be the wiser."

"I know." I sniffle. "It was . . . it was such a bad idea. I'm sorry."

I almost wish a tiger *had* eaten me so I wouldn't have to feel so crappy now. I can already imagine the whispers that will follow me if anyone catches wind of what happened last night.

In Bangladesh one stolen kiss is enough to brand you with a scarlet *A* for life. Never mind that Akash has been cheating on his *fiancée*, that he's probably broken a hundred hearts before I ever handed him mine.

Ever the playboy, never the slut. The patriarchy strikes again.

Halima sets a hand on top of my head. "It's fine, Bibi."

"It—it *is*?" I gawk at her. "Who are you and what have you done with my sister? That time I spilled pasta sauce on your Princeton hoodie, you didn't talk to me for weeks."

She smiles ruefully. "What else am I supposed to say? It's not like you listen to me." I duck my head, then blink at her quiet "I'm just glad you're okay."

"Thanks, Afu."

She shrugs, and I almost don't catch her muttered "It's not like I have any room to talk, anyway" as she turns back to the table and starts clearing our plates.

"What do you mean?" My little-sister senses begin to tingle. "Wait, what did you want to talk to me about last night?"

Halima falls still beside the table. All at once I notice that there's a tan line where her glitzy engagement ring has been all summer. Before my tired brain can figure out what that means, she says, "I'm starting to think it would be best if . . . I called off the wedding."

The whole world tilts on its axis.

"What?" I breathe, a roar in my ears. "You are?! Is it because of last night?"

Because of *me*?

"It's not your fault," she murmurs, as if reading my mind. "It's a lot of things. Everything. Yesterday just . . . Maybe I needed yesterday to help me make up my mind."

I stare.

Like a robot she stacks plate on top of plate, glass inside of glass. If I didn't know any better, I would think she was talking about the weather, not her engagement. Except her shaking hands tell a different story.

"Maybe you should sit down," I tell her, bolting to my feet. "Is it— Do you not love Sunny after all?"

If so, that's good, right? All I've wanted this summer is for her to come to her senses. If she has . . . If she has . . .

She collapses into my abandoned chair, and the tears dripping down her cheeks pierce an arrow of guilt through my heart. "No, I . . . I *do* love Sunny. Or . . . I did."

"What happened?" I kneel next to her, chin on her knees. "Did he say something last night?"

Halima shakes her head. "No. We haven't talked. We couldn't with so many people around. He left right after."

"Is that why?" I ask. "He—he should have been there."

"He's not my Sunny," she whispers. "The Sunny who made me laugh, who respected my choices, who's been my biggest supporter and friend. He hasn't been since we arrived. I thought we loved each other enough that I'd be okay giving up my dreams for him if it meant we got to be together. But I didn't understand what it would mean to be his wife until we got here. Last night, right after his parents and grandfather left like they couldn't stand to even look at me, his aunts began asking me how soon I could give him *children*. An heir."

"Oh." I cringe at the thought.

Her glistening eyes shoot to my face. "With the way life is here, I might have to give up *everything* for him, Bibi—my home, my goals, my family—and I'm not sure I'm ready for that. Not if he'll leave me to fend for myself."

"First of all"—I snatch her hands with my own—"you could *never* give up our family, no matter what you or anyone else says otherwise. Hell, you could banish us from ever coming to see you again, and we'd be on the next flight to Sylhet to kidnap you."

That evokes a watery laugh from my sister, but it doesn't last long. "I—I don't know, Bibi. I love Sunny, but maybe love's not enough. What if I'm being selfish with all my wants and keeping him from his needs? I'm majorly freaking out."

"It's okay," I say, comforting her. "I think that's a perfectly normal reaction to learning your future husband's family is expecting a baby machine, but what does *Sunny* Bhaiya expect? Have you talked to him about all this?"

Halima's lips contort into a bitter smile. "How can I? We haven't been alone for more than a few minutes since we got here. You know I don't mind being accompanied by a chaperone, but we *never* have the privacy to just talk. Either he's stolen away on business by his father, or I am by his swarm of aunties. I see now why their mother seems so beaten down—she *never* speaks up for herself, no matter what they say. If she isn't brave enough after so long, how can I be expected to?"

"You shouldn't," I rebut. "That's *his* job. Sunny Bhaiya needs to pull a Prince Harry and defend your honor against them."

But would he do that for her?

If he won't, this might be for the best, right? My sister will get over her heartbreak someday and find someone better. Won't she?

It's exactly what I wanted, so why do I feel so crappy all of a sudden? Why do I desperately want to be wrong about Sunny after spending all summer trying to drive a wedge between him and Halima?

"Don't worry, Afu. I'll take care of everything."

THE GREAT BIG BOOK OF BIODATAS

(B: I don't even wanna look at these anymore ☹)

(S: I'm starting to
worry about you. . . .)

Bishnu Jilani

DOB: 11-20-2002
(S: why are there so many old guys?)

Address: Born in Uttarbhag, Rajnagar,
also resides in New York City
(S: Wow, he's not far from you at all.)

Height: 173 centimeters
(S: That's about 5'7" or 8" for you Americans)

Education: B.Sc. IT

Career: IT for a Wall Street firm

Blood type: O negative, very rare
(S: . . . Well, that's new. You seeing this, Miss America?)
(B: who cares? all of these guys suck, all men suck)
(S: Oof, someone did a number on you, huh?)

Father: Abdul "Jillu" Jilani

Mother: Umme Begum

Ready for marriage: Yes
(B: sorry, I'm not)

Ready for children: Yes
(B: children???!!!)
(S: Let's just go ahead and slide this one over
to the no pile, shall we?)

CHAPTER TWENTY

News of Akash's engagement spreads like wildfire and rapidly becomes the talk of the town—perhaps even the *country*. I'm confronted with constant pitying glances and hushed whispers since everyone was aware a courtship was brewing between us.

I do my best not to show that it affects me, keeping my head high, but Abbu doesn't get the memo. The second he learns the truth—from an announcement in the *paper*, of all things—his face cycles through several shades of blue, purple, and red before he booms, "I'll kill him!"

"Abbu, I'm okay!" I try to convince him.

He isn't listening to me. "How dare that boy! Does he think because he's a Mamun, he can do whatever he'd like with impressionable young girls? And he had the nerve to show his face at our Halima's gaye holud?!"

"We should discuss this in private," Ammu tells him. "This is a family matter."

I'm relieved that she provides a voice of reason, because

he flings his Bangla patrika away and rushes to his feet, chair screeching across the wood. Halima wraps an arm around me as we all follow his stomping footsteps into his and Ammu's room.

He whirls on his heel the instant the door is shut and tugs me into his arms. I don't resist, my eyes burning for some embarrassing reason, even though I mumble, "I'm fine."

"Did he do anything to hurt you, my Bibi zaan?" he asks insistently.

I think of the kiss.

It's just a kiss, but I hate him for stealing it.

Abbu might legitimately murder him and get sentenced to a century in Bangladeshi prison if I tell him about that, though, so I shake my head against the fabric of his shirt.

Thathu sets a hand on my shoulder and squeezes. "I know it hurts, moyna, but perhaps we should be grateful we learned the boy's character so early on?"

"Our Bibi will be okay. It's not as if she was seriously considering marriage," Ammu reasons. "She's not even seventeen yet."

"That's beside the point," Abbu growls. "I know boys like him, and men like his father. They think they can use everyone else as chess pieces on a board because of who they are."

Ammu tuts in pity. "If he's ready to take that step himself, that's well and good for him. I'm more concerned for the Baig girl. I hope he learns to be loyal to her."

"I'd be heartbroken if I learned something like that

about Sunny," Halima whispers from the doorway.

"It would be a shame if someone informed the Baig family of the other games Mr. Cricket likes to play," Thathu mutters darkly.

That makes me snort.

Untangling myself from Abbu's arms, I gaze around at my anxious family, take a deep breath, and summon a smile for them. "I'm honestly okay! We went on two dates. So what? It's not like I was in love with him or anything. He can do whatever he wants."

"Attagirl," Halima says. "You will find someone so much better, Bibi."

I'm not so sure about that, but I nod. Abbu, on the other hand, scoffs. "No! No more dates! I knew this was a terrible idea!"

Ammu must expect me to kick up a fuss, because she adds, "I'm afraid I'm in agreement with your father about this, Bibi. Your birthday is coming up, and there's so much left to do for Halima. You shouldn't be stressing about boys, too."

"You're right," I agree quietly. The two of them exchange a perturbed look but don't object when I continue, "If it's okay, I wanna get some fresh air in the tea garden for a bit."

"I can come with you," Halima says.

I shake my head. "I'll be okay. I want to be alone for now."

She nods. After allowing them all to give me a few more hugs, I leave the guesthouse with a bag of water, an umbrella, and some fruit—Sohel must be rubbing off on me. As if thoughts of him have manifested the boy into being, he sniffs me out within ten minutes of my stroll and falls into step beside me. He doesn't speak, but I can read his mind.

I break the silence first. "If you're here to say 'I told you so,' I will actually punch you."

"I didn't say anything," he says, holding his palms out between us.

"You were *thinking* it," I accuse.

He darts out of my warpath with an airy laugh. Then his expression softens. "I *am* sorry my cousin hurt you. I could punch *him* if you want."

"Why do you care so much?" I ask. "Just—just to one-up Akash?"

"I . . ." Sohel frowns at the path ahead. A breath snags in my lungs as I wait for the answer. "I'm sorry. I was caught up in my rivalry with him, but I swear, if I'd known about his arrangement, I would have told—"

"It's fine," I interrupt, waving a hand, though I'm touched by how upset he seems on my behalf. "I'm not sure I would have believed you. I'd rather forget about Akash."

He makes a lip-zipping gesture and pitches an imaginary key somewhere into the brush. "Happy to do that. I can leave, if you want?"

"Actually . . ." I try to swallow the hard lump rising in my throat. This might be even tougher to discuss than Akash. "There *is* something else I wanted to talk to you about."

"What is it? Mr. Ahmed?" he asks.

"It's about Operation Breakup."

Sohel's brows pinch together when I lower myself onto the ground and pat the grass beside me, but he obligingly drops down too. "What about it?"

Playing with the straps of my bag to avoid his scouring gaze, I explain Halima's conundrum to him, as well as my plan to get them some privacy.

A tempest of emotions storms across his face, before settling into one resembling betrayal, his jaw clenched tight. "You're serious? You're going to back out now when we're so close to finishing this thing? When it was *your* idea in the first place?"

"Sohel . . ."

"No. I should have known you'd flake." He lunges to his feet like he can't bear to look at me. "I don't know why I expected anything else from you."

"That's not fair," I whisper. "It's just—after talking to my sister—I—I think I jumped the gun." I try to dredge up a sheepish smile. "You know me. I meddle first, ask questions later."

"But *I* don't," he snaps. "In case you haven't noticed, my brother and I don't get along very well, and that's for a reason. After everything that went down with my cousin, you don't think I might know Sunny a little better than you?"

I flinch at having Akash thrown in my face but try to keep my voice level. "I have, in fact, noticed your very *one-sided* hostility toward him." This earns me a venomous glare. I stand up too. "How come you don't like him, anyway? You're always attacking him, but even in private, Sunny's never had a bad word to say about you. He brags about how you're so smart and seems genuinely proud of you."

Sohel scowls down at the ground. "You don't get it. *Nothing* bothers him. Nothing ever makes him say, 'Enough.'"

"I've only known him for this summer." I choose my words carefully. "But even if I still have my doubts about him being right for my sister, he seems like a legitimately decent guy. Do you think he's lying about loving her?"

He shakes his head, an inkling of frustration bleeding into his tone. "I'm not saying he's a bad person. My brother never sets out to hurt anyone. *Everyone* thinks he's such a nice guy. But he just looks the other way if people end up hurt, even when he's responsible. In that way he's a chip off the old block, just like my father. How nice can that be?"

"How could he notice something was going on with Halima Afu if they were always kept apart?" I ask, trying to understand.

Sohel presses his face into his hands. "You don't know him like I do. Blame my father all you like, but at some point you have to accept that Sunny runs from his problems because *he* wants to. Because it's easiest for him." The next few words are almost incomprehensible in the breeze that rustles the tea leaves and plucks at my skirt. "I've certainly accepted the kind of person he is by now." But then he gets angry again, dropping his hands to point at me. "And you know what the worst part is?"

"What?" I whisper.

His smile is all edges. "That I'm the *only* person in the world who sees it. He can abandon us a hundred times, screw up a thousand, but my family will always welcome him back with open arms. Because he's the *beloved* first son, so this place that means nothing to him and everything to me is *his* birthright."

There's some deeper-rooted hurt there that I don't think I'll fathom anytime soon. Even if I've sometimes felt inadequate compared to Halima, instead of taking Sohel's approach of setting myself on fire in the hopes that my parents would praise the warmth, I chose to be Bibi. Chose not to care if I'm a little bit *less* than my older, smarter, more beautiful sister.

I try to imagine the Rahman brothers over the years. At some point, I guess Sohel, who seems to care about so many things so very much, came to the conclusion that his brother didn't care at all, even about him.

"You're right." I surrender at last, grateful when he allows me to close the distance between us and set a hand on his back. "You know your brother better than I do. Maybe better than anyone else. So don't do this for him. Do it for Halima. You *like* her. I know you do." My voice softens. "You want her to be happy."

"I do like her," he allows. "That's why I think she's better off without him. This is how my family *is*. I've watched them tear my mother down my entire life. My brother is like my father—anything to keep the peace. Perhaps Halima Afa should get out while she still can."

Now that I've come to know Sohel, I know he means this in earnest. This is his way of expressing concern for my sister. I can appreciate that, but . . .

"She *loves* him, Sohel," I tell him softly. "Don't they at least deserve a chance to work things out?"

He ruminates over my words for what feels like forever. I hold my breath until he says, "Fine. I'll help."

"Thank you." Sohel looks at me intently, and I suddenly realize his eyes are very close to mine, locked in a deep, unspoken understanding that he's doing this for me. In that moment I feel completely seen. The intensity of it surprises me so much that I have to look away and crack a joke. "If I'm wrong, I'll never doubt you again, O Wise One."

"Yeah, yeah." I catch a glimpse of his scarlet cheeks as he marches toward the manor house. Did he feel it too? Whatever *that* was? "Let me go find my oaf of a brother and come up with an excuse to get him away from Baba." He's already halfway back when he stops in his tracks. "Hey, Miss America?"

"Yeah?" I blink at his back.

He turns to flash me a smirk. "Just one other thing . . . I told you so."

That shocks an incredulous laugh out of me. I toss him two thumbs-up in return.

CHAPTER TWENTY-ONE

It's surprisingly easy to make the pieces fall into place once I've recruited Sohel.

"How'd you swing this?" I ask him as we spy on our siblings from the top of a little hill overlooking a small waterfall in a private copse of fragrant orange trees that I've never seen before because of a locked gate.

"Just asked him to lunch." Sohel shrugs. "I never ask him for favors, so he tripped over his big bungling feet to make time."

"See?" I bump our shoulders together. "He *loooves* you."

"Shut up!" he mutters with a light shove. "What about you?"

I shrug, drawing my knees up to my chest. "Told my folks I needed some sister time because of my broken heart. They bought it."

Swapping devilish grins, we return to our observation of our siblings. Mist from the waterfall glitters in the air and grass. Sunny and Halima sit on a blanket spread out over the banks below, but only have eyes for each other, not the food or Insta-worthy scenery.

I almost go cross-eyed in an attempt to lip-read while Sohel pours tea out of a thermos and hands me the screw top that doubles as a mug. I accept it from him and offer half of a finger sandwich I pilfered from the picnic basket, which he begins to nibble on delicately.

When I take a distracted swig of the tea, my eyes widen. "It's sweeter this time!"

"Right." He makes a face as he tries some, then switches out the flask for my makeshift cup, giving me the bigger portion, seeming not to notice or care that we've both already taken sips. "I have no idea how you take it like this. It's more sugar than tea!"

"*I* have no idea why you made it this way if you're going to complain," I rebut with a raised brow. "It's not like I asked you to, mister."

He chokes on another sip, then coughs into his fist, scowling at me when I pound his back hard to help him get it down the right pipe. "Just didn't want you whingeing again."

"*Whingeing*," I repeat, imitating his ridiculous posh accent. He opens his mouth to defend himself, but I end up smacking his arm in my fervor while pointing with my mug. "Look, look, something's happening!"

We both careen forward on the ledge to watch as Sunny places an imploring hand on his chest, his eyes red-rimmed with remorse. He gestures in the direction of the manor, past the orange groves, and shakes his head.

Halima's hands shoot up to cover her mouth, her own eyes glassy. After a long minute that feels like an entire eternity, she nods, tears glimmering like crystals in the sun. Sunny reaches out to hug her, his lips whispering a mantra I recognize even from so far away—"I love you, I love you, I love you!"

"I think they made up," Sohel murmurs.

"I guess this once we don't have to tell if things aren't strictly halal," I reply, averting my gaze in order to grant them more privacy. I don't know how she did it, but my sister miraculously managed to avoid PDA with Sunny until now. Not for the first time in my life, I think hijabis are stronger than the US marines. "They're practically married anyway."

"Mm," Sohel hums in agreement.

After a moment our siblings spring apart, clearly flustered. Sunny waves up at us to signal that everything's moving forward as planned. When I turn to Sohel, he is smiling too, an expression so soft and affectionate, I'm not sure he realizes he's doing it. "See, aren't you glad you decided to be a good brother for once?"

He snorts. "We can't all be such doting siblings, Miss America. I'm probably the one person in the world who doesn't coddle my brother."

I set my finished tea aside and draw up my knees, cocking my head at him above them with a besotted smile. "You know how much I love second chances."

He quirks a smile at me. "Do I. I have to admit, I went along with your chaperoned dating thing because I thought it would be fun to mess with you—"

"Thanks." My good mood dims. "Your generosity knows no bounds."

"*But*," he continues, ignoring my sarcastic jab, "I never could quite wrap my head around why you wanted to do it in the first place. Now I think I might get it. You're a hopeless romantic, aren't you?"

"Well, maybe a *tiny* bit," I concede. "Abbu calls me boy-crazy, but the truth is, I've always just wanted to feel noticed by someone."

"I find it hard to believe you don't draw *every* eye in the room," Sohel scoffs.

"You don't know what it's like having Halima for a sister," I answer, smiling down at the sibling in question. "I mean, don't get me wrong. It's not her fault. She can't help being who she is either. *Everyone* has paid attention to her all our lives. Aunties would say right to my face that it was a shame I didn't have her complexion or her brains."

"What?" His hackles rise. "Have they even *met* you?"

Heat floods my cheeks, but I do my best to keep my words from garbling together. "Thanks. I know I'm special in my own ways, but when I was younger, I guess I tried to become the exact *opposite* of her. I started going by Bibi instead of Habiba so teachers would stop confusing us. I got really into fashion and dance, in part because I knew Halima never would. And

I noticed that boys noticed me, no matter how much my dad tried to chase them away."

"You *are* very noticeable," Sohel says, relenting after a moment.

I elbow him playfully again. "Keep talking like that and you might give me a big head."

"Too late," he teases, then laugh-grunts when I catch him in the ribs.

"Maybe, somewhere along the way, I became kind of a romantic, both for myself and others." I shake my head, surprised by the revelation myself. "It just seemed like something I could be good at."

"So, *that's* why you're into meddling in everyone else's love lives," Sohel guesses before thrusting up his arms to shield his midsection. When I only roll my eyes, he grins. "On that note, I think I tracked down one of our Mohammeds. He doesn't live too far away, if you want to go meet him with me tomorrow."

"Really?" I exclaim, whirling so fast toward him that I almost knock us both flat onto the grass. He catches me at the last minute, arms around my back, stiffening when I take it as an excuse to wrap my own around his shoulders.

After all, being on a personal romance cleanse doesn't mean I can't poke my nose into *other* people's love lives. Look how much I've already helped Halima and Sunny!

Abbu may have banned me from dating again, but he *never* said I couldn't play matchmaker.

CHAPTER TWENTY-TWO

Sunny and Halima are giggling like schoolkids on Valentine's Day when we make our way down the hill to help them clean up their picnic. The sight warms the cockles of my heart, since I haven't been given many opportunities to see them like this.

"Everything okay with you lovebirds?" I ask just to be sure.

My blushing sister nods, while Sunny proclaims, "Better than ever, Alhamdulillah!"

"The wedding is still on, and"—Halima shares a solemn glance with her fiancé—"we'll be doing things our own way, at our own pace. We want to start a family someday, but on our own time."

"Thank you both for making this happen." Sunny beams at Sohel and me before settling his gaze solely on his brother. "Sohu, it means a lot to me to have your blessing."

Sohel crosses his arms and casts a practiced aloof look over at the waterfall, but his tinted cheeks bely his true feelings. "Just take care of your wife, and we won't have a problem."

"Because if you don't—" I cut in, dragging a thumb across my neck and waggling my eyebrows as villainously as I can manage until my sister no longer looks like she can decide between muffling a laugh or scolding me. "Lots of places to bury a body out here."

Sunny rubs the back of his neck with a self-conscious smile, which grows more genuine when he turns it on his bride-to-be. "Thank you both for being on Team Halima. Because I am too. Always and forever."

"I love you, Sunny," Halima whispers.

Sohel and I let them walk home a couple of feet ahead of us so they get a few minutes of straggling in private.

The next day, Sohel and I turn our attention to the missing Mohammeds.

Mohammed Z. Ahmed, the only one who used his middle initial, ends up not being our man. When I interrogated a befuddled Thathu about what the *Z* stood for over tea one morning, she informed me that her Mohammed's middle name was Ziarul. The Mohammed we found was Zamil. But another one Sohel tracked down ticks off a bunch of boxes.

"He's a playwright and director at Moulvibazar's newly opened Kazi Nazrul Islam Theater," Sohel informs me while we sit on the fountain in front of the manor, a bag of fish food in my lap for the koi and his sketchbook in his lap. "Since he often wrote your grandmother poems in his letters, I thought that the playwright might be a strong contender."

"Moulvibazar's pretty close," I muse. "Why don't we go ask him ourselves?"

"My thoughts exactly," he agrees. "But Sunny and Halima asked our parents and grandparents to dinner at an Indo-Chinese place in Moulvibazar, presumably to discuss their plans for the future, and they're taking Ekhlas Sasa."

I frown. "So? Don't you Rahmans have a fleet of private drivers?"

"The rest would *immediately* run to my parents to get permission," he replies with an exasperated sigh.

"So, what's the plan?" I ask. "You always have a plan B, right?"

A smirk slowly spreads across his face. "I always have a plan B."

Less than an hour later I pick my chin up off the ground when Sohel pulls up the road leading out of the estate on a glossy red-and-black motorcycle.

He slows to a smooth stop right in front of me and slides off his helmet, a breathless grin beneath, his dark hair all fluffed up. "What do you think?"

"Are—are you even allowed to have this?" I wonder, eyes darting all over him and the bike to inspect them for scratches.

Sohel snorts. "Do you think I stole it, Miss America? It was an eighteenth-birthday gift from Sunny Bhai—a month late, I might add."

"A birthday gift?" I run reverential fingertips down the

metal sides of the bike, staggered by this fact. "Do you know what my family got me last year? Makeup. Do you know what they'll probably give me for my birthday in a few days? Clothes."

Don't get me wrong, I never mind either, but it's *not* the same.

Sohel's brows pinch together. "It's your birthday this week?"

"Yeah, my seventeenth—but it's no big deal!" For some reason the question makes me redden and stammer. "With all the wedding stuff, I didn't want to make it into a huge thing."

Sohel's eyes search my face, before he distracts himself with retrieving a second helmet from the trunk space under the passenger seat. He cocks an eyebrow up at me as he holds it out. "You comin' or what?"

I gulp as I gaze between him and the *very* small space remaining on the bike, my knuckles blanching around the helmet. Sucking in a deep breath, I stick the helmet on and take the hand he offers to help me up.

We are incredibly close together all of a sudden. I can feel heat emanating from his body and smell the citrusy spice of his cologne as my arms reluctantly wind around his waist. He goes rigid in my grasp, and I wonder if perhaps I should let go, but I tighten my grip when his next command reverberates right through his back into the cheek I'm resting against his spine, even through the helmet: "Hold on tight, Bibi."

The motorcycle zips into action.

A choked-off scream tears out of me as the world transforms into a blur of green and brown, my heart skipping several beats from the speed of the bike. I can hear my heart—or Sohel's—thundering in my ears, louder than the roar of the engine.

There's an open road out of the tea garden. Sohel pitches his body forward and steers the motorcycle along at full speed, dodging the occasional car trundling leisurely along the path, until we reach the traffic feeding into Moulvibazar.

The bike is so sleek and swift that he easily skirts around bigger vehicles and swarms of pedestrians, seeming not to mind the force with which I squeeze his ribs. Wind whips all around my body, ripping at the frilly bottom of my Celine blouse, making me glad my hair isn't long enough to stick out much from the helmet and lash us across the face.

It's more exhilarating than any roller coaster I've ever ridden.

All too soon he slows in a busy square, in front of a grand stone building. Vaulted windows are carved into the smooth gray surface, elaborate swirling patterns adorning each, turrets on every corner of the roof.

An awning with a balcony above it hangs over our heads, from which a marquee states the title of a play in Bangla. There's a man pacing near the wrought-iron railing, but he doesn't pay us any mind. The sound of drums and flutes streams from within.

"I—I think they might be in the middle of a performance,"

I croak into Sohel's back, breathless for some reason, my eyes not yet readjusted to the stillness.

Although I haven't yet released him or removed the helmet, he seems to understand what I mean, since he jerks his chin at the ticket stand. "I'm sure they'll let us in if we pay."

I nod, but my limbs are jelly.

A gentle hand—gloved, I realize distantly—sets itself on mine and carefully pries my fingers apart, but Sohel doesn't release me. Clutching the errant appendage, he painstakingly climbs off the bike, then helps me get down, holding on to me until I'm steady again.

"Okay?" he whispers. I nod, thankful for the helmet hiding my furiously blushing face. When I work up the nerve to remove it, Sohel chuckles at my helmet hair. "You look like a poodle after it's been blow-dried."

I scowl up at him. "Yeah, well, you—you—"

He has the nerve to be perfect.

His golden cheeks are rosy from the thrill, and one comb of his long fingers through his fluffy hair makes it rest artfully around his face. Between that, the black jacket, and the gloves he wears, he looks as if he's walked right off the set of a *Teen Vogue* motorcycle modeling shoot.

"Me . . . ?" he presses, crossing his arms.

I can tell he already knows, so I shoulder past him while doing my best to smooth down my own hair, steadfastly ignoring the barely stifled chuckle behind me.

"Ji, ma'am?" the ticket boy asks at the counter where I've

arrived first, Sohel making sure his bike is properly parked and locked. "Dekhana tho arombo oigese."

Soon my partner in crime returns to step in front of me and takes over the task of explaining our plight. Peeking around him, I catch Mohammed's name and assume Sohel is asking where we can find the man we're looking for.

After listening for a few minutes, Sohel turns to me. "Apparently they're having some kind of problem. One of the actors fell ill right before they could commence act two. I think Mr. Ahmed might have been the guy on the balcony we saw on our way in." To the ticket boy he says, "Thuita ticket thilao."

Although he seems confused by why we'd want to attend an already in progress performance with behind-the-scenes drama, he and Sohel exchange money for tickets, and the two of us enter the dimly lit building. The heavy red curtains are shut. Over the instrumentals of the band visible on either side of the stage, we hear the discontented mutters of the audience.

Before I can find a seat, Sohel grabs me by the wrist and jerks his thumb in the direction of a side entrance with a sign. "That's the balcony. We should go."

"Wouldn't it be better to wait until the performance is over?" I hiss back.

He motions toward the complaining spectators. "At this rate it might already be."

"Okay," I allow, shadowing him to the door with paranoid glances over my shoulder to ensure no one catches us.

It's not locked and he quickly slips inside, then takes the

stairs two at a time to a second entrance, this time to the balcony itself. When we open the door, we find the man from earlier now crouching on the ground with his head in his hands, fingers grasping at steel-gray curls.

Could this be Mohammed Z. Ahmed?

"Excuse me, sir," I call out. "Are you okay?"

His head whips up. "What are you two doing here?"

I take the lead and start explaining. "We're looking for a Mr. Mohammed Ahmed who attended Dhaka University between the years 1969 and 1971. Is that you, sir? Please, it's very important!"

The man makes a vexed sound as he dusts himself off, already indicating for us to get out of his way. "I have no time to reminisce with you children. My directorial debut is proving to be enough of a disaster without a stroll down memory lane."

"Because an actor got sick?" I ask, recalling what the ticket boy said.

"Not only that but he got his *understudy* sick," the man who has yet to deny he's Mohammed Ahmed bemoans. "How does one accomplish such a virulent feat? Both of them are now vomiting up their very souls backstage. The show must always go on, but how can it under these circumstances?"

Sohel makes a sound in his throat that resembles a choked-off laugh. Elbowing him in the side to shut him up, I continue, "Can *we* help somehow?"

"And how exactly do you propose to do that, young lady?"

the old man challenges, taking a step in my direction with a finger outstretched.

I stumble into Sohel, who tows me behind his frame and frowns down at Mr. Ahmed. "I get that you're upset, but don't take it out on—"

The man gawks up at him. "You—you're—how tall are you?"

That throws us both for a loop.

Before Sohel can so much as stutter "W-what?" Mr. Ahmed is circling him with shrewd eyes, like an auctioneer surveying a prime piece of antique furniture at an estate sale.

"My . . . ," he mumbles beneath his breath, stroking his white goatee. "What fine bone structure. A dancer's physique. Are you classically trained, by chance?"

"Ummm," Sohel replies, horror dawning in his eyes. "I-I'm not even *un*classically trained. Whatever you might be thinking right now, sir, please don't."

I gape at the two of them, unsure how to arbitrate, but Mr. Ahmed refuses to be deterred. "It's not a problem! The complicated parts of the story are over, but you would be a perfect stand-in for the sick actor. You would only have to die!"

"D-die?" Sohel goes pale. "I-I'm not sure I'm ready for that."

Neither of us expects the man to then throw himself at Sohel's feet and lunge for his ankles, sobbing, "Please! A producer from Dhallywood is rumored to be in attendance, and it would ruin my career as a director before it ever takes off if I can't finish my first play!"

Sohel eyes me helplessly above the man's bawling form. I shrug and mouth, "Sorry."

Grimacing, he kneels to help Mr. Ahmed rise to his feet even as he mutters, "You said I just have to . . . die, right?"

"You die almost instantly," the man promises, all traces of tears gone. "If you help me with this, I will owe you my life, young man."

"We don't need your life, sir," I pipe up, giving him a little wave to remind him of my existence. "Just a few minutes of your time to ask you some questions."

Mr. Ahmed gazes between the two of us, then snatches up Sohel's hands, staring deeply into his eyes while he squirms. "I vow to answer all of your questions."

Sohel shoots me another panicky look. Although it kills me to give up on this, I slice a hand across my throat to let him know he doesn't have to do anything that makes him uncomfortable. Maybe once the show ends, Mr. Ahmed will find it in his heart to speak to us when we tell him about Thathu—not that I'm sure she needs such a melodramatic co-star.

Sohel takes a deep breath. Both Mr. Ahmed and I hold our own breath, then utter a collective sigh of relief when he says, "I guess if all I have to do is die, I can at least try."

"Dhonyobad, dhonyobad, onek dhonyobad!" Mr. Ahmed declares.

I'm ushered backstage with Sohel after a brief misunderstanding, during which the theater staff try to direct me into the audience instead. Before they can, he catches my hand in a terrified vise and grits out, "Thai amar loghe thakbo."

"We're a package deal," I confirm, tipping my chin high.

Mr. Ahmed pinches the bridge of his nose but shoos away the hovering costume designers, muttering something about divas. I wait outside Sohel's dressing room while they get him ready, snickering to myself when I hear rustling cloth, loud thumps, and his familiar voice cursing in English and Bengali. Eventually the costume designers leave the room looking like they lost a fight with a mangy cat.

One of them says, "He wouldn't let us touch his face."

"Miss, can you?" another implores, presenting a makeup brush to me.

Although the rest of the actors meandering about backstage don't wear overly exaggerated costumes, and all of the designers are staring at me with such hope, I've never done theater makeup or any other professional looks before.

If Sohel is doing such a massive favor for me, however, I guess this is the least I can do in return. Hoisting the makeup brush aloft like a weapon, I announce, "I'm coming in," and enter his dressing room, not quite sure what to expect on the other side of the door.

Sohel sits in front of a vanity with a baleful expression. "Do. Not. Laugh."

That makes me want to dissolve into a giggling fit even

more, but I manage to shove the laughter down my throat with a palm as I make my way over to him. He's got a hideously fluffy white robe tied tightly at his waist and an orange pagri crowning his head, a garland of fake marigolds around his neck.

"Oh no," I whisper. "Don't tell me it's your death *and* wedding day."

He sniffs derisively. "Watch how you speak to me. Apparently I'm a prince."

That does it—I snort.

Sohel's lips twitch reluctantly. "You owe me big-time for this."

"Anything you want, Your Majesty," I retort with an angelic smile, shifting my attention to the scattered makeup on the vanity. It's mostly face paint, probably to evoke a more dramatic effect for the audience members furthest from the stage. "Close your eyes."

He does.

There's so little distance between us that I can tell he's hardly breathing. I'm not sure I am either as I squirt primer into my hands and begin gently applying it to his angular, blemish-free face, tracing the sharp curves of his cheekbones, the stark lines of his jaw. I whisper what I'm about to do before I do it so he's not startled. His long eyelashes still flutter when I grasp his chin to lower his head, bringing the nib of a kohl liner to his eyes. I'm careful, ever so careful, not to poke him in the eye.

When I'm done, I ask, "Can you open them?"

He blinks a few times, then gazes up at me through the moist fan of his lashes, now darker and fuller, his brown eyes honeyed by the bright bulbs in the vanity. "Do I look bad? I've never worn makeup before."

"You look great," I assure him with an affectionate smile, my chest brimming with too many emotions to name. "I always did love when Bollywood leading men used to wear kajol. It's such a shame toxic masculinity makes them do it less often these days, because you literally look like a sexy pirate when you do." Sohel's cheeks flush even without any of the powder blush, and I realize what I've just confessed. "I—I mean the royal *you*—not you-you, or even royal-prince you sitting here right now, but the—"

"I know what you meant," he interrupts, a little strangled. "Can we finish up?"

"One last thing," I say, and bend closer with another brush, using it to dab a bit of red onto his lower lip. His sharp intake of breath makes my eyes flick to his. Suddenly I'm hyperaware of how close we are, how little it would take to breach that distance. Instead, as he stares into my eyes, I use the pad of my thumb to smear the red across his mouth until it's no longer so vibrant, but a subtle tint a mere shade or two darker than his natural dusky pink. I pull away at last. "Th-there! All done!"

Sohel is still looking up at me in a way that makes me want to—

I don't know.

He parts his lips like he might say something, but before

he can, I hold my ear up to the door and exclaim, "I think I hear Mr. Ahmed! Let's go!"

Like a coward, I escape from the room, but the old director thankfully does arrive right after to spirit his newest rising star toward the curtain.

Although he now looks the part, Sohel is far from a good actor. Mr. Ahmed guarantees he doesn't have to worry about memorizing any lines—his character is only meant to stare soulfully into his lover's eyes with a hand cradling her cheek and then get swarmed by enemy soldiers who stab him a bunch of times.

"It's an homage to Shakespeare," Mr. Ahmed explains with pride.

Sohel and I exchange a mystified look, before he's all but shoved onto the stage, now decked out in a billowing orange fanjabi with baggy white harem pants and pointed wooden shoes that are a size too small, borrowed from the sick actor.

Rather than gracefully lowering himself onto his knees in front of an actress in a bridal shari, Sohel stumbles, lands heavily on his palms, and looks up at her with bafflement rather than adoration on his frowning face. She manages to guide him into the proper position with a hand on his cheek, something else he forgot, and soon commences her passionate monologue.

They're attacked by armored actors swinging wooden swords who manifest from every side of the stage before she can kiss him—which I tell myself I'm only relieved about because I feel guilty enough for roping him into this in the first place. One evil soldier lifts Sohel to his feet by the scruff of his fanjabi's collar when he's too slow to rise himself, then wedges his prop sword under his armpit so it might pass for a genuine stabbing to the audience.

Mr. Ahmed, meanwhile, is furtively mouthing "Die! Die!" to Sohel.

Upon noticing the man, Sohel frowns but dutifully lifts an arm to the heavens while pressing his other hand to his wound. He grunts out an "Ami shesh! Mara ghesi!" that wasn't in the script and does a wormlike writhing collapse onto the ground.

His fake bride weeps over his body, then grabs a fallen dagger to exact vengeance, while he's supposed to lie there, dead, until the scene ends. I'm pretty sure I catch him impatiently cracking open an eye at least once over the next fifteen minutes, and then he's so motionless, I wonder if he's taken the opportunity to nap.

Mr. Ahmed buries his face in his hands. "He's awful. What a tragic waste of a face." Tears are streaming down my own at this point, but I squeeze the fingers of both hands over my jaw hard enough to leave imprints so the man doesn't hear me laughing at his magnum opus. He catches my faint gasps regardless and eyes me suspiciously before saying, "Well, I suppose if you and the audience are moved to weeping, that's all that matters."

To his credit, there are a few people applauding and wiping away real tears. They give an unenthusiastic standing ovation when the actors and Mr. Ahmed take a bow, a gloomy Sohel in their midst looking like he wishes he'd actually died.

I whistle and clap, and when a vendor selling roses passes the stage, I even purchase one from her basket to present to a tomato-red Sohel upon his return. It's my turn to flush when he tucks the stem behind my ear instead, brushing away a loose lock. Mr. Ahmed clears his throat before the two of us melt into puddles of embarrassment.

"Although there was room for improvement," he starts, before backpedaling at Sohel's withering glare, "I'm very grateful to you for your help. What is it you wanted to ask?"

"My name is Bibi Hossain," I explain to him as I pull up Thathu's photo on my phone. "This is my grandmother. When you were a student at the University of Dhaka, you may have known her as Shuki, but her name is Khadeza Khatun." He frowns down at the photo. I wish with all my might for him to recognize her. "Is this you with her here? If so, she's been wondering where you've been since the war began, worried because you stopped writing so suddenly."

"Khadeza . . . The war?" Mr. Ahmed shakes his head. "I'm sorry to be the bearer of bad news, children, but I'm afraid the man you're looking for isn't me. I'd already completed my degree at the university before the war heated up, and I decided to get my master's at an institution abroad. I've never met your grandmother."

"Oh," I whisper.

Sohel squeezes my shoulder, and I lift my hand to clasp

his. Even though the logical part of me knew our first pick probably wouldn't be the right one, a surge of disappointment swells inside me. "Sorry for wasting your time, sir."

"Please, no, you saved the day," Mr. Ahmed replies. "If you lovebirds ever want a date to another show, get in touch anytime. Theater used to be the height of romance, but the forsaken youth of Bangladesh have no appreciation for cul—"

"Thank you, sir." Sohel cuts him off pointedly.

The older man snaps his jaw shut. "Right, well . . . Good fortune to you on your quest, young thespians. I shall away."

"Don't look so down," Sohel tells me once we're alone. "He was just the first one. It would have been too convenient if he ended up being the right Mohammed."

"I guess you're right." Shaking off my disappointment, I brandish a smirk at him. "We should *away* too, young thespian, before we get caught. Your aunties would be horrified to hear about your budding acting career."

He gusts a long-suffering sigh. "I'm never gonna live this down, am I?"

"Never."

Even though we didn't get what we came here for, I can't help smiling against his back all the way home, delighted that I got to witness a side of Sohel Rahman no one else in his life has ever seen before.

CHAPTER TWENTY-THREE

The next morning a knock on my door wakes me.

"Morning, sunshine!" Halima says, all bubbly, taking a seat next to me on the untidy bed. "How's my almost-birthday-girl?"

I groan and burrow my drooling face back into the pillow, tempted to tug my satin eye mask back in place. Although I've gotten used to early starts because of my shifts at the garden, I am *not* a morning person, especially on my day off.

She gives me a none-too-gentle shove. "Wake up already, sleepyhead! Don't you want the tea about dinner with Sunny Bhaiya's family?"

That gets my attention. I spring up like a Whac-A-Mole, rolling onto my stomach with my head in my hands and my legs kicking. "Ooh, yes please! Do tell!"

A luminous smile dawns across her face. "Dinner was wonderful. And by 'wonderful,' I mean complete chaos—but in a good way! Oh, Bibi—watching Sunny stand up to his father, grandfather, and aunties for me may have made me fall in love with him all over again. I've never seen him so fired up about *anything*."

"Go, Sunny Bhaiya!"

Halima utters a soft laugh. "That wasn't even the most surprising part."

"It gets *better*?" I exclaim. "I'm starting to regret not begging to come along."

My sister shakes her head like she can't quite believe it. "When Sunny said he'd be flying back and forth for the next three years, until I finished my law degree, his parents were quiet at first. I could tell his father was upset, but I couldn't get a read on his mother. His grandfather and aunts, on the other hand, started attacking me at once, furious that I hadn't already submitted the withdrawal paperwork. Of course Ammu, Abbu, and Thathu couldn't hold their tongues, so soon it became a total free-for-all."

My jaw drops. "Now I *really* wish I were there," I mutter under my breath, balling my fingers into the sheets. "I hope Sunny made them eat their words."

"He was amazing," Halima promises me. "He even told them they'd never see his face again for as long as they lived if they tried to create problems between us."

I whistle, blinking at his audacity. "Never thought he had it in him, but I like it."

"I was starting to get worried, though," my sister replies, pulling one of my pillows into her lap to fiddle with the corner. "I have never wanted to be the reason he fought with his family. I was terrified we might end up having to elope. I couldn't do that to Sunny and was about to apologize when— oh, it was incredible—*Mrs. Rahman* stood up and told everyone to have some decorum. His aunts were shocked silent as she told her husband, and only her husband, that she had held her tongue for too long. She could do it for herself, she could give up her own family to be part of his because she loved him that much"—now Halima's eyes glaze over—"but while she still breathed, she would never let her son and his wife suffer the scrutiny and judgment she had for the past twenty-five years of her marriage."

I slap a hand to my open lips. "Sohel's mom did *what*?"

"I misjudged her." Halima meets my gaze somberly. "Oh, Bibi . . . She took me aside after and told me everything. How she was born the daughter of tea laborers, but then she and Sunny's father met and fell in love in the gardens after he snuck into her village with some friends for a festival and saw her dancing. How his parents didn't approve and hers were terrified of backlash. They almost ran away to be together, but in the end Mr. Rahman was their only son. His parents begged him to stay and take over, even if it meant having to accept her."

"But they never really did."

It's not a question.

All at once the pieces of a scattered hundred-piece puzzle finally slot into place. The way Sohel's mother fades into the background around her in-laws. All the times he's implied that his mother isn't happy. How he rarely ever talks about her side of the family without hastily changing the subject. How much he wants to improve conditions at the tea estate. It makes sense, because the tea laborers are the other half of his family. His and Sunny's and their mom's. What his grandfather said about not letting history repeat itself clicks now too.

Halima shakes her head sadly. "She was only allowed to stay if she cut off ties with her own family. Sunny's thatha didn't want his grandchildren raised around them. All her husband could do for her was try to reform things when he inherited the estate."

"That's not enough," I assert, eyes ablaze. By doing that, all he ever ensured was that his wife—and Sohel, perhaps even Sunny—endured in silence. It wasn't prioritizing them at all but forcing them to prioritize him.

"No, it's not," my sister concurs, "but she accepted it to keep him and the new family they made together for this long. Now, though . . . Now she's choosing her son. And me. She'd rather fight for us than let it happen again."

I exhale a shuddering breath. This whole time Mrs. Rahman has been almost a nonentity to me. I can probably count on one hand how many times I've heard her speak. Sohel is clearly protective of her, but I just thought she was a willing mat for the Rahmans to walk all over, that the trade-off for their wealth kept her compliant.

It's obvious now how wrong I was. How strong she is. A woman who gave up everything, even her family, for love, only to find herself caged by impossible expectations and a thousand watching, judging eyes, unable to even seek comfort in the husband she braved so much misery for, because she didn't want him to have to choose between her and his family. It must have taken so much love and courage to break that cycle at all.

"I had no idea."

Halima squeezes the pillow to her chest. "Neither did I. Mr. Rahman said nothing while she spoke. His face was so stony, I was afraid I would be the reason Sunny's parents were fighting. But before Sunny's grandfather could breathe a word, Sunny's father told them all he had chosen love for himself and would let his sons do that too. He said that Sunny was an adult and could make his own choices. Not another word was spoken on the matter for the rest of dinner."

"I don't even know what to say." I sit up to hug her. "I'm just—I'm so glad everything worked out."

"Me too," Halima answers with a contented smile. "In fact, Sunny and I decided the two of us should head into town to give everyone some space today. He was hoping Sohel might want to come along, and I wanted to ask you."

"Oh." I chew my bottom lip, my heart hammering at the prospect of seeing Sohel again after our excursion to the theater.

Halima notices my hesitation and adds, "We're only doing a few last-minute chores for the wedding, so I understand if you'd rather stay at the estate. It might be boring, but—"

"You don't have to convince me," I object with a laugh.

"I never say no to getting a chance to spend time with you. Especially if we're shopping."

Halima beams and gives me a hug, only pushing me away with a wrinkled nose when I try to kiss her cheek. "Let's pick up where we left off *after* you brush your teeth."

Sunny and Sohel are waiting for us in front of the guesthouse, a Rolls-Royce idling behind them. I sneak peeks from behind Halima as we draw nearer, trying to avoid Sohel's gaze. The Rahman brothers aren't chatting or laughing much together like me and my sister, but they also don't seem to be at each other's throats.

There's a faint blush on Sohel's cheeks as Sunny says something to him, and he doesn't dodge his brother's hand—at least not for the first two seconds—when Sunny ruffles his hair.

The sight makes me inexplicably happy.

In spite of my nerves, I move forward to hook one arm with my sister while waving at the brothers with the other. "Hiiiiii, Rahman boys!"

Sunny's smile in return is a given, but the one that lights up Sohel's face seems to surprise us both enough that we end up with our siblings between us in the car. It's only as we exit it in town that Sohel falls back to walk with me and says, "One of the other Mohammeds responded to my email."

"Really?" I ask. *"And?"*

He shakes his head. "I wish I had better news, but he said it couldn't be him."

"I-it's okay." I fight to hide my disappointment, not wanting to bring down the mood. "I guess it was never going to be easy, right?"

"That's true," Sohel concedes with a frown, "but don't give up hope just yet. There's still one more person I've reached out to. I heard he's been living in Singapore. As *soon* as I hear back from him, I'll fill you in."

Although I'm disheartened by yet another dead end, the earnestness in his voice makes me smile. "Thanks, Sohel. Even if we don't find him, I'm . . . I'm glad we got to know each other better because of this."

His cheeks redden. I expect him to blow off my comment, but he swallows, smiles, and says, "Me too."

My mouth falls open, but then we're bumping into each other in the entrance to a sweet shop, the doorway too narrow to fit us both at once.

Our bewildered siblings watch our brief squabble to free ourselves from the constraints of the door and then have to subdue laughter when Sohel ends up teetering back a few steps while I trip forward and nearly land flat on my face, Halima steadying me at the last second.

"Don't get so distracted by boys," she scolds, but there's a teasing note in it.

Sohel fares a little better from Sunny, who must know to hold his tongue while his younger brother pretends to be stoic and unaffected, hands in his pockets, even with his face blazing bright red and his clothes rumpled.

I quickly attach myself to my sister's side, helping her pick out candies and pretty packaging for wedding favors. "Ooh, these golden ribbons with tiny flowers on them are adorable! And what about these rose-shaped chocolates?"

"Hm, I'm not sure about the gulafzol flavor, though," my sister mumbles. "It's great on kalajam, but sometimes a bit too strong."

We each make a face and simultaneously mutter, "Rooh afzah," recalling a rose syrup drink our father forced us to try one Ramadan that we both despised.

Sunny chuckles and turns to the curious lady at the counter. "Sample ki ase?"

She removes four delicate chocolates for us to try. This elicits Sohel's curiosity enough for him to join us, but we both end up reaching for the same chocolate and snapping our hands away from each other as if shocked by static.

"S-sorry, you can have it!"

"N-no, you take that one!"

Sunny and Halima trade another meaningful look, and then all four of us are demurely nibbling on the chocolates until we come to the consensus that the flavor is subtle enough to be a hit even with someone who doesn't have a big sweet tooth.

Outside the shop it's Sunny who asks, "Hey, you okay, kiddo?" in a surprisingly gentle voice that's uncharacteristic of him.

I fake a laugh. "F-fine of course! Sorry I'm such a klutz. I know you and Halima Afu haven't been getting much time together, so pretend I'm not even—"

"You're the reason she hasn't stopped smiling," he replies, gazing fondly up ahead where Halima and Sohel are perusing the wares of a shingara vendor, inspecting the heavily stuffed triangular pastries with amusing severity. "I'm so grateful you and Sohel kicked my ass—uh, butt; Lima probably wouldn't like it if I cursed—into gear, or I would have lost her."

"Give yourself some credit," I refute with a friendly nudge. "Halima Afu loves you *so much*. Everyone gets cold feet before their wedding—she just needed a reminder of how much you love her back. No one could prove that better than you."

And now that he has, there's no point letting on how much I doubted him myself. They're happy together, and that's all that matters.

He grins unsuspectingly. "How'd you get to be so wise, kiddo?"

"That is not typically a question anyone asks me." I laugh.

He grows somber and shakes his head. "No, seriously. I'm glad you're going to be my little sister, Bibi. You've made my life so much better since we met. Thank you for accepting me into your family and for befriending Sohel. I haven't seen him act his own age in years. He can let his guard down around you." His smile is tinged with a hint of sadness. "I always worried about leaving him here to fend for himself, but when he's with you, he cares about something other than the gardens for once. Maybe you can keep encouraging him to get out of his head, think about what's best for him sometimes rather than just what's best for the estate."

"I'm glad you're going to be my big brother too," I whisper back, touched by his sincerity but also thrown by his claim. "About Sohel . . . I think you're overestimating my influence on him, but I'll try."

Is Sohel truly so different with me?

Our siblings soon return from their street food detour with hefty shingaras in their hands, one for each of us. Sohel frowns at me and an equally choked up Sunny, as cynical as ever, but Halima merely smiles.

As my sister and I venture into another shop, I catch the Rahman brothers speaking in hushed tones, and then Sunny says, "We'll be back in a bit. There's something I wanted to check on for my groomsmen."

Halima shoos them off. I wish I could be relieved that they're gone—no Sohel means no more awkward moments. I don't think I can afford those after the way things transpired with Akash. It was one thing for that to crash and burn, but Sohel . . . He's Sunny's brother, and we're becoming friends now. If another silly crush ruins that, not only would it be much harder to avoid him than Akash, but Halima is the one who'll suffer.

My heart hurts when I remember that. I can't let it happen, not now that she's so close to getting everything she deserves.

"They're talking again because of you, you know," my sister says, interrupting my spiraling thoughts.

I whip my head toward her. "What do you mean?"

She smiles sadly. "Sunny . . . He's always regretted that he and Sohel weren't closer. He blames himself for it because he should have tried to be there more for his brother. You gave him the chance to make amends."

"I'm glad, but I think you both give me too much credit," I answer her with a nervous laugh. "They're brothers. Family. I used to think Sohel was hard to read, with that scary glare, but I think he's wanted Sunny to reach out just as much. All I did was give them a tiny push."

"Don't be so humble," Halima tuts. "You have this uncanny ability to take someone's hand and help them find even the tiniest light in the darkness, Bibi. It's one of a million reasons why I love you and why so many people get sucked into your orbit." I shuffle my feet, at once embarrassed and pleased, but only half-heartedly resist when she pulls me into a hug and lands a big, wet kiss on my cheek—most likely revenge for this morning. "Seventeen! I can't believe my baby sister has grown into such an amazing young woman."

"I love you, Afu," I reply, and mean it. "But please don't talk like that, or you'll sound like a middle-aged empty nester sending the last of her children off to college."

Halima smacks my arm.

The boys join us again outside the shop, all of our arms laden with bags and boxes. Before we can return to the car, I feel a tap on my shoulder and turn to find Sohel. Sunny and Halima have already gone ahead, and though the car loiters with the engine on, neither pokes their head out to tell us to hurry up.

"W-what's up?" I ask Sohel, my pulse beginning to gallop again.

He gazes down at the ground, before flicking his eyes up to mine with determination as he shoves a plastic bag with the name of an unfamiliar boutique into my hands. "Here."

"What's this?" I whisper, even as I open it up in a daze and peek inside.

A gasp escapes me. Sohel watches wordlessly while my jittery hand enters the bag and retrieves a golden hair ornament in the shape of a comb. Ten small leaves made of emeralds glint around a bee studded with topaz, clear white crystals forming its four wings. Dainty golden chains dangle from each leaf.

He clears his throat. "Do you like it?"

I nod fervently. "But what's it for?"

"Your birthday's tomorrow, right?" he asks, before quickly clarifying, "I asked your sister about it while getting food and figured I'd— It's not a motorbike or anything, but I thought you might like the bee since you're always making fun of me over them, and also, a memento from Sreemangal might be nice—"

"I love it, Sohel!" I assure him before he can devolve into anxious rambling. I clutch his gift close. "I can't wait to wear it!"

He quirks a relieved smile. "I think it'll suit you."

Something about those tender words makes me swallow, abruptly lightheaded and parched beneath the sweltering rays of the sun. He starts to head back to the car, but as I watch him go, the tines of the comb digging into my palm, I have a revelation.

I can't lie to myself any longer.

I have feelings for Sohel, and I don't think I can keep ignoring them.

CHAPTER TWENTY-FOUR

My birthday comes and goes. Although it's much less splashy than last year's epic sweet sixteen that ended with the police called to our street, I find I somehow don't mind the quiet contentment of time spent with my friends and family.

Then, faster than I can say Dolce & Gabbana, the day of Halima's bachelorette party arrives. As her maid of honor, it's my job to throw it for her.

"Nothing wild, Bibi," she told me when I asked what she wanted. "I haven't seen Sunny's aunts since that dinner, and I don't need to give them another reason to hate me."

"Soooo," I snarked, "no strippers, is what you're saying?"

It took a while to convince her she could trust me with the task after my joke. Although I know my sister would be more than satisfied with a simple tea party in the gardens—*she* certainly never got her birthdays shut down for noise complaints—we've *already* been doing that all summer. I want her bachelorette party to be special. Sunny agrees with me and helps me make the arrangements to book the entirety of a gorgeous restaurant with patio seating in Sylhet.

We even ensure that all of the serving staff are women so Halima can let her hair down—both literally and figuratively, since hijabis aren't comfortable unveiling around men outside their immediate families. I want to make amends for screwing up her holdi.

The restaurant turns out to be as marvelous as I hoped.

Unfortunately, the van ride over is anything but. In my eagerness to arrange the bachelorette party of her boring dreams, I forgot that it takes ages to travel from Sreemangal to most other places in Bangladesh, even Sylhet City.

Halima, Ammu, Mrs. Rahman, and I sit on one side with my sister's friends, our aunts, and our cousins, while Sunny's side of the family sits on the other.

At least, part of his side does.

Despite not wanting to create any more friction with Sunny's snobby aunts, Halima asked if it would be okay to invite some of Mrs. Rahman's family members and the other girls from the tea garden we've gotten to know all summer. When her future mother-in-law swept her up into a bone-crushing hug, there was only one answer: Come hell or high water, we'd include Mrs. Rahman's family in the festivities from now on.

Mrs. Rahman's siblings declined but permitted their own daughters to go. Now Nganu, her sisters, and other female relatives sit beside their aunt, Ireima, Yumjao, and Khoibi. They all anxiously eye the rest of the party bus like they're not sure they'll survive the night. I decided to invite Jui along as well, since the Tea Girl Gang isn't quite complete without her.

Whenever I attempt to ease the tension by blasting some music from my phone and encouraging the others to sing or dance along, Sunny's stone-faced aunts cluck among themselves, noses in the air.

The younger Rahman cousins are only marginally more conversational, although they've inherited their mothers' superior airs. We're treated to endless backhanded compliments like "I respect Sunny Bhai for being *so* open-minded" that prompt the Tea Girl Gang to sink into their seats, ashamed for daring to breathe the same air.

I *hate* it, but I don't want to make things worse by confronting anyone.

Halima's American friends make up the remaining passengers of the bus, albeit awkwardly, sensing the tension that separates the groups like a heavy curtain, even if they don't understand the internal politics of the tea estate. At one point I catch Halima's best friends whispering that the situation is more fraught than *Downton Abbey*. I can't disagree.

Once everyone steps out of the bus, my sister snatches up my arm and says, "Maybe I shouldn't have had a bachelorette party to begin with. I can't see it ending well."

"It'll be *fine*," I promise her, although I'm not confident that's true. "They're just, er, hangry right now. You're not you when you're hungry, right?"

"Bibi, that's a Snickers commercial," my sister replies blandly.

"Still," I chirp, trying to convince myself as much as her. "If they get some good food in them, it'll bring everyone together."

It does not, in fact, do that.

A kindly hostess welcomes us inside and takes us out to a patio garden. In the photos on Google, there were mood lights turning dinner visits into a dreamscape, but it totally slipped my mind that they wouldn't have the same effect during the day.

"She brought us all this way when we could have had better in Sreemangal?" I hear two of the Rahman aunties complaining as we are led to our seats.

Halima slumps next to me.

"I guess they're kind of right," I allow, "but hopefully everyone likes the food."

The restaurant serves an eclectic mix of any kind of fare you can imagine, including American, Mediterranean, Mexican, and Chinese food, as well as a diverse menu of fancy coffee, tea, and mocktails.

One of Halima's future cousins-in-law, if that's a thing, flags her over as we're all ordering to say, "Is this *all* they have? I'm currently pregnant, you see, and *foreign* food doesn't sit well with me. I spent all of my honeymoon in Venice throwing up."

"Oh." Halima shoots a glance at me.

Although I'm not sure my sister will approve, I decide to intervene with a bubbly, "Sorry to hear about your delicate constitution, Afa, but there's only one option otherwise—tandoori chicken. That'll be okay, won't it? Even the white people back home don't struggle with that."

The woman's lips flatten. "I see."

"You're the one Akash Bhai was dating, aren't you?" a girl around my age asks, giving me a once-over with a smirk on her lips.

"I wouldn't call two dates *dating*," I rejoin, bottling my reaction.

Everyone at the table swaps suggestive looks. The girl who posed the question turns to speak into another girl's ear right in front of me while the latter snickers into her palm.

The pregnant woman from earlier kisses her teeth. "You poor thing."

"Please, don't feel bad for Bibi," my sister says with a rigid smile. "Alhamdullilah, we learned the truth about his dalliances early on. I don't know about you, but if my family was that serious about getting me engaged, I wouldn't play with someone else's heart like that—or my fiancée's. I can't imagine how she'd feel if she knew."

"Thank goodness Sunny Bhaiya is a gentleman," I add, playing along.

That shuts the snooty shit-stirrers right up, since they don't have an excuse for Akash's deceitful behavior. But it doesn't stop them from being killjoys for the rest of the meal. Although there's an outdoor stage for karaoke, our family in Bangladesh is clearly afraid of painting themselves as gauche country bumpkins around the pretentious Rahmans, while none of our American guests want to break the ice first.

The Tea Girl Gang, meanwhile, does their best to blend into the background the same way they do when they're serving the Rahmans back at the estate. Karaoke is probably the farthest thing from their minds when Sunny's aunts shoot dirty looks their way anytime they so much as reach for an appetizer. The rest of us do our best to form a barrier between the two factions of Sunny's family, but it twists my stomach into knots, seeing firsthand the way his mom's side is treated like they're not even people, on or off the estate. More and more I understand why Sohel gets so fired up about the topic, and I wish we hadn't invited the Rahmans at all.

I'm tempted to brave the stage myself and begin singing a rousing rendition of "We're All in This Together" from the *High School Musical* soundtrack—except I'm not sure how much Halima would appreciate the gesture.

She doesn't look like she's having much fun either. As we finish up with our meals and sip our beverages, staring blankly up at the empty stage, she pops up in her seat and declares, "Bibi and I need to use the bathroom now!"

"We do?" I ask while everyone else side-eyes us in consternation.

She drags me off without elaborating, then spins to face me the second we're in private. "This is an absolute disaster!"

"Don't look at me," I plead. "There's only so much I can do with that crew out there."

"It's not your fault." She sighs. "It might be mine."

My eyes widen. "No way! Sure, you wanted to keep things simple, but the Rahmans would sabotage everything no matter what kind of party you set up. You can't blame yourself."

"I know," she whispers, fiddling with her sleeves, "but I feel terrible for our friends and family. So many of them came from so far away, giving up time at work, to be here for this. And Sunny's other cousins! I know how scared they must have been about coming here. I feel like I'm letting them down with this snoozefest. I can't even protect them from the insults."

I pat her arm as I puzzle over a solution. It hits me all at once. "Leave it to me!" Before she can react, I'm already sending several text messages.

Once we're back at the table, Halima and I concentrate on downing our drinks as quickly as humanly possible. Inevitably one of Sunny's aunties says, "This has been . . . pleasant, but don't you think it's time to return home? There's so much to do."

Mrs. Rahman steps in. "Why don't we let the girls enjoy themselves for a while longer while the rest of us head back to the estate?"

"What about the bus?" the auntie asks.

"Sunny is sending another," I reassure her.

"Please, feel free to go home and rest if you're tired," my sister adds. "I appreciate you for gracing me with your company today."

They don't object.

Before long, most of the older women are piling into the bus and bidding us unenthusiastic adieus—good riddance. Before she and Mrs. Rahman follow, I give Ammu a hug and ask her to let Halima's skittish mother-in-law-to-be know that my sister and I will defend her nieces with our lives. A few of the Rahman cousins remain, but that should be fine since they'll be outnumbered. Not fifteen minutes later, Sunny texts to let me know he's arrived with another bus.

I turn to the curious gathering and proclaim, "Ready? It's time for the *real* party!"

CHAPTER TWENTY-FIVE

"The boys and I are spending the day at Adventure World," Sunny informs us from the driver's seat. "We had lunch first, so we haven't been there long. Perfect time to join us!"

"That sounds awesome!" I exclaim. "Is Sohel . . . ?"

Sunny chuckles. "Yes. He called it childish, but Amma made him come."

The prospect of seeing him gives me butterflies.

Or is it buzzing bees?

"Adventure World?" one of the Rahman cousins echoes, sounding perplexed but not entirely opposed. "I haven't been there since I was a child."

"Neither have I," one of our own cousins says. "I heard they've added lots of rides."

When Ireima murmurs that she's never gone at all, with nods from her sister and the rest of the Tea Girl Gang minus Jui, several of our American guests chime in encouragingly that they haven't seen it either, and won't it be great to try it together?

"You'll like it," a Rahman girl says, tentative but polite. "It's not Disney World, but it's a lot of fun."

"I bet we will," Aracely agrees, wonderment in her eyes. "I'm from Minnesota, the state fair capital of the world. Trust me, we don't need anything fancy to have a good time."

"I *love* a good carnival," Tameka adds.

Adventure World is a riot of colors. Cheerful music flows out of a giant fountain. Although it's not the biggest amusement park I've been to, there are so many different kinds of rides, games, and stands for food that even the most wet-blanket Rahman cousins are letting loose, if the childlike awe on their faces is anything to go by.

"I left Sohel in charge," Sunny explains. "He and the others are at the stadium with some snacks they got from vendors. Let's meet up with them there."

We follow him over to a series of massive stone steps. When I spot Sohel, my heart leaps into my throat. I wonder if it would be possible for us to get time alone together at the park, then shake the thought from my head. It's Sunny and Halima's bachelor/ette party, and we should focus on them, right? The way Sohel's eyes land on me like a homing beacon the second our two groups reconvene tests my willpower.

"We should pick some group activities," Sunny tells us all. "Anyone have any ideas?" My hand shoots up and he chuckles. "Yes, Bibi?"

"I saw a bumper car raceway on the drive in," I burst out eagerly, bouncing on the balls of my feet. "What if we have a race? Boys versus girls—losers have to carry prizes around for the winners the whole time we're here."

Another rush of excitement rolls through the group. When no one puts forward a better alternative, Sunny and Halima nod at one another. "Let's do it."

To be objective, the bride and groom stay out of the matchups and judge instead—along with anyone else who declines to participate—but have me and Sohel as their stand-ins, other competitors positioned around our cars at the starting line.

"Hey, listen," Sohel says from the car beside me, almost indecipherable over the roar of revving engines. "There's something I wanted to—"

My hand tightens around the steering wheel of my pink car. The race hasn't even started, and adrenaline is already pumping through my veins at the prospect of being close to him. But with Halima preparing to wave a makeshift race flag, I'm not sure now is the best time for a heart-to-heart.

I aim a smirk at him. "You can tell me whatever you want when you're carting around my stuffed animals, Astronaut Boy. I hope you saved some room during lunch to eat my dust."

Sohel's jaw drops. Before I can determine if I've gone too far, a familiar competitive glint lights up his eyes. "You're on. Better not whinge when you can't see over the mountain of prizes I make you carry, short stack."

We set the trash talk aside when we hear, "Ready—"

Both of us lean ever so slightly forward.

"Set—"

I touch the tip of my foot to the pedal.

"Go!"

And we're off!

Straightaway I swerve to the right, slamming Sohel into two other boys. His indignant squawk makes me cackle like a witch and speed up until I'm out of his range, although I've fallen behind the other girls thanks to my ploy.

"I didn't know we were allowed to sabotage each other, you cheat," he calls after me.

"They're called bumper cars for a reason," I shout back. "Keep up!"

"Oh, we're definitely no match for Bibi," one of my cousins on the boys' side bemoans with a hysterical laugh. "She is the *Mario Kart* queen."

"Princess Peach all the way, baby," I chant, pumping a triumphant fist and grinning wider because of the wind making my cheeks flap. "Got what it takes to catch me, Bowser?"

"You did *not* just call me that," Sohel gasps.

I smirk. "You prefer the short Italian plumber?"

Whatever he says gets lost in another garbled croak when I collide into his car yet again and run him off the track in a spiraling crash—at this point more than content to slow him down rather than come in first. In the end, Sohel puts forth a valiant effort, but the girls win 6–4, with a surprisingly ruthless Ireima taking the gold. We're all breathless and giddy, our legs jelly, when we ultimately reach the finish line. Despite getting last place, Parek trails Ireima like a duckling that's imprinted.

Sohel offers me a hand to help me out of my car. Hoping my palm isn't too sweaty from gripping the wheel with all my strength, I arch a brow. "Seems you're all set to be my butler for the day, huh?"

He rolls his eyes, but there's a smile twitching at one corner of his lips. "Yeah, yeah, laugh it up. Let's see who actually wins the most prizes."

Before the group can break up into smaller ones of varying sizes, Halima and Sunny have a private debate and then suggest a ride on the Ferris wheel.

"Sohel, ride with me?" Sunny asks, surprising us both.

Halima and I enter one cabin as they disappear into another. We're both anxiously anticipating their return throughout our ride, despite the panoramic view of Adventure World—and even parts of Sylhet, greener than any other city I've known—from high above.

After the ride, Sohel and Sunny depart their cabin, talking quietly between themselves. I hold my breath and cling to Halima until Sunny slings an arm around his shoulders that Sohel doesn't shrug off. We both deflate in relief.

When everyone scatters, I think about sticking with my sister, but Tameka, Aracely, and the Tea Girl Gang are already there to keep them company, joined by some of Sunny's groomsmen. Before I can slip into the fray, Sohel clears his throat. A breath hitches in my own.

"Yeah?"

"I was thinking, maybe we could explore the place on our own for a bit," he suggests with a jittery glance. "I wanted to talk to you."

"Okay." I succeed in sounding calm, even though my heart is ratcheting into my belly. A million scenarios run through my head. Does he have bad news about the final Mohammed? What will it mean for us if we don't find him? Or even if we *do*?

Can I think of other excuses to be around him?

Will he even *want* me to?

After the wedding will there be an *us* anymore?

Sohel is lost in his own thoughts as we make our way over to a gun range game where we're supposed to shoot water guns at bull's-eyes. My nerves ramp up the closer we get. The moment he parts his lips, I blurt, "Do a lot of people bring dates here?"

Sohel blinks, caught off guard, but manages a nod. "Sure. Dating is technically taboo in Bangladesh, but that doesn't stop people. Lots of married couples come here for their honeymoons too."

Oh . . . so that means people might assume *we're* here on a date, then? The prospect makes me gulp and fiddle with the water bottle Halima made me bring along. "Have *you* ever come here before?"

"Yeah," he answers, though the line of questioning clearly stumps him. "Came with my family for a birthday once. Sunny accidentally lost me and got a proper earful."

I crane my neck so I can scrutinize his face. "Have you ever been here with a *girl*?"

"Oh." Red suffuses his cheeks, but he shakes his head. "Miss America, you know I've only ever attended all-boys schools, right? They weren't madrashas, and I'm not exactly a model Muslim, but it didn't leave much room for dating regardless."

"That never stopped Akash," I mutter before I can talk myself out of it.

He frowns down at me. "I am *not* my cousin."

There's a note of *something* in his voice, in his deep, unwavering gaze, and in response I stammer, "I—I know that," before I get sucked into the heady brown of his irises. I force a laugh and unscrew the cap of my bottle, twisting it open and shut just for something to keep my hands busy. "What about a co-worker? I heard rumors you were popular among the tea garden girls. Did you seriously never notice?"

Has he never reciprocated any of their feelings?

He answers with a shrug. "We all grew up around each other, so I can't help thinking of them like sisters."

"Okaaay . . . A pretty tourist at the tea garden, then?" I suggest, frowning up at him. "I don't know if I believe that a guy like you has never been interested in anyone."

Or that no one's ever been interested in *him*.

"A guy like me?" he repeats, crossing his arms and sounding amused now.

I blush. "You know what I mean. Don't deflect."

"Tourists are usually . . . entitled," he says, distaste twisting his lips.

"Oh," I breathe, not quite sure whether to feel relieved or disappointed.

"But . . . ," he continues.

My eyes snap to his. "But?"

His voice drops to a decibel so soft, I almost don't catch it over the carnival music coming from the gaming booth. "That doesn't mean there's never been an exception." His eyes drop to my lips, then dart back up to my eyes. "Among the pretty tourists, that is."

"Oh." I swallow. "Sohel . . . what did you want to—"

Before I can finish, the woman manning the water gun game coughs pointedly. "Sir, ma'am, apne ki line ke astha theen hold up khorbe? Na apne khelaithe chain?"

"Other people are waiting, Romeo," another customer pipes up.

We bound apart, red-faced and hyperaware of the small crowd that's been gathering around us while we were trapped in our own world. They giggle and whisper. A few even wink and blow kisses. Thankfully, the Rahman cousins aren't in the throng.

Sohel clearing his throat brings my attention back to him. He pays no mind to our onlookers, his eyes locked on the target ahead instead, a water gun now gripped in one hand. "Hey, Miss America . . ."

"Yes?"

"If I *did* want to bring a girl here for a date," he continues, and my heart leaps into my throat, "do you think she'd say yes if I gave her *that*?" I follow the jut of his chin to a humongous tiger plush that hangs from the stall, the biggest one there. Mutely I nod. A smile slowly spreads across his full lips. "Great."

The crowd around us begins to whoop and whistle as he shuts one eye, aims the gun, and shoots a perfect bull's-eye for each of the five rounds he's paid for. I hold my breath until he's done, then empty my lungs in one big *whoosh* when I find my arms full of striped fluff.

Sohel plucks me out of the line by my free hand. We don't speak for a few seconds, this moment between us as wispy and ephemeral as cotton candy. He watches me squeeze the tiger. I watch him rake his fingers through his hair until it's deliciously mussed. I have to bury my own fingers in the tiger's fur out of jealousy.

"I know you've given up on dating," he says at last, "but, Bibi, do you think you might want to go out with—"

"Yes!" I blurt before he's even done saying, "—me."

A smile brightens Sohel's face, so radiant, it could chase away every cloud in the sky. My heart skips a beat. If there weren't so many people around, I would stand up on my tiptoes and kiss it off right then and there, letting the tiger tumble from my grasp.

Instead I settle for extending a hand to him again. "Should we see who can win the other the most prizes?"

"Game on," he replies, still beaming.

CHAPTER TWENTY-SIX

I wear Sohel's hair comb to the mehndi party.

The emeralds and gold perfectly complement the embroidered golden blouse and shimmering pastel-green shari of Halima's bridal party. As her sister, my shari is unique in that it has hand-sewn golden flowers and green leaves all over the pleated skirt.

I smile at my reflection in the mirror, lifting my fingers to the ornament and letting them brush through the dangling gold chains.

What will Sohel think when he sees?

A knock on the door stirs me out of my daydreams. "Bibi zaan, are you ready? I thought we could go over together."

I hurry to open it and do a dramatic twirl for my grandmother. "Ready! What do you think?"

"Oh my go," Thathu breathes, the Bengali equivalent of "OMG." "Thumi tho khubi shundori! The bride won't be the only one turning heads tonight."

I giggle, but there's only one head I want to turn.

Together we make our way to the sidewalk in front of the guesthouse and clamber into one of the waiting baby taxis. The entire garden is a fairy wonderland at night, especially now that it's been festooned with additional decorations for the wedding, every tree strung with lights or floral garlands, the fountain aglow, wooden signs set up for the wedding procession.

The baby taxi slows to a lumbering stop in front of the teahouse behind several others, with more and more lining up behind us. I'm surprised to open the door and find Sohel, who greets Thathu and holds out his crooked elbow to help us both out one at a time.

"What a bhadro young man," Thathu croons, patting his arm.

"I try, ma'am," he replies with a pink-cheeked smile, looking incredibly attractive in a fanjabi the same shade of mint as my shari, with a similar glimmering texture and golden buttons.

She gazes between the two of us, a knowing twinkle in her eyes. "I'll head inside and make sure your father is keeping his cool, Bibi. Get some fresh air while you can."

Once she withdraws into the greenhouse with other attendees, Sohel and I are briefly alone, standing off to the side of the entrance. I tuck a loose strand behind my ear and peek up at him through my lashes. "Hi."

"Hi," he replies breathlessly. "You look—you *always* look beautiful." My lungs stop working when he reaches out to gently stroke his knuckles against the delicate, dangling chains of the bee comb. "I knew it would suit you, but you're just . . ."

"Just?" I prompt, hardly daring to breathe.

His throat bobs as he swallows. "Beautiful."

My hand rises to the comb, almost touching his. A smile claims my painted lips. "You mean . . . bee-u-ti-ful?"

That startles a laugh out of him. "You are such a dork."

"So you don't want to bee mine?" I joke.

"May-bee I do," he banters back.

Warmth surges from the tips of my ears all the way down to my toes, but before I can give him a more heartfelt thanks for his gift, or return the conversation to where we left off last night at the amusement park, Abbu meets us at the door. "Why are you standing out here, Bibi? Sohel, you too—your mother has been looking for you."

"R-right." Sohel indicates for me to enter the building first. When I cast a look at him over my shoulder, he smiles. "We'll talk soon."

Abbu drags me over to the gazebo, where Sunny and Halima have been set up, now completely enveloped in marigold and rose garlands, with hanging garlands forming a curtain around them. They wear a matching forest-green shari and sherwani set, but jeweled flowers grace my sister's neck and collarbones, fresh blossoms winding around her heavy bun through the veil of her shari, so she resembles some sort of fairy queen on her wedding day.

Her face lighting up at the sight of me, she proffers the

blank canvas of her arm. "Bibi, I wanted you to be the first to put mehndi on me."

"Okay." I drop onto the cushioned bench at her side. "But I'm going to use one of these stencils so I don't mess it all up before the professional henna artist gets to you." I point at the table in front of us, where henna tubes have been laid out into a flower shape inside a clay bowl, next to stencils, and of course plenty of treats for the bride and groom.

"Don't worry, I can wash it off," she laughs.

I shake my head. "Nuh-uh. I want it to get as dark as possible because I know that's how deep Sunny Bhaiya's love for you is."

"She's right, babe," Sunny answers with an infatuated grin. "If the henna knows what's good for it, it's not washing off for at least a week."

Halima rolls her eyes, but there's a good-natured smile on her red lips. Although she's ticklish, she does her best not to move an inch while I trace the petals, stem, and leaves of the carnation on the stencil, all the while manifesting it to turn a deep, dark crimson.

"It's perfect," my sister pronounces when I peel the stencil off.

I preen, then glance at Sunny. "Can I do one for you, Bhaiya?"

"I'd be offended if you didn't," he replies, flexing open his large palm. At the center of it I use a different part of the stencil to draw a perfect heart with petals lining the fringes, then improvise to write *SR + HH* in the center. A tender smile softens his face. "Thank you, Bibi." He looks past me. "Sohu, you gonna do my other hand?"

I turn to find Sohel hovering.

He ducks his head but nods, and I hasten to make room for him in front of Sunny, watching with wide eyes as he flips the same hand over and paints an elaborate pattern from Sunny's wrist, up his knuckles, all the way up to his nails.

His brother whistles. "Maybe we should have hired you instead of a professional, Sohu. These are incredible."

"They're not that good," Sohel denies before frowning up at Sunny. "Some of our aunts and uncles have arrived. Amma's siblings. She's with them right now."

Sunny trades a look with Halima. "Can you two invite them up?"

Sohel nods seriously. I fall into step with him and try to gauge his expression as we relay the message to his uncles and aunts, who seem jumpy but hopeful. When they're gone, I say, "This is good news, right?"

"It's . . . it's great news," he replies, quietly disbelieving. "I never thought this would happen."

I grin at him. "I like this new, optimistic Sohel."

"Maybe you're rubbing off on me," he teases, but there's something in his eyes that makes my mouth grow dry. They remain on me as he pulls out a henna tube. "Would you . . . I can do your mehndi . . . if you want?"

I suck in a breath. "I-I'd love that."

The entire party is so distracted by the surprise appearance of Sohel's mother's family that no one notices the two of us slipping out of the building. The area outside is quiet now, tranquil at night, with stars glittering above and dew glistening on the grass. Only the dueting song of crickets and cicadas surrounds us.

We take a seat on the bench in a nook beside the greenhouse. When he holds out his hand, I place my own in it, palm facing the sky. Sohel's eyes flit to mine before he lowers his head and brings the tube down to my skin. I shiver at the cool moisture beading against my skin.

His breath raises goose bumps along my wrist when he murmurs, "You asked me if I've ever dated. And I haven't, really. But I never told you why." I gasp but can't bring myself to interrupt. He draws a careful line down my arm, following the faint green of my veins, then adds leaves to the painted vine. I can hear him swallow. "I grew up hearing about my parents' love story but never seeing anything besides the aftermath. I always knew my mother wasn't happy."

"Oh, Sohel . . ." I bite my lip. "I—I understand. We don't have to—"

He shakes his head. "I don't think you do, actually. I'm—I've always been scared of putting my heart on the line the way she did, because it seemed to me that love could only be about sacrificing and suffering for someone else. I didn't want that . . . and I've never wanted to put anyone else through that either. That's why I was against Sunny Bhai's engagement at first. I love my brother, I really do, but I wasn't sure he would be any better, any less careless than our father, and I didn't want that for your sister or anyone else." His voice drops to a scarcely audible whisper that I feel more than hear. "I don't want to be that way."

"You won't be," I reply fiercely, cupping his cheek with my free hand. "I have never met *anyone* who cares as much as you. You try to act all tough, but I can see how much it hurts you whenever someone else is hurting, how much you go out of your way to help others whenever you can. How can someone like that ever be careless?"

"Bibi . . ." His hand moves to cover mine. A wary smile curls his lips as he confesses, "I tried to be careless with you. I told myself you were hasty and impulsive, that looking for love was a fool's errand at our age. I tried so hard not to care when it became clear Akash would break your heart, told myself it was your fault for letting him, but I—I . . ."

"Couldn't?" I finish for him.

He nods, looking away. "It's impossible not to care for you, Bibi. When I finally stopped fighting your orbit, I realized . . . well, maybe I'm a coward, but *you* are brave."

"I'm starting to realize I can be a bit reckless," I admit with a contrite smile.

"A bit?" He shuts his eyes in disbelief. "It's—it's more than a bit, but I like that about you. I like *everything* about you, even when you make me want to tear my hair out. When I'm with you, I want to try to be brave too, because I . . . I like you. I like you a lot. Too much to want to be just a summer fling."

"Sohel, no. . . ." I shake my head fervently, shocked he could ever believe that. "There's no way I could see you as *just* anything. You're so much more than that."

Sohel is an entire garden. As stubborn as a weed. As beautiful as a rose. You might prick your fingers on his thorns if you aren't careful, but if you take your time, if you water and prune and care for him, he can blossom into something entirely unexpected. As lovely and complicated as the tea gardens he belongs to.

My eyes fall to his lips. Before I can make sense of the jumble in my mind, he pitches forward to graze them against mine. His are soft and featherlight, tasting ever so faintly of citrus and sugar, the rich coffee-chocolate scent of agarwood imbuing my senses. I rock forward more urgently, dropping my hand from his cheek to his collar. His mouth shapes into a smile, his puff of laughter no more than a single breath as the hand that held mine rises to pet my hair, playing with the dangling frills of the comb.

The motion jerks the tube in his other hand. I jump at the cold squirt of henna on my skin. Sohel pulls away to frown down at the blob spreading across my palm, before grimacing at me. "I can fix that." I giggle but reluctantly allow him to redirect his attention before the henna can stain. Without looking up from the roses he's drawing on my skin, he says, "I—I think we should keep this between us for now."

Reality comes crashing in the moment his words register.

"O-of course," I stutter with an awkward laugh, but the words taste bitter on my tongue as I forcibly disperse silly thoughts of telling my friends, fantasies of him visiting for prom.

Before I got here, I didn't want to be in love, but with him, it feels like it could be a possibility someday. Perhaps it's still too early to believe that, but from the second I met Sohel, he fascinated and infuriated me at every turn. He's probably the prettiest boy I have ever met, but beneath the porcelain mask he sometimes wears, at once fragile and sharp, he's also sensitive and kind.

"I'm sorry, Bibi," he whispers. "I like you more than I know what to do with, but you're leaving after the wedding, and I—I don't want us to be the reason anything else goes wrong."

"I understand," I make myself say, dredging up a smile. "We wouldn't want to distract from Halima Afu and Sunny Bhaiya's big day. Besides, my dad has had me under a renewed dating ban since the Akash incident. He might not take the news too well."

Sohel peers up at me with equal parts yearning and hope. "So, it's okay if we take things slow?"

"I can do that," I promise, caressing the curve of his cheek with the pad of my thumb.

After all, what's one more thing to pretend about? Once the wedding is over, we can figure out how to move forward together from different continents, but for now it's sort of romantic to have this secret, with only the moon and stars as our witnesses.

This time I close the distance between the two of us, and Sohel lets me.

CHAPTER TWENTY-SEVEN

A couple of mornings after the mehndi, the golden rays of the sun rouse me, warm and almost ticklish across my scrunched face. Not my parents or sister, not Abbu's rooster, not Ireima, not even my alarm. After I turn the latter off before it can ring, I creep out of bed to open my curtains so more sunshine saturates the room.

It dawns on me that this has somehow become a familiar routine. If you told me at the onset of the summer that I would one day happily wake up at five thirty, excited for another day at the tea garden, I would have laughed in your face. But now that my time is running out with my friends here—now that my time is running out with Sohel—I can't help missing something I haven't actually lost yet. Part of me never wants the summer to end.

But that's silly—going back home doesn't mean I won't be able to stay in touch with my Tea Girl Gang or my—my—

With Sohel.

Is he my boyfriend now?

We haven't exactly had that talk yet, but we spent hours strolling hand in hand through the tea gardens yesterday, with him showing me all the secret copses no one else knows so we could steal kisses and talk about the future.

Even if we can't tell anyone about our relationship yet, he thinks we *have* a future, and that's what matters most, right? That he wants to try, despite the eight thousand miles that will come between us at the end of this month?

I hold on to this hope while I change into my uniform for one of my last shifts ever here, finding that I no longer mind the drab outfit as much—although, I will totally suggest some upgrades for a more breathable material and extra pizazz to Sohel the next time I catch him in a good mood.

By the time I'm dressed, there's a knock at the door. I open it and blink at Yumjao, who has a saucer and teacup in her hands. The sweet smell of a perfectly brewed cuppa—as my insufferably posh boy calls it—permeates the air, a cake rusk on the saucer beside it.

"Yumi, what are you doing here?" I ask as I accept it. "Where's your sister?"

"Afa pawned off all her morning duties on me but refused to tell me why," she answers with a shrug, braided pigtails bouncing around her round face.

"Jeez, girl, do you ever sleep?" I grumble.

As always, I'm awed and a little envious of how peppy and daisy-fresh she manages to look at the crack of dawn. In spite of my new habits, I still have a looooong way to go before I hatch out of my egg into a proper early bird.

"I've been up for at least an hour." She grins toothily at me. "See you down there when you've woken up, Bibi Afa!"

"Yeah, yeah," I call after her, before taking a long sip of the tea and immediately feeling the last vestiges of sleepiness melt off my shoulders. I will never tell Sohel because his ego will grow too big, but he's so right about the benefits of a good cup of tea.

Halima is too busy, with the wedding mere days away, so I drain my cup, munch on my biscuit, and take the scenic route to join the other girls on the hill we were assigned to work. Along the way I can't help marveling at how exquisite my henna is, as vibrantly dark as an actual rose. My heart sings whenever I remember what it's supposed to symbolize.

Silly again.

Sohel and I aren't the ones getting married, after all.

Jui spots me first and jumps up and down. "Bibi, we're over here!"

"About time!" Yumjao shouts with her palms raised around her mouth.

Her older sister isn't yet back from whatever errand she's running—and Sohel is missing too, which is only a little odd, since he's probably with a different set of employees—but Khoibi and Nganu are there. Ever since their family began to reconcile, the latter's daughter spends more time with her grand-aunt, Mrs. Rahman, in the manor while her parents and grandparents work. The boys are also operating tractors not far from us. Even as he digs a small trench with his, Parek keeps shooting concerned glances our way.

"Our girl's not back?" I ask loud enough for him to overhear us.

"She said she'd be back by lunch," Yumjao explains.

Jui shakes her head. "Ireima would never skip work if it wasn't important. We'll get her to spill all the tea later." She looks to me to see if she's used the phrase correctly and beams at my approving nod. "It might be about university. She was telling me the other day that she'd start researching requirements for enrollment, even though she won't be able to attend for another two years. Not many tribal girls go to university, so she's trying to be proactive."

"Really?" I exclaim, a frisson of excitement running through me at the prospect. That's something else I never would have expected, once upon a time: feeling thrilled that someone else wants to go to college of all places. "Maybe she's getting the scoop from Sohel. He'll know all about enrolling at Dhaka University."

A chuckling Khoibi chimes in then. "All right, girls—let's get to work for now so you can gossip as much as you like later, achaa?"

Sheepishly we stoop to follow her lead, but there's something meditative about picking tea with the other girls while we chat and listen to music. Humming under my breath, I lose myself in the ministrations until the sun changes positions in the sky.

Ireima still hasn't returned when our break rolls around.

When a flash of worry crosses Yumjao's face, I pipe up, "Why don't you and the others go check if she went home? If she's not there, you can bring the food I know your mom made back here, just in case she skipped lunch."

"Thank you, Afa!" the pigtailed girl cries out. "We will be back in a gif!"

I don't bother correcting her, leaving the task to Jui while I rearrange all of our baskets so there's room for the picnic blanket they'll come back with. It's far from the first time we've taken our lunch this way, but something wrenches in my chest when I realize it might be the last.

"Need help?" a quiet voice asks me suddenly.

I leap to my feet. "Ireima! We've been waiting for you! Your sister and the others went to check if you were in the village!"

"I thought about going back to my room." Her voice wobbles, and it hits me all at once that her eyes are red-rimmed, the tip of her nose ruby red as well.

"What happened?" I demand, guiding her onto the grass with my arm around her shoulders. "Is it—is it about coll—I mean university?"

A watery laugh bursts out of her. "Sort of, but no."

"You don't have to tell me if you don't want to." I rub her back in time with my words. "We can just sit here until your sister comes back. We don't have to talk at all."

She stares at me for a second, before shaking her head. "Afa, I . . . confessed."

"Confessed?" I repeat. "To what?"

"To Sohel, Bibi Afa," she replies with more patience than the situation calls for.

"Oh."

Ireima doesn't know about me and Sohel, because no one does, but I've been aware of her feelings for him for so long and never even considered them before he and I got together. I would have talked to her if I could have—I would have told her I was starting to fall for him too, begged for her understanding—but I promised Sohel I would keep us a secret.

Because of that, I had to violate the girl code.

Am I the worst? Do I even deserve to call her a friend?

"Yeah," she mumbles, fussing with the torn stem of a tea leaf she must have plucked when I wasn't looking. "He—he shot me down. Said he only saw me as a little sister and—and apparently he's in love with someone else?"

My eyes bug out, and the ground begins to spin below me. If I wasn't already sitting, I'd probably fall over from the shock.

"In love?" I choke out.

She nods and muses softly, "I wonder who this girl is. His voice sounded different when he talked about her. I could tell he was heels over head even if he didn't give much away."

"Did he really say that?" I press, reaching for her hands and not even bothering to correct her mistake. "He said 'in love'?"

Ireima grimaces. "I—I don't know. I think so? After he rejected me, I sort of blacked out." She digs her palms into her eyes to dry them, inhaling a long, sniffly breath through her stuffed-up nose, before releasing it through her lips.

"Whatever!" she says in an admirable impersonation of me, pumping her fist. "He's not that hot anyway, right, Bibi Afa?"

"R-right," I agree, not sure whether to cringe or be proud.

Luckily, she doesn't appear to notice, a determined expression brightening her ebony eyes with something other than tears. "Forget Sohel Bhaiya! I am going to focus on getting into a good university and meeting lots of new people! Perhaps I will fall in love while I'm there like Halima Afa, but even if I don't, I will be self-sufficient! I will take my family and leave the tea gardens someday so we can see what else is out there!"

Although my mind is reeling from the revelation she foisted on me—Sohel is in love with someone? And that someone might be *me*?—I manage to muster up enough enthusiasm to pat her on the back. "Attagirl!"

"At . . . ta?" she repeats, not having heard that phrase before. "Like wheat? I think I cried so much, my brain is no longer functioning well. English is hard right now, Afa."

"Don't worry about it," I answer with a weak giggle. "Don't worry about Sohel or anything else right now, except getting that bread so you can accomplish all your dreams, okay?"

"Okay," she replies, her smile resolute, even though I can tell my dough metaphors have flown right over her head and confused her more.

As I watch her shuffle off toward her empty basket to wait for the others, I spy another familiar face hovering nearby, half-hidden behind his tractor. Parek tenses when I wander over and ask, "You didn't go with Jui to the village?"

"I—" He swallows, eyes skirting past me to follow Ireima's distant figure. "I was worried about her. I wanted to be here when she came back."

"I've watched you watch her all summer," I remark, then smile when he flinches. "It's all right. I think it's sweet. Have you told her you like her?"

He rubs the back of his neck, shaking his head.

Exactly as I expected.

Parek has faded into the background for most of the summer, especially when compared to fiery Sohel and jovial Taamba, but he's actually pretty cute, with the same curls and baby-deer-brown eyes as his cousin Jui. Perhaps he's what Ireima needs—a loyal shadow to support her while she pursues her dreams. Perhaps she doesn't need to wait for college to find that.

"You should tell her," I continue. "I can't promise she'll return your feelings, but you'll never know until you try, right?"

He exhales the breath he's been holding. "Okay, Bibi Afa. I-I'll try."

"Attaboy!" I tell him, just like I told Ireima.

Later that day, when I catch him carrying her basket for her while she smiles and blushes, nothing in the world can bring down my triumphant mood. Not even all the questions I want to ask Sohel about the girl he's supposedly in love with.

CHAPTER TWENTY-EIGHT

My henna dries into an even darker red over the next day, a physical reminder of everything that happened with Sohel that makes my head spin whenever I look down and see it or catch a glimpse in my reflection. Although I still haven't worked up the courage to ask him about what Ireima confided in me, I know Sohel can't tear his eyes away from my henna either.

Halima's is even more striking. I catch her admiring it with a smitten smile while we both dress for the rehearsal dinner before tomorrow's wedding.

The real ceremony will be much more involved, but tonight only the bridal party, groomsmen, and closest family members are invited. It's the final opportunity for everyone to practice their toasts and get a rundown of the following day, but also to receive gratitude in return from Sunny and Halima for helping them cross the finish line.

I wolf-whistle at my sister. "Bhaiya must love you *a lot*. I've never seen henna so red."

"That's the work of a professional henna artist for you," she retorts with a laugh, pointing at my arms. "Yours doesn't look half bad either." My cheeks darken, but thankfully, she returns her attention to the elegantly simple lantern-sleeve white gown she's wearing tonight. I almost don't catch her murmured "I do love him a lot, though."

I smile at her in the mirror. "I'm happy for you, Afu. By this time tomorrow you two will officially be husband and wife."

"I'm happy too," she replies with another beam of her own. "Sunny's already found us an apartment with a guest room, if you ever want to come visit. He's hoping Sohel might be willing to leave Bangladesh now and then too."

She doesn't have to tell me twice. "Unlike him, I will *definitely* take you up on that the next time me and Abbu fight."

Just then the man himself pounds on the door to come collect us, and we both burst into laughter, prompting him to demand, "Is everything okay in there?"

"Everything's fine!" we call back simultaneously.

Arm in arm we exit the room and join our parents and grandmother, striding down to the baby taxis together on our way back to the teahouse. There's barely enough room for three people in one auto-rickshaw, so I reluctantly release her and follow Abbu and Thathu to another.

Once the ride down has kicked off, my father says, "You've come so far this summer, Bibi."

"I have?" I blink.

It doesn't feel like it, since I'm ending the summer in much the same way I started it. As far as Abbu is concerned, I'm prohibited from dating again, after the Akash fiasco crashed and burned, but he doesn't know I'm doing exactly what got me into hot water in the first place—sneaking around behind his back with a boy.

"Yes." His firmness surprises me. "You've made a few mistakes, but have been there for your sister and proven yourself to be more responsible than I ever imagined. I know we weren't seeing eye to eye before we got here, but I'm proud of you, Bibi. You've earned back my trust."

Thathu reaches over to squeeze my hand.

"Th-thanks, Abbu," I stammer, even as my palm grows clammy in hers.

A blade of guilt wedges deeper into my chest at his fond smile. Although it's nice to not be in trouble for once, if he knew about Sohel, knew how we almost derailed Halima's happily-ever-after, he wouldn't feel the same way, would he?

Is it okay to let sleeping dogs lie and keep him in the dark about those things? It's not like I want to hide anything, but there's no point in rehashing old drama when things are going well, right? Moreover, I promised Sohel I wouldn't tell anyone about us, and I suspect Abbu will be unhappy no matter what if he learns the whole truth.

Oblivious to my frenzied thoughts, my father continues, "I'm sure you're disappointed things didn't work out with the Mamun boy—"

"It's okay," I cut in. "I'm fine. *Really.*"

"I know you are, but I want you to know it's not such a bad thing to take your time," he says, taking my other hand. "As I watch you become a young woman, I never want you to feel that I'm the reason you have to pressure yourself. *Especially* about something like dating."

A lump rises in my throat at his words, but I shake my head. "I know you'd rather I stay away from boys forever."

"It's true that there are very few boys I would trust with my Little Nugget," he admits gruffly, "but while things haven't always gone smoothly since we've been here, Sunny and Halima's love has proven to me that a few good ones exist."

I curl against his side and mumble, "I'd still be your little girl no matter what."

At the same time, the lump of remorse I swallowed sours in my stomach. Sohel wants to keep our relationship a secret, and after Abbu's heartfelt speech about trusting me again, I'm not so sure I can keep lying to everyone I love. I'm not sure I want to hide how I feel about Sohel for much longer.

Will he want to break up if I tell my family?

Maybe. . . . Maybe if he does, it's not actually meant to be.

When the baby taxi stops, I allow Abbu to help me and Thathu out, then dither behind them as they congregate with my mother and sister. While Abbu and Thathu check in with Halima about the wedding the next day, Ammu notices my out of character silence and asks, "What's wrong, moyna?"

"N-nothing," I reply. "I'm just thinking."

"What has you thinking so hard?" she presses. "It will wrinkle your pretty face."

I huff a laugh. "We wouldn't want that."

"Bibi," she urges. "Tell me."

My eyes stray to the rest of our family, then return to her. "Um. I guess, because Halima Afu's marriage is tomorrow, I'm just thinking about love."

"Oh?" she replies, eyebrows arching.

I rub my arm, face heating up. "It was hard for Afu sometimes, and I'm just wondering how you know when it's worth fighting for. Was it tough for you when Nana and Nanu didn't approve of Abbu?"

Her lips unfold into a genuine smile as she follows my gaze to my father, who is booming a laugh over whatever joke he's cracked, while Halima shakes her head. "It was hard," she allows at last, "but for me it would have been harder to let him go, even if it made your grandparents unhappy at the time." She nudges my shoulder. "These days they tell me they're glad I was too stubborn to listen to them, because your Abbu has made this wonderful life and family for us."

"That makes sense," I murmur.

Ammu drops a kiss onto my cheek. "Come find me if you're still worrying, moyna. I have to go check on something for your sister now."

I nod and watch her hurry over to the head chef, but my thoughts haven't yet quieted. A tap on my shoulder brings me face-to-face with the boy haunting them. "O-oh, hey!"

"Hey," Sohel replies with a bashful smile that makes my heart pitter-patter.

"I was looking for you!" we both say at once, then do a double take.

Squirming from foot to foot, I ask, "How come?"

"There's something I wanted to show you," he tells me.

Before I know it, my hand is in his.

When I glance over my shoulder, no one else seems to notice, but I'm sure he can feel the thudding of my pulse in the flat of my palm. I hold my breath as we melt into the flora of the greenhouse, separated from the restaurant area by a gate crawling with vines that he releases me to unlock.

The instant we step inside, we're surrounded by the butterfly garden. Colorful wings flap all around us, boasting different sizes and patterns, but Sohel kneels in front of a particular plant. As I stoop beside him, I gasp and clutch at his sleeve. There are even more butterflies hanging from husks.

"Did they just . . . hatch out of their cocoons?" I ask.

He nods. "Something like that. Those are their chrysalises. Moths have cocoons. I thought . . ." His eyes rise to meet mine. "Butterflies usually enclose before the rainy season, but because the greenhouse is temperature controlled, they're safe here. I know you're a little scared of bees, but butterflies are pretty and harmless, so I hoped you might like to see."

I let my head fall onto his shoulder. "You are so strange." He goes rigid, which makes me giggle and trace a pattern on his sleeve. "I like it, though." I turn my face so I can look up at him, shifting ever so slightly. "I like everything about you, Sohel."

"Bibi . . ."

I can almost hear his rising apprehension and shake my head. "No, I—I'm not kidding. The very first time we met, when you gave me that umbrella, I think I might have started developing this massive crush, Sohel."

"You shouldn't have," he mutters. "I was such a prat to you."

"I can't think of anyone else who would have entertained my ridiculous idea to find Thathu's lost love—"

"It's not ridiculous! We might still find him."

His vehement interruption makes me grin. "See what I mean? I know we might seem like complete opposites, but I like that about us . . . don't you?"

"I—I do," Sohel confesses, blushing again. "But why are you telling me now?"

I turn my attention back to the butterflies, who are slowly stretching their bejeweled wings, not quite ready to join the others that are already in flight.

Exhaling a breath, I say, "I like you Sohel. Enough that I can picture a future together. But my parents *finally* trust me again. I don't want to hide us from them or my sister. I don't want this to be like it was with Akash."

"It's not like that at all," Sohel insists, facing me and catching me by my arms. "I'm not—There's no one else, Bibi. There never has been. I just know what my family is like, and isn't it okay to be happy with you for a little while before we let all of that pressure in? We've seen firsthand the way it's affected our siblings, and they've been together for so much longer. I'm not sure you understand what might happen."

"I understand perfectly," I reply, cradling his face so I can search his apprehensive eyes. I miss the Sohel he is when we're alone, the one who is so playful and funny, but if the two of us are going to last beyond a single summer, we need a foundation stronger than secrets. "I know exactly what I feel for you, and I already know what your family is like. Those two things don't cancel each other out, but I'm scared you're not as sure about me."

"I've never been *more* sure about anyone." He raises a hand to cover mine over his cheek, and I hate the way it shakes ever so slightly. "It's just . . . I'm afraid. I don't want to lose what we have."

"We won't," I promise. "If—if you really mean it, then we'll find a way together."

In response he lowers his lips to mine, his free hand moving to the small of my back to brace me. He kisses softly, and I sink into it, sink against him. His cheek is warm beneath my touch, my fingertips tingling from the flush that encompasses them. My other hand crumples the cotton of his button-up shirt, and if I were in a more logical state of mind, I might worry that everyone will be able to tell what we've been up to when they see how disheveled we are.

I guess that's answer enough.

He pulls away, and I feel his soft breaths ghost across my lips. Before he can speak, a bloodcurdling scream accompanied by the clang of a teapot crashing to the ground forces us to spring apart, and then we find ourselves surrounded by our entire family.

CHAPTER TWENTY-NINE

The butterflies are escaping.

Despite the train derailment in my mind, all I can think is that I know it will make Sohel sad if they do. As the two of us are marched out of the butterfly garden by our angry parents, I can't help but stammer, "C-can someone shut the gate?"

One of the many onlookers scoffs—perhaps even the auntie who caught us in flagrante and shrieked like she'd just seen Shaytan himself manifesting out of hell. Sohel's oldest fufu wags a finger in her brother's face. "What did I tell you, Anwarul?"

"Not now, Afa," he clips out.

But she continues to rave, her sisters and a few of their children nodding and whispering. "These American girls are floozies, and your wife played right into their hands! Do you know how unwelcome your bow ma made us feel?" She swings a hand in Halima's direction, eliciting a flinch from my sister even as Sunny and her friends step in between them.

"This isn't about her—"

Before I can defend my sister, Abbu growls, "How dare you throw these accusations around about my daughters?"

"What else are we supposed to believe?" Sohel's grandfather interjects. "Our family has operated a certain way for years, taken care of this tea garden for centuries, and suddenly *your* daughter barges in to steal Shariq away so *she* can study. Because of that, she can't give him a child? What else will he have to give up for her to have a career?" His beady eyes narrow at me next. "Meanwhile, this little witch won't rest until she's wrapped every eligible bachelor in Bangladesh around her pinkie finger."

I feel like I've been slapped. At this point Halima starts to cry. Everyone is watching us both with judgment as if we're some sort of thieves.

While her friends comfort her, Sunny says, "She was never the reason I left. I couldn't stand this place *before* Halima ever came into the picture—and is it any wonder, when our family is like this? When you first told me I could only be with her if I came back here, I should have given up my claim entirely and eloped."

"Shariq," his father reprimands sharply, making him snap his jaw shut.

My own eyes well with tears that creep down my cheeks as I mumble, "I'm sorry, I didn't want you to find out like this.."

"Find out what?" Sunny's aunt barks. "That you've been sneaking around with our Sohel, trying to sink your claws into him, too, you behaya, beshorom girl?"

"You never should have allowed the boy to think it was

fine to mix with the riffraff," her father adds. "The best place for him was at Eton."

For the first time since we were dragged out here, Sohel's head snaps up, his eyes blazing, jaw set, fists balled at his side, but he doesn't refute his aunt or grandfather.

"Th-that's not true," I stammer, before his temper gets the better of him and he sets alight the fuse of the bomb between us all. "Sohel and I, we're, we're not—"

"Mind your tongue!" Thathu intervenes much less kindly, the warning in her voice directed at the Rahmans, while Ammu comes to wrap protective arms around me. "I will take off my sandal and teach you a lesson, should another word about my granddaughters leave your lips."

"My go," Sunny's aunt gasps, paling and clutching her chest. "Anwarul, are you going to let your in-laws speak to me this way?"

"Who's to say we want anything to do with your family any longer?" my mother asks coolly. "You might believe you're so superior to us in bongsho, but my bright, beautiful, compassionate daughters can do much better than a family who slights them like this."

"Wait, please," Sunny says, trying to salvage the situation.

My heart plummets to my feet like a meteorite at the realization that I might be the reason things end for him and my sister once and for all.

Tearing myself out of the human shield my parents have formed around me, I spin toward Sohel and reach for his sleeve. "Sohel, this is—this is being blown completely out of proportion, isn't it? We were about to tell them about us, weren't we?" A hint of hysteria bleeds into my voice as I shake him by the arm. "S-say something."

"Bibi . . ." He swallows audibly. "I'm sorry. I can't do this. This estate means too much to me to lose over something like this."

"W-what?" I whisper, brain failing to register the words. "What are you saying?"

A cruel smile twists Sohel's grandfather's lips. Looking sickeningly pleased with himself, he taps his cane on the ground. "Enough of this foolishness, Sohel. Your parents never should have let you run wild like you were no more than one of your mother's uncouth brood, when you're a Rahman. Come here."

Sohel wavers for too brief a time before he loosens my listless fingers. He doesn't move, but he doesn't meet my gaze either. My heart shatters into a million unfixable pieces, my clenching fist empty and cold.

Abbu yanks me behind him even as he rounds on the Rahmans. "Do you see? First your nephew, now this. I didn't bring my daughter here for your boys to take advantage of her."

"No, that's not what happened," I exclaim, instinctively coming to Sohel's defense despite his unwillingness to defend my honor in return. The bite of my tone evokes a shuddering breath from him, drawing my gaze back. "Why are you listening to your grandfather, Sohel? Why aren't you saying anything?" The floppy bangs I loved so much obscure his eyes. My fingers twitch with the urge to brush them behind his ear, but instead

I clench my hands until my nails dig into the soft flesh of my palms. "Is this—do you want things to end this way?"

Want *us* to end?

He turns away from me altogether, voice so quiet, I almost don't catch it over the incessant whispers. "I'm sorry that I hurt you, Bibi. But given the way things are, it's better for you if you forget about me."

I stare at him in disbelieving horror while Ammu and Abbu try to lead me away. It feels like the world is spinning beneath my feet, cracking into a yawning abyss that will swallow me whole, separating us forever.

But he's okay with that.

He let go of my hand so easily. Let me fall for him and get crushed.

"H-how can you say that?" I manage to whisper at last. "You're exactly every awful, cowardly thing you feared you were. You're no better than Akash."

Except, that isn't true. He and Akash are not the same. He and Sunny, who he railed so much against, are not the same. At least Akash was eventually honest about what he wanted from me and let me go when I had no interest in messing around behind his fiancée's back. At least Sunny ultimately fought to be with Halima and is fiercely protective of her even now. I thought Sohel loved me enough to stand up to his family for me. To *fight* for me. Instead he just stood there and said *nothing*.

No, Sohel isn't like Sunny or Akash.

Sohel is so much *worse*.

CHAPTER THIRTY

It's raining when we make our way outside.

Dark, heavy sleet dims the ethereal beauty of the tea garden.

My mind is too foggy to notice when Abbu removes his jacket to place it over my head so I can make it into the baby taxi relatively unscathed, because I let myself cry with abandon, unable to work up the courage or voice to call out to Halima, who is with Ammu and Thathu.

"It's all my fault," I sob into my father's already soaked shirt when we're inside. "I was so stupid to think Sohel could like me, and now I've ruined everything. I'm *always the one* who ruins everything."

Enzo didn't choose me.

Akash didn't see me as anything but a plaything.

Sohel gave me up at the first sign of opposition.

Why am I so easy to give up?

"Don't cry," Abbu says in a much gentler tone than I'm used to from him. "Everything will work out, Bibi zaan."

I shake my head without lifting my face. It's not even that he means to yell sometimes, so much as that his default volume is loud, and this tender voice, these sweet words of comfort, only make me feel crappier about myself.

"It won't, though," I rasp out. "I broke your trust, and because of that, Halima Afu and Sunny Bhaiya are suffering the consequences. She's going to hate me forever. You all should."

"Oh, Bibi . . ." Abbu tips my chin up, using his sleeve to wipe away tears, snot, and raindrops alike. "How could I ever hate my baby?"

"But Halima . . . ," I whimper, chin wobbling.

My father sighs. "Your sister . . . She will be angry for a time, and that's her right. You understand that, don't you?"

Another fat teardrop slips out. "You don't understand. This whole summer I've been trying to break her and Sunny up, because like *always*, I got it into my head that I'm right and everyone else is wrong. It took me so, so long to figure out the opposite was true."

She *keeps* suffering because of me.

When she finds out the truth, *all* of the truth, won't she hate me for life? Won't she be right to do it? Maybe that's why I've kept that secret to myself for this long, but after everything that's happened with Sohel, I am *so* sick of always hiding things.

"Bibi . . . ," my father whispers, hand stiffening on my head.

"You were right about me before, Abbu," I mutter. "I'm

the screwup. I deserved to be punished all summer because all I ever do is think about myself. I'm selfish and self-centered and—and—and—"

He yanks me into his arms once again, murmuring, "Hush, my Bibi zaan," into my hair.

I can't help it: I start bawling again.

Abbu runs his big hand up and down my back for a long time. The baby taxi comes to a stop, but the driver just bows his head and steps out, granting us more privacy. I wish I could muster a smile to thank him.

Only when my sobs have become tiny hiccups does Abbu say, "You made a mistake, it's true. I understand. I made plenty at your age too. You've always been too much like me."

"Yeah, right, Mr. American Dream." I snort wetly. "We could not be more different."

"You think I had it easy?" he asks with a faint chuckle.

I shake my head, unable to look him in the eye. "I *know* you didn't."

That's what makes everything worse.

Thatha and Thathu struggled to take care of their family. When my grandfather passed, my grandmother worked so hard to raise enough money to send Abbu to America, where *he* worked his butt off not only trying to help his family back home but to take care of us. Even when Nana and Nanu didn't want to let him be with Ammu because he wasn't as educated and established as her other suitors, he proved everyone wrong and became a monumental success—fast-food royalty, in fact.

Despite the fact that he and Ammu have unrolled the red carpet to a much easier life for me, I'm a royal screwup who trips over her Louboutins every step of the way.

I'm not like Halima or Abbu or my mother. Not like Thathu. I'm not even passionate about anything the way Sohel is about the tea garden.

All I do is make things harder for everyone around me with my schemes and antics. My family loves me because they *have* to, but that must be the reason everyone else walks away.

"Bibi . . ." My father's fingers under my quivering chin force me to meet his gaze. His eyes are overflowing with so much affection that I almost burst into fresh tears right then and there. "You have only ever known your old man as I am now, and honestly, that's the way I wanted you to see me. The reason I never told you about my time working at this tea garden is . . . I always felt small here, felt small during so many moments of my life. Being back reminded me of that."

Hearing the almost brittle shift in his voice makes my eyes narrow. "The Rahmans have no right to make you feel that way. So what if they're old money and we're not? That just means everything has been handed to them"—like it was for me—"while *you* worked for it. To me, that will always be more impressive."

"Thank you, my Bibi zaan," he replies with a smile. "But I'm starting to think perhaps I shouldn't have hidden so much of my past from you."

"What else is there?" I whisper, suddenly struck by nerves.

He tugs me closer. I feel a sigh reverberate through him. "Your old man may seem like I have everything together right now, but when you were still a baby and Halima was only five or so, I almost lost everything. Do you remember our first house, on Elm?" I nod, although the memory is fuzzy, mostly contained in old photos of that time that Abbu wasn't often present for. "Back then, before Royal Fried Chicken, I had a different restaurant. I poured all my savings into it, and because of my pride, I couldn't ask your mother's family or anyone else for help. Instead I . . . I took a second mortgage out on the Elm Street house."

"Is that why we lost it?" I ask.

"It was 2008," he says, "and the financial crisis was tearing through the country. Because of rising interest rates, it became impossible to keep up with my loans—for the house *or* the restaurant. When debtors came knocking, your nana and nani were so angry, they told your mother to come back home to them. I have never been more ashamed in my life."

"What happened?" I mumble, only distantly noticing the way my fingers bury in his shirt the way they used to when I was a little girl. "How did we go from that to everything being okay?"

He places his hand over mine and squeezes. "More than okay, I like to think. Your mother absolutely *refused* to go, even when I told her perhaps she should listen to her parents so you girls wouldn't have to realize how dire things had gotten. She said . . ." He swallows, choked up from the memory. "She said you and Halima would never want to be without your daddy and that she wouldn't either, no matter *what* happened. That's when I knew I couldn't simply give up. Not when it meant losing more than just a house or restaurant, but losing my *real* home—my family."

Sniffling, I burrow deeper into his side with my arms around his waist, almost missing the french fry smell I got so used to. "I'm glad you told me. I'm *so* proud of you."

"You were *always* on my mind," he rumbles, his other hand on my head. "You, your mother, and Halima—when the restaurant and house foreclosed, when I was forced to look for new work, and then eventually your mother encouraged me to chase my dream again. She wasn't the only one. Other people in the community came together to help me when I needed seed money for RFC. Your grandmother ended up selling some property here. So many people believed in me that I couldn't possibly let them down again. That's why I never moved out of Paterson, why I always try to pay things forward when another down-on-his-luck young gun with a whole lot of gumption turns up on my doorstep."

I nod against his shirt. "I think—I think I understand why you're telling me that story now. You and Ammu and Thathu believe in me the same way. Maybe Halima Afu did too. But after the way I messed everything up, how can she ever forgive me?"

"While you could have done things differently," he replies, rubbing his hand down the knobs of my spine, "the tension between our family and Sunny's, the things Sunny's aunts believe about your sister . . . they would have always come to a head, with or without you. I personally believe it's better for it to be out in the open, what they think about her, because it gives Sunny a chance to prove what kind of man, and kind of husband, he can be."

"I like them together." The confession catches in my throat. In spite of so much time spent trying to break them up, I don't want to have to see my sister go back to the shy, lonely person she was before Sunny. "I don't want to be the reason things end."

"I like them too," Abbu admits. "It took some time, but once I got to know him, I couldn't help rooting for Sunny. Although I hope that he will fight for your sister and prove he deserves her, she is my daughter, so if he can't stand up for her sake, Halima will always be my priority. No matter what, your sister will be fine. She'll have us." I nod. "So will you, Bibi zaan. If that Sohel boy isn't brave enough to stand by your side, to hell with him and the entire Rahman gushti! You will be fine without him! You have your father's magic touch and your mother's stubborn streak."

"I'm surprised we could talk like this," I blubber into his shirt, half giggling, half crying. "I thought you'd be super mad and ground me forever."

"Oh, don't worry," he answers with a cheerful tap on my snotty red nose. "There's plenty of time for that. Forever is a long time, Bibi zaan. This may be the age when you make the most mistakes, but I will always be here to help you learn from them, the easy way or the hard way."

In spite of myself, and my promised eternity of banishment from all things social life, another laugh bubbles out of me. "I guess that's fair. Love you, Abbu."

"I love you too," he says into my hair after dropping a peck into it. "No matter what happens from here on out, you will always be my Bibi."

CHAPTER THIRTY-ONE

When we finally exit the baby taxi, we find Thathu waiting outside with an umbrella open over her head and a second in her hand.

I dissolve into a fresh fit of giggles when I recall her threatening Sohel's auntie, and as if she's read my mind, she winks. "I meant every word I said. If you want me to teach that little cad and his mouthy aunt a lesson with this umbrella, I will. That grandfather of his has been grating on my patience since we met."

"I'd rather not have to bail you out of prison, Ma," Abbu retorts, but he's also chuckling.

The three of us walk into the guest house together, with me between them both, their arms around me, umbrellas held over all of our heads.

Ammu comes running to meet us at the entrance, her eyes frantic, something clutched in her white-knuckled hand. "Is Halima with you? Sh-she said she wanted some privacy when we got here, so I suggested she take a nice bubble bath, b-but when I knocked, she, she didn't—"

Realization hits me like an earthquake.

My sister has run away.

Before I can freak out, Abbu's phone rings. He listens to the distraught voice on the other end for several minutes, then tells us gravely, "The Rahmans want us back in the courtyard."

Mrs. Rahman is holding a letter of her own when we arrive.

I've already read my sister's neat cursive more than a dozen times in the last ten minutes, enough that I have her message memorized:

Dear everyone,

I'm sorry it's come to this. We wanted you to be there with us, celebrate with us. But even though we love you, we've decided against a wedding here and will be married when we get back to New Jersey.

Someday, inshallah, I hope we can all be a real family, but until then, all Sunny and I want is each other. Please, don't think too badly of us or give us bodwa. We'll need your prayers now more than ever.

Love,

Halima

Sunny's letter is even more forthcoming.

Ma, Baba:
Being home for long has never made me happy. Not
the way Halima does.
I know I'm much luckier than others here because I'm
your son, know that I'm only next in line because I'm
the firstborn, but the constant reminder that I should
be grateful, the constant expectation of perfection, has
always felt suffocating to me. I escaped abroad every
second I could, even when I missed you, because it
meant I could be free, could be just like everyone else.
When you said you would only support our marriage
if I came back, I did it only for Halima, because I knew
she would be sad if you refused to be part of our lives.
I tried so hard to please you, please our whole family,
and almost lost her because of it. We both see now
that it isn't possible to stay.
I'm sorry.
Sunny

P.S. Now that I'm leaving, I hope you'll consider how
much more Sohel cherishes the estate. If anyone should
take over after Baba, it's him, not me. I hope he knows
I always hated how much the family business came
between us.

As the last dregs of lightning flash in the sky, even the rumble of rolling thunder is drowned out by the shouting match that ensues between our families.

"This is all your fault," Abbu is screaming at Mr. Rahman, jabbing a finger at his chest. "How could you let your son steal my daughter away under your nose?"

"The same could be said of you, couldn't it?" Mr. Rahman parries.

"Why does he even want her, after all the disgusting comments his aunts and grandfather made to dishonor her?" Abbu replies with stony sarcasm. "Isn't your beloved son too good for our daughter?"

Mr. Rahman has the good grace to wince while his conniving sisters squawk in offense, but he merely shakes his head. "He hasn't forced her. Everything he's done since they became engaged has been to make her happy."

"Even at his own expense," one of the witches chimes in.

"Happy?" Abbu spits. "You call that happy?"

Both of their wives and even both sets of grandparents join the fray, but I listen from afar, frowning down at the fountain. Raindrops disturb the water and make the fish swim off. It's like Abbu said in the baby taxi. The problems between our families are so entrenched that even causing Sunny and Halima to elope can't make them get along.

Is my sister right to get as far away from this place and all of us as she possibly can? What will this mean when the two of them need their families next time? Will we never get our acts together enough to be there for them?

I'm so lost in thought that it takes me a few minutes to notice that the rain has stopped. I look up to find a familiar umbrella, then glare over my shoulder at Sohel.

"What do you want? Haven't you done enough?" I snap.

He ducks his head. "I—I know this is happening because of me."

"Because you should have never dated me, right?" I throw this back into his face, crossing my arms and scowling down at the koi.

"You don't understand." His voice is almost imperceptible over the downpour. "Your sister doesn't deserve this, but it's the inevitable outcome with my family. I care about you, but I could never walk away the way Sunny Bhai did. I didn't want this"—he waves an arm toward the other Rahmans—"for you."

"*You* don't get to choose for me," I snarl before kneading my fingers into my temples. "It doesn't matter anyway. You made your choice. And now everything is ruined." The wounded way his face crumples shoots a traitorous twinge through my chest, and I *hate* how much I still care. What I hate more is that it's not entirely his fault.

Sohel may have stomped on my heart like it was bubble gum under an Italian leather oxford, but even *if* he'd stayed by my side, even if he'd proclaimed his undying loyalty to me in front of both of our families, what would have changed?

The problem is bigger than us, or Sunny and Halima.

Ignoring him when he calls after me, I pivot to stomp toward our families, shrieking in the highest pitch I can manage, "Enough already!"

That shuts them up.

They're too stunned to chew me out for being disrespectful. Good.

I march right past our mothers and grandparents toward our fathers, my hands on my hips as I glare daggers up at them. "The truth is, it's *both* of your faults. *All* of our faults. And standing around here bickering isn't going to change anything."

"Young lady—" Mr. Rahman begins, a warning in his voice.

"Uh-uh, no sir," I cut in. "Your son *loves* Halima Afu, but you've never made her, or any of us, feel welcome here. She has constantly had to hear how little your family thinks of her, despite doing her best to keep the peace. I know I'm far from perfect, but my sister has gone out of her way to make things work. Your silence while she was being treated so badly let her and Sunny Bhai know exactly where they stand with you. How can you force him to choose between you and the person he loves? Hypocritical much?"

He parts his lips to answer, then presses them shut, even as Mrs. Rahman comes to take his arm and adds softly, "I told you, Anwarul. I don't want our children to have to live like us. You kept me away from my family for almost thirty years. I can't let the same happen to my son's wife." Her eyes, so like Sohel's, flicker to me for a fraction of a second. "Either of them."

"I know." He sighs, raising a hand to hold hers.

My eyes widen as I watch them, surprised that it actually worked, but when Abbu reaches for my shoulder, I twist toward him instead. "And you!"

"Me?" Abbu proclaims, pointing at himself.

"You could make things easier for Afu too," I remind him. "Sure, the Rahmans haven't been the most hospitable hosts, but you can't decide it's over for Halima, no matter how much you want to protect her. We may be your kids, but that doesn't mean you can control us forever. The world is changing. Parents can't just play with their children like pawns anymore."

I turn to the rest of them, squinting at Sunny's grandfather and aunts in particular. "That goes for all of you. Sunny Bhaiya and Halima Afu are adults. If they choose to be together, you either support them or shut up and stand aside. This isn't the past, where you could decide to marry them off to whoever you wanted. *They* have a say too, and they can decide to ghost you forever. I wouldn't even blame them if they did, but would you honestly want them to elope instead of celebrating their love with us all like they deserve?"

Another eternity of silence reigns as everyone goggles at me. When I meet his gaze, Sohel is grinning under his umbrella even as the rain begins to trickle to a stop, and I don't quite know what to make of that, or the way my treasonous stomach does a backflip. I settle for glowering at him until he stops tormenting me with that smile that always worms its way under my skin.

Then Ammu rushes to the rescue, waving Halima's letter, while Mrs. Rahman clutches Sunny's to her chest. Exchanging a nod with the latter, my mother says, "What matters right now is stopping our children from making a mistake. If we leave right now, we may make it to the airport in time."

CHAPTER THIRTY-TWO

I grab Sohel by the hand to stop him before he can skulk after everyone else toward the garage. His face brightens, but I shake my head before he can speak. "This isn't about us; it's about our siblings. If you genuinely feel bad and want to fix things, give me a ride."

"A ride?" His eyes grow round in realization, then narrow. "The bike?"

"They have maybe an hour's head start on us," I explain, "but your bike was able to swerve through traffic much faster than any car last time we went to Moulvibazar."

"The Sylhet airport is much farther away," he warns, "and the rain may have stopped, but the roads are still slick from the storm."

I set my hands on my hips and level a challenging frown at him. "I don't care. We *have* to stop them, and there's no other way. Unless you fancy Rahmans have a chopper?"

He chews on his thumb, but I know he's smart enough to come to the conclusion that I'm right. I've already tried calling and texting my sister a hundred times, and he must have done the same with Sunny, but neither answered. They must have turned off their phones.

Determination alights in his eyes. "Okay."

He runs to speak to our parents, who frown between the two of us, obviously gearing up to protest. Their voices swell together into a choir of disapproval I can't make heads or tails of, but Sohel's firm voice cuts through it like a bell.

"I promise I'll keep Bibi safe," he says, with a hand on his chest, "and that we'll bring Sunny Bhai and Halima Afa home."

Our families barter conflicted looks. Abbu breaks the silence by squeezing Sohel's shoulder. "You'd better keep your promise, young man."

The "or else" hangs between them.

Sohel nods, then hurries to retrieve the bike. I accept a helmet, spare jacket, and gloves from him, trying to pay no mind to the fact that they smell like him. Once I wrap my arms around his midsection, we speed off, one of the Rahmans' Rolls-Royces not far behind.

Between the recent rain and the clear, dark sky, now aglow with stars, the road is emptier than it was the last time I rode with Sohel, but he has to steer more carefully, avoiding any hard turns so that our bike doesn't flip over on the slick road or get trapped in the mud.

Bangladesh is a veritable paradise at night, but I can't pay the view any mind when every inch of my head is filled with a mantra, willing Halima and Sunny to be there when we arrive. Since this is a last-minute trip, it will ideally take them some time to secure a good flight, acquire tickets, and get through airport security.

Please don't go, please don't go, please don't go. . . .

We make it in record time.

By this point we've lost the car, thanks to a few creative shortcuts Sohel took. He doesn't even bother to properly lock or park the motorcycle, letting it tumble sideways onto the asphalt of the parking lot as he lobs his keys at an alarmed valet and charges into the airport, pulling me by the hand.

"Sunny Bhai!"

"Halima Afu!"

We're shouting in unison, whipping our heads in every direction in an attempt to find them in the busy terminal.

When a security guard runs up to us, Sohel tells the man without looking, "We'll buy tickets to be here if we have to, just, please, help us—"

"Sohel?" a voice calls.

We turn to find a skeptical Sunny. Halima hovers behind him, peeking out past his muscular bicep, each of them holding a single, hastily packed piece of luggage.

"What are you doing here?" my sister bites out.

Her voice is unreadable, so stoic that it makes me flinch, but before I can apologize, Sohel intervenes and says, "Please, don't be angry with Bibi for anything that happened. It was all my fault, and I take full responsibility. I don't want to be

332

the reason you're forced to do this, so if it fixes anything, if it means you can have your wedding as planned, you don't have to go. I—I can go back to my dorm in Dhaka early. I'll even go back to England if you decide you want to stay at the gardens after all. I don't mind."

"Sohu, why wouldn't I want my brother at my wedding?" Sunny asks.

Sohel shrugs, but his shoulders are tight and shaky.

I step forward, gazing up at my sister with watery eyes. "For what it's worth, I'm sorry too, Afu. I let my feelings get in the way of yours. I should have been honest with you. I never should have done anything that put your wedding in jeopardy."

"Bibi . . . ," Halima whispers. "I'm mad at you. Madder than I've ever been. You've made so much of this summer harder for me with your stunts."

I throw out an arm to stop Sohel before he can come to my defense again, mumbling, "I know, and I deserve it" as I fight back tears. "You don't even know the half of it."

"*But*," she continues, making my eyes snap to hers, "you and Sohel are not the reason Sunny and I decided to do this. Yes, what happened earlier tonight was the straw that broke the camel's back, but the camel's been collapsing beneath the weight of all these family expectations and arguments *anyway* since we got here. We realized that if we stayed, we wouldn't be able to stop it from affecting how we feel about each other, so we . . . we have to go."

"No, you don't," another voice rings out.

We whirl to discover our parents surging through the airport entrance together, out of breath from having run to meet us. Sunny's father strides over to them, but it's Halima he speaks to. "Halima . . . Bow Ma, I have failed you as a father-in-law."

"Sir . . . ," she gasps, speechless.

He shakes his head. "Let me finish, please. The truth is, I have always chosen the tea garden over everything else. Over my wife, over my children. I love and respect my sisters and my father, but I shouldn't have lost sight of what matters most because of them—this wedding is meant to be a testament to yours and Shariq's love, to the union between our families."

"Please, come home and have the wedding ceremony as planned," Mrs. Rahman begs. "I promise you, Bow Ma, I will do my best to ensure you don't repeat history."

"Even if that means setting boundaries with the rest of my family that I should have put into place decades ago," Mr. Rahman adds, taking his wife's hand and squeezing it. "I want my sons to be happy, to feel as though they have a home with us that they can visit whenever they please, a home where they find peace rather than having to run thousands of miles away to escape it. Escape us."

"What more can I say?" Abbu drops an amicable clap onto Mr. Rahman's shoulder, while Ammu asks, "Will you please come back with us?"

Halima and Sunny search one another's faces, then nod, breaking out into faltering smiles when all of us erupt in cheers.

🍃 🍃 🍃

I can't stop grinning from ear to ear as the rest of the night unfolds. Sunny, Mr. Rahman, and Sohel chat among themselves as they lug the bags out of the car while our mothers and Thathu accompany Halima inside.

Abbu slings an arm around my shoulders as we stare up at the guest house. "You did it."

"It wasn't all me," I respond, blushing. "They wouldn't have come back without Mr. Rahman being willing to eat a slice of humble pie."

That makes Abbu snort. "He's not the only one. But, Bibi, none of us would have looked past our egos in time, if ever, were it not for you. You saved the day tonight, and I couldn't be more proud of you if I tried, Little Nugget."

I swallow, moved by his words, but attempt to hide it beneath humor. "Does that mean you'll reduce my sentence?"

"It means the court may consider a partial commutation due to your service to society," he concedes, then considers me with something akin to wonder, rubbing my cheek with his thumb. "You truly are more like me than I ever knew, Bibi zaan. I should have seen it all along and trusted your instincts a little bit more. You have such a way with people, perhaps more than I ever did. I can't wait to see what you accomplish with that someday."

I beam.

Perhaps not everything is figured out yet, but it feels good to be understood and appreciated by Abbu for once, to feel like everyone is where they should be.

He hugs me close, and I let him.

CHAPTER THIRTY-THREE

There's nothing else quite like a Bangladeshi wedding.

Early the next morning, in the company of their closest family and an imam, Sunny and Halima have their akth, officially pronouncing them husband and wife in the eyes of Allah.

Then the rest of the festivities commence.

It's absolutely, utterly perfect and feels even sweeter after the many obstacles they've had to overcome to reach their happily-ever-after.

Wearing a blush-pink tulle Tarun Tahiliani shari beaded in crystals, I carry Halima's long red veil while she sashays forward beneath a beautiful phoolon ki chador—a canopy heavy with all manner of red, white, and yellow flowers with tiny streaming garlands hanging around it, hoisted high by our male cousins, her bridal party following in our wake.

Ammu, Abbu, and Thathu ride just up ahead in a slowly moving baby taxi piled high with more flowers, the lead float in our parade to the teahouse. String lights illuminate our path through the night, distant music growing closer and closer.

When we reach the teahouse, we usher Halima over to the gazebo-turned-stage, where she's meant to await her groom. She looks like a doll in her classic crimson-and-gold shari, with ruby-studded gold bangles running up her arm, henna peeking out on the skin beneath, the elaborate pearl-and-gold headpiece from Sunny's mother's family perched atop her head.

The bridal makeup I helped with is the best I've done yet!

Once she's safely cloistered away, our cousins, her friends, and I hurry over to the entrance of the greenhouse, which we bind up with red ribbons and rose garlands, before picking up signs we created that morning that say NO TAKKA, NO HALIMA; PRADA OR NADA; WE DEMAND $10K FROM THE THAMAND; GIVE US MONEY, SUNNY; BRIDE 4 A BRIBE, and other catchy slogans.

When Sunny's procession arrives—the groom himself aloft in a canopied howdah on top of an actual *elephant*, looking as regal as a prince in his gilded sherwani with a matching pagri on his head and a hand-woven stole from his maternal cousins draped over one arm—they're trapped outside.

My brother-in-law—because that's what he is now—guffaws when he spots me at the front of the line. As he dismounts the elephant with Sohel's help, he tells him, "Careful, Sohu, this one will be tough to negotiate with. I might end up missing my own wedding."

"Damn right. What will you offer for my sister?" I ask with a devious smile.

It flounders when Sohel replies, "What do you want?" His voice is quiet, like we're the only two people in the universe and not surrounded by hundreds of family members.

He looks painfully handsome, in a silver sherwani with sapphire trim, and suddenly I have to fight the urge to blab, "N-nothing from you, kiss thief!"

Thankfully, one of my cousins taps on the monetary amount on his sign. "No money, no honey, thulabhai! Cough up some cash!"

Like this, the negotiations go back and forth, until Sunny and his groomsmen have emptied most of their wallets, leaving us cackling and fanning ourselves with banknotes in their wakes while they enter.

I don't let myself stare after Sohel for too long as he lopes after Sunny toward the gazebo, instead distracting myself with my sister and her husband's reunion on the thrones where they sit. Pure, unfiltered love dawns on her face at the sight of him. Although I'm staring at Sunny's back, I suspect that his own expression matches.

There's a tradition that Bangladeshi brides cry when they marry—not because they're emotional about one of the happiest moments of their lives but because in the past many of the brides were meeting their husbands for the very first time, and marriage meant abandoning their own families to become part of his. I never liked the idea of that particular tradition much, so I'm glad Sunny and Halima have chosen to seek joy together instead, especially since Sunny's aunties are wisely keeping their smart comments to themselves tonight.

Sohel and I climb onto the stage to hold a red urna over their heads while they peer at one another in a mirror and are asked what they see.

"I see . . . the most beautiful woman in the world," Sunny answers first. "Beautiful inside and out, with the most brilliant brain and the most generous heart."

Halima swipes at her kohl-lined eyes, even as she giggles down at their reflection. "I see a man who would do anything to make me smile, no matter how hard things get. A man who will be the most incredible husband, friend, and father."

It takes every ounce of my willpower to keep from bawling right then and there, but when even Sohel chokes back a sniffle, I figure it's okay if I let a few teardrops slip out.

Nganu's daughter, Sunny's niece, doubles as the ring bearer and flower girl. When she reaches the gazebo, at long last, our siblings exchange rings and the garlands made by Sunny's mother's side of the family, carefully placing them around one another's fingers and necks.

Dinner service kicks off after. While the adults bound onto the stage to feed the bride and groom assorted treats from an array of trays, I huddle with the rest of the bridal party in a corner and whisper, "Next we have to steal Sunny Bhaiya's shoes, hide them somewhere good, and ransom them back to him when it's time to go. That's how you get the big bucks."

"Ransom his *shoes*?" Tameka parrots.

Aracely whistles. "These Bengali weddings are wild! I love it!"

"But it won't be easy," my cousins and I warn them and the rest of Halima's clueless American friends. "We have to get them without him catching on *and* hide them where none of the groomsmen can sniff them out—they'll be looking."

With that, we salute each other and split apart to accomplish our mission.

It's not long after that Sohel finds me and says, "Bibi, can we talk?"

I frown at him, forced to speak around the growing lump in my throat. "Look, Sohel, I . . . I'd rather not have anything else go wrong today of all days."

"Just for a minute?" he pleads, pulling something out from behind his back—Sunny's pearl-and-gold shoes with curling tips.

"You'd betray your own brother just to talk to me?" I ask, eyeing him suspiciously.

He rolls his eyes. "Like Sunny Bhai said, you're a demanding negotiator."

I begrudgingly nod, accepting the shoes from him to pass off to one of my cousins. After directing her to hide them somewhere on the grounds where the groomsmen will never find them, I turn back to Sohel and cross my arms.

"Fine. Just for a minute."

As he escorts me back to the butterfly garden, my chest grows tight. This was the place where it all happened—where we got caught, where he broke my heart.

I'm scared to go back.

Scared of an encore.

Even if my feelings for him haven't yet faded, I'm not sure I can trust him not to toss me aside again the second it gets inconvenient.

He stops just short of entering the enclosure and turns to me with the butterflies behind him. "I made a mistake, Bibi. I thought—I *hoped* I could forget about you. That we could forget about each other and you'd be better off, but I can't."

"What does that mean?" I grind out. "I don't exactly love to hear how often you try to convince yourself to hate me, you know?"

"I could never hate you," he professes, then swallows audibly. "The truth is, I think I love you."

"W-what?" Try as I might, I can't make sense of the words. "You . . . love me?"

"I understand if I blew it," he answers with a miserable nod, not denying the fact. "You were right—I was a coward, and I was every bit as bad as I always blamed my father and brother for being. If anything, I was worse, because despite everything I believed, Sunny Bhai fought for your sister in a way I didn't for you. I'm sorry, Bibi. It hit me when we got caught, how deeply I feel for you. How, fifty years from now, I could still be thinking about you. And I just—I got scared. It terrified me to realize how much those feelings could come back to haunt us both. I couldn't forgive myself if my family became the reason you lost everything that makes you, *you*, the way my mother did, but I was also afraid of disappointing my family."

"Sohel, I . . ." My heart flutters like the butterflies but not in the way it used to before our families discovered us together. A sickening, nauseous flutter. "I don't know what to say."

He shakes his head. "You don't have to say a thing. I know it's not fair to spring this on you after everything I put you through, but I . . . When I think about having nothing left of you except the memory of this summer, I hate myself more for not choosing us. I would have left you alone tonight, but if this is good-bye forever, then I at least wanted to leave you with one last gift before letting you go. So someday, you might look back and smile too."

"A gift?" I search his face. "What kind of gift?"

"Let's go get your thathi," he responds, already moving toward the rest of the guests.

An epiphany widens my eyes and makes me gasp his name as I reach for his sleeve. "Sohel, you . . . you found him?"

He flashes me a beautifully tragic smile and nods. "I found him by seeking out his poetry. He responded to my e-mail a few days ago. He's always wanted to see your grandmother again too, but he lives abroad and I wasn't originally sure I could fly him in before you left."

"But he's *here*?" I ask, needing him to confirm that I'm not hearing things.

"He's here," Sohel vows.

Together we rush over to Thathu, who sits close to the main stage, clapping while others take photos with Sunny and Halima. The protective expression that claims her face diminishes when I tell her, "Thathu, there's someone we want you to meet."

"Oh?" Her forehead puckers. "Who is it?"

We follow Sohel with her elbow crooked in mine, painstakingly making our way through the many guests. When I spot Mohammed, seated with a young woman I don't recognize, I somehow intrinsically know it's him—with the same dark, pensive eyes as in the original photo, even with one side of his handsome face bearing old scars, a thick head of steel-gray hair, and a wheelchair it must have been hell to heft through the garden.

"Shuki?" the man whispers.

Thathu gasps, her hand tightening around my arm. "Ziarul?"

And just like that, nothing in the world seems impossible anymore.

CHAPTER THIRTY-FOUR

Later that night Sunny brings Halima with him to stay at the manor for the first time.

Early the next morning all of us gather to bid them good-bye, since they're departing for their honeymoon trip to Türkiye and we won't see them again until they return to New Jersey in a week, not leaving much time before classes start.

In the Rahmans' case it might be much longer.

I watch, fastened to Halima, our parents around us, as Mr. and Mrs. Rahman pat Sunny on the shoulder and cup his cheek, reminding him to take care of himself. When they move on to their new daughter-in-law, Sohel shuffles over to his brother awkwardly, but Sunny doesn't hesitate before pulling him into a bear hug, which Sohel returns with equal fervor after a second.

"Maybe, if I get very good grades this term, I can apply to a school in America?" I hear Sohel ask his brother, who breaks away only to beam at him. "Baba thinks it might not be a bad idea to leave home for at least a little while before I come back to take the reins."

"Of course, kiddo!" Sunny drags him into another embrace.

Sohel laughs into his shoulder. "Let's see if I even get accepted."

"They'd be fools not to take you," his brother replies. "You're the second-smartest person I've ever met."

Once they separate, I get a chance to give Sunny a hug of my own. "See you on the flip side, Bhaiya. Take care of my afu—she gets shy around strangers."

"Will do, Beebs," he vows, ruffling my hair with a laugh. I decide I'll miss him so much that I won't carp about him committing two of my personal deadly sins this once. "You come by and visit too, eh?"

Soon we're left staring after the car they've driven off in.

Once it's no longer in sight, our families start to go their separate ways for the last time, but Sohel and I linger, everything left unspoken last night hanging in the misty air between us. By the time I tore my gaze away from my grandmother and her lost boy at the wedding, my own had slipped off to give me space to collect my thoughts.

Seeing Thathu and Mohammed find each other after so long certainly gave me plenty to think about. In the decades they'd been apart, they'd had two marriages, many children, and even more grandchildren between them. Entire lives not knowing where the other was. Now they were a widow and a widower, but that didn't mean things would be simple.

When I asked Thathu what she planned to do, she only

smiled at me gently and said, even if she and Mohammed decided not to try again, Sohel and I had given them a sense of closure because they knew at last what had happened to each other. They were both happy and safe and didn't regret falling in love or the lives they'd lived apart until now.

"Perhaps we'll write letters again," she mused. "We'll see how it goes from there."

If Sohel and I say our farewells with things as they are, will we find each other again someday too? Will I always wonder where he is and what he's doing?

Do I want so many unknowns?

"Bibi, what are you doing?" my mother calls when she notices I'm not right behind her.

"Can I please say good-bye?" I call back.

Ammu hesitates. "Hurry back. We have to finish packing for our flight."

"Good-bye, huh?" Sohel whispers when she's gone.

My heart contracts, but I make myself nod. "Take one last stroll through the tea gardens with me before I go? For old times' sake?"

He nods, and together we amble into the rolling green hills of tea. The estate is breathtaking and eerie so early in the morning, the sky painted gold, the reflection of the sun glittering across dewdrops. There's an inkling of rain in the wind, the aroma of it surrounding us. I close my eyes for a minute, breathing everything in deeply, writing it into my memory.

"Thank you for finding Mr. Ahmed," I tell him at last.

Sohel nods. "Of course. I don't expect anything in return because I found him, though. I just—I know how hard you worked to do it, and I wanted to be able to give that to you before you left, if nothing else."

"I know."

I turn to face him. A gossamer drizzle mists the air. In the rain, Sohel's dark, somber eyes are truly beautiful, his hair like silk as it slips into his face. He sucks in a sharp breath when I reach to smooth it back, even as I use my other hand to open the umbrella I've been carrying, and raise it over our heads.

"Y-you—"

"It's the rainy season," I tell him with a hint of a smirk curling my lips. "I remember."

"Bibi," he breathes. "What does this mean?"

I stand up on my tiptoes, close enough that he must feel my breath ghost across his lips, because they part in surprise as I inform him, "It means I forgive you."

"R-really?" he sputters. "You don't have to. I know I messed up."

"You did," I agree, "but, Sohel, even though our families might be completely different in so many ways, I understand exactly what it's like to try to be someone you're not because of pressure and expectations."

His eyes jerk away from me. "I should have stood beside you, come whatever may."

"Maybe," I acknowledge, "but I don't want to wonder if

we made a mistake fifty years later. I'd rather make all our mistakes *now*. So, if you want to try again, it's not too late?"

He leans his forehead against mine, his hands coming up to clutch my waist, steadying me against him. "I do. I—I love you, Bibi."

"I think I might love you too, Sohel," I whisper back, tilting my chin higher to press our mouths together at last. We kiss while the rain begins to pour harder and harder around us, kiss until the umbrella slips from my grasp and we're drenched by the storm, knowing that it's as much a kiss good-bye as it is one for a new beginning.

After all, who knows what this next year will bring?

This wild, wonderful summer alone has already changed me so much for the better.

Six months later.

THE BIODATA OF SOHEL RAHMAN, ACCORDING TO BIBI HOSSAIN

(B: happy almost bday to my favorite pisces-aries cusp!
we are SO compatible!)

DOB: 03-21-2007

(S: Again with the horoscope mumbo jumbo 🙄)
(B: you LOVE my mumbo jumbo)
(S: . . . No comment.)

Height: Annoyingly difficult to kiss
(S: I promise I'll bend more)
(B: that's the sweetest thing you've ever said 😍)

Education: Cornell University, babyyyyy
(S: You don't know that yet . . .)
(B: I have a sixth sense for these things
😊 😉 😋)

Career: Professional lover boy
(S: Didn't SOMEONE just complain I was too tall to kiss?
So which is it?)
(B: awww are you pouting baby? I'm willing to get a crick to kiss it better)
(S: Oh, are you? How romantic . . .)
(B: why don't you come find out? 😉)

Single orrrr . . .

SORRY, LADIES. This one is taken!

(S: All right, you've had your fun.)
(B: you know you love it)
(S: I don't. We should be doing homework instead of messing around.)
(B: you know you loooooooove ME)
(S: . . . I plead the fifth.)

CHAPTER THIRTY-FIVE

Seven months later . . .

I'm spending my spring break at Royal Fried Chicken.

What else is new?

Luckily this time my sentence is a brief one—looking after the place for a week while Ammu and Abbu attend a nephew's wedding in the UK. Not even a punishment, since I did the mature thing and volunteered to train some new recruits for Abbu.

How's *that* for character growth?

Halima is supposed to drive over and help me, except when I look away from my English Lit IV packet toward the clock on the wall for the third time, I realize she's half an hour late. Tossing my pencil aside, I text her again.

Where are you?

She replies immediately. **Sorry, Beebs. Got hit with a surprise test tomorrow that I have to meet a few classmates to study for . . . but I've arranged help.**

What the hell does that mean? I type back.

Before I can hit send, the bells above the door jingle, and I start to say, "Welcome to Royal Fried Chicken, where your wish is our—" The last word dies on my tongue when I realize who's grinning back at me, a bag slung over his shoulder. "S-Sohel?"

"Surprise," he declares.

I vault over the counter and launch myself into his arms, eliciting an *oof*, even as I begin to interrogate him with a million questions, my legs wrapped around his waist like one of the baby monkeys we used to see at the garden. "What are you doing here? Does Sunny Bhaiya know? Do your folks? Did you run away from home to be with me? I—I thought we were supposed to video chat later today. Why didn't you tell me you were coming, you meanie?"

"Will you ever take a breath?" he quips. "Will I ever get to answer?"

Unenthusiastically I release him long enough for him to settle in at the counter while I lock the door and pull down the curtains to give us some privacy. A thousand different thoughts swirl in my head. Over the past school year Sohel and I haven't had much of a chance to see each other in person, aside from his college interview visits and a brief trip to Bangladesh for winter break at the tea estate.

I've missed it and him, missed Ireima and the other girls, and no amount of texting or e-mailing or even seeing their faces on video chat has kept me from wanting to go right back to the place I'm starting to consider a home away from home. Enough so that I might not mind moving there forever someday.

However, Sohel had been determined to help me turn things around for my senior year, and so, despite the time zone difference between the US and Bangladesh, we've been studying together every minute we can. Somehow, through mostly virtual charms, he managed to win over all my friends and even Rosho Gulla—though whether he'll ever get Abbu's full stamp of approval remains to be seen.

Not long ago each received a packet in the mail, the culmination of all our efforts, and were supposed to open them together tonight on video.

"Did you come to open the letter with me in person?" I ask, batting my eyelashes at him.

Sohel smiles and retrieves it from his bag. "Since we're on break at the same time, I asked Sunny Bhai if it'd be okay for me to visit. I wanted you to be the first to know, Bibi."

"I left mine at home, you goof," I complain, even though there's a smile tugging at my lips and my voice is tremulous with emotion. "You could've given me a warning."

He laughs. "We both know that if it's a packet, the answer is yes."

To be fair, I wasn't able to resist checking my status online, though I kept the envelope in pristine condition as promised— but Sohel already knows I like to bend the rules.

An acceptance from the Fashion Institute.

Upon much deliberation, Sohel chose to transfer after his

first year at Dhaka University and apply to Cornell's school of agricultural science, with a minor in sustainable agriculture, in addition to a few other safety schools like Princeton. I, on the other hand, am still a fashionista through and through, but in the last year alone I have pushed myself beyond my wildest expectations and tried so many different things I never thought I could do.

New sports (still a big nope, dance aside). Debate club (Sohel thinks I have a knack for arguing). Even an upcoming internship at one of my favorite fashion start-ups, Luxe Lotus, after all of his ranting about ethical, sustainable farming made me take a deeper interest in what that could mean for the fashion industry.

For the first time ever, I'm excited for what the next four years of school might bring.

I know, right?! Who even *am* I?

For now, though, I plop myself down next to Sohel and poke his arm. "Go on! Open it! The suspense is killing me!"

"Your father would tell you to be patient, *Little Nugget*," he teases with a smirk before laughing and waving the packet out of my reach with his annoyingly long limbs when I attempt to make a grab for it. "All right, all right, settle down." In spite of his bravado, he holds his breath while tearing open the envelope. I lean my head close to his and hold my breath, too, until the contents of the letter materialize. "I . . . got in."

"Of course you did, boy genius," I respond with a wide

grin. "Now you'll only be four hours away. I got a car for school so I can come see you."

"Only four, huh?" he asks with a huff.

"Better than twenty," I retort without missing a beat.

He answers me with a lingering kiss, pulling away only to murmur, "Thanks, Bibi."

"For what?" I answer breathlessly. "I'm not the reason you got into Cornell."

If anything, he's the reason I got into the school I wanted, since he never let my *whingeing* and tricks to distract him with flirting deter him from making me study. Then again, Sunny claims I've been a good influence on Sohel, too, since Sunny was afraid Sohel would never give life outside the tea gardens a fair shot before we met. Even his parents approve of him broadening his horizons before he returns to the estate.

We're good for each other like that!

"For not giving up on me," Sohel responds. "For not letting me give up on my family and what it could be."

I smile and press my lips to his again, dragging him closer by the collar.

So much has changed in so short a time.

Our next adventure, we're embarking on together.

ACKNOWLEDGMENTS:

First and foremost, I am so grateful to the readers who not only picked up yet another of my books, but have also made it all the way here, past *the end*! A sophomore novel is no joke, but we did it. We reached Bibi's happily ever after—and I hope the journey brought you joy too!

Always Be My Bibi was a fun new challenge for several different reasons. I was inspired to write the book because of my visit to a tea garden in Bangladesh a few years ago, but being born and raised in America, it was a little scary to tell a story set somewhere I'm an outsider to, no matter how proud I may be of my family's heritage. Plus there's the fact that I consider being the eldest daughter and sister in my family a defining part of my identity, while Bibi is quite the opposite—brash, reckless, free-spirited, and the youngest. It's not easy writing a troublemaker when you're usually the responsible one.

So of course, I owe a debt of gratitude to everyone who helped get this book past the finish line. Above all, thank you to Dainese Santos and Laura Barbiea for your brilliant editorial insights, especially when it came to doing justice to the characters who work in the tea garden. Tea estates like the one in the book are ethereal settings to visit, but their colonial history is so complicated that I appreciate you knowing how important it would be for me to write about them with sensitivity. I also always defer to your expertise when it comes to making one of my rom-coms as funny, swoony, and heartfelt as possible—and you never lead me astray. (The same goes for my kick-ass agent, Quressa Robinson, who lets me write whatever I want, to the point that I'm somehow now on track to publish THREE stories that have almost entirely South Asian casts, in an industry where it is still pretty rare to get even ONE Desi protagonist!)

In general, I struck gold with the wonderful Simon & Schuster team! Thank you to Justin Chanda and Kendra Levin for your leadership; to Jenica Nasworthy and Morgan York for catching all the silly mistakes that made it through draft after draft so that the final book is as polished as possible; to Sarah Creech, Tom Daly, and Shazleen Khan for the absolute stunner of a cover that positively glows whenever readers photograph it; to my lovely publicists Alex Kelleher and Maryam Ahmad for getting me so many opportunities to talk about bookish things; to Chrissy Noh and Erin Toller for getting Bibi into so many readers' hands; and finally, to Chava Wolin for taking my document and transforming it into a real book, an act that feels like nothing short of magic every time!

In addition to having a stellar publishing team, I have been so fortunate with my family, which includes Paterson's Bangladeshi community. They all came together to make the launch of *The Love Match*, my first book, as marvelous as possible. They're also the reason that my books are often complimented for having likable side characters and poignant platonic relationships, because I have lived a life surrounded by so much love. As Rabindranath Tagore said, "I seem to have loved you in numberless forms, numberless times, in life after life, in age after age, forever." So—thank you to my mother and father, my brother and sister (this book dealt a lot with sibling bonds, after all), and my many, many aunts and uncles and cousins (blood-related or otherwise) for cheering me on throughout this adventure. I'm trying to keep things short and sweet this time, so I won't mention everyone by name, but specifically, thanks to Anik and Anmoy, because I forgot you by accident last time.

To my found family, my writing friends, thank you for keeping me sane in this tumultuous industry. Tammi, Adiba, you two are practically my sisters, even if my parents claim we're NOT somehow related the way all Bangladeshis seem to be. (P.S. Thank you for blurbing *TLM* too, Adiba!) Tana, Alisha, Cassandra, Cindy (who even came all the way across the country for my launch!), you're my safe haven, the first people I wake myself up enough to talk to on any given day, as well as some of the last people I say good night to after an evening of writing sprints. Jen, Lyla, I'm so blessed to have you as authors I admire in addition to being able to call you friends. Thank you as well for blurbing my debut! Thank you to *all* the authors who took the time to blurb *The Love Match*, in fact, particularly because I was and still am obsessed with you as a reader— Axie Oh, Farah Heron, Nisha Sharma, Lillie Vale, and Farah Naz Rishi. To the folks in the debuting class of 2022 and 2023 books, I know we don't keep in touch as much anymore, but I will eternally cherish everyone I met there. To other talented author friends like Gayatri, Elizabeth, Eunice, Brian, Soumi, Petula—honestly, more folks than my little goldfish brain can recall with these acknowledgements due tomorrow—I'm the luckiest person in the world because I get to be your fan and your friend. Love you all!

Last but certainly not least, thank you to the librarians, educators, booksellers, trade reviewers, and bookish influencers who took the time to champion my first book. I have adored every post, every video, every interview, every visit—however you chose to support me and my work. Although I won't be able to list everyone here, I'd like to shout out at least a few readers who made my day every time they spread positivity about my debut: Tazrin, Ayushi, Amani, Maya, Sami, Sel, Rita, Paige, Moukthika, Irin, Taha, Jill, Sarah, Nihaarika, Lisa, Veronica, Star, Thya, Brenna, Zai, Dedra, Zahra, Katie, Trishla, Basma, Laura, Maha, Emma, Jay, Shiela, Daniela, Kylie, Becka, Sam, Nyla, Shincy, Sahana, Jesse, Emily, Bren, Kess, Yz, Vivi, Ri, Monet, Jazelle, Mahek, Sumbal, Sasha, Sunny, Zainab, Daaria, Chitti, Nicole, Janelle, and so many, many others who I'm sorry I can't list here! It isn't easy being an author of color, especially one who often writes all-brown casts. Publishing still tends to prefer books that are more "palatable," in which characters of color are lighter or have white love interests. There are an innumerable amount of hurdles when it comes to support of books like *The Love Match* and *Always Be My Bibi*, so it means that much more when readers go out of their way to shout from the hilltops about them. I hope that you will also love *Always Be My Bibi* as much as you did *The Love Match*.

THANK YOU! You'll always be some of my favorite people!

XOXO,

Priyanka

PRIYANKA TASLIM

Priyanka Taslim is a Bangladeshi American writer, teacher and lifelong New Jersey resident. Having grown up in a bustling Bangladeshi diaspora community, surrounded by her mother's entire clan and many aunties of no relation, her writing often features families, communities and all the drama therein. Currently, Priyanka teaches English by day and tells all kinds of stories about Bangladeshi characters by night. Her writing usually stars spunky Bangladeshi heroines finding their place in the world—and a little swoony romance, too.

X ⊙ @BhootBabe
PriyankaTaslim.com

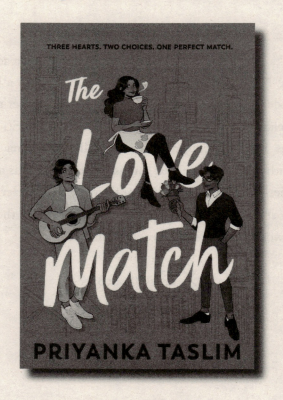